Twilight of the City

A NOVEL OF THE NEAR FUTURE

○ ○ ○

CHARLES PLATT

Macmillan Publishing Co., Inc.
NEW YORK

Macmillan Publishing Co., Inc.
866 Third Avenue, New York, N.Y. 10022
Collier Macmillan Canada, Ltd.

Library of Congress Cataloging in Publication Data
Platt, Charles, 1949–
Twilight of the city.
I. Title
PZ4.P718Tw [PS3566.L285] 813'.5'4 76–40913
ISBN 0–02–597620–6

First Printing 1977

Printed in the United States of America

*For Dr. Michael Linnett,
without whom this might never
have been written*

and

*For Ellen Couch,
without whom this might never
have been published*

PART ONE

The End of Summer

1997

Twilight on a summer Saturday evening, and Michael had some time to kill. He adjusted the climate control and turned on the magic fingers in his seat, settled back in the sealskin upholstery, and took the vintage '66 customized Toronado up a wide, empty avenue toward the lights and crowds of midtown.

Through the armor-glass windshield he watched movie theaters swing past, pedestrians overflowing the sidewalks onto the pot-holed street. Color and life and activity: the city still had vitality, and it fed him. And yet there was something depressing about the neon and the crowds. Too many people looked pale under the lights, their clothes shabby. Long lines waited outside the state-run community food outlets. And the faces that watched the Toronado murmur past were brooding and resentful.

Irritated, he turned onto a cross-street, away from the urban energy he'd deliberately sought out. Whatever it was that he needed, it wasn't there.

He spun the power steering idly and drove up another block. Because he was preoccupied he didn't notice that the light ahead was red. When he did see it he hit the brakes clumsily, already into the intersection. And then he saw the other car coming and he swerved to avoid it, but it was too late. He heard rubber screaming across asphalt, glimpsed the other driver's surprised face, flinched as the other car skidded toward him.

There was a crash of metal on metal. The seat jerked under him, throwing him against the door. The cars bounced apart and slid to a standstill. In the aftermath, the other vehicle's horn blared in the night.

Michael got out quickly, cursing, rubbing his shoulder. He noted the damage: dented rear panels, but the Toronado was still drivable. The other car was an old station wagon loaded down with furniture and possessions. It was in bad shape— smashed in at the front, steaming water trickling from its radiator. Its horn blared on and on.

The girl who'd been driving it got out and stood staring at him. She was ragged, disheveled, looked as if she came from a ghetto zone. In which case, how come she was driving a car?

"You went through a red light." Her voice was loud, angry, yet nervous.

He stepped quickly over to her. "Yeah, well, look, I'll pay all the damage." He glanced around uneasily. The blaring horn was attracting a crowd. People were looking at his expensive, fashionable clothes and his fancy car.

"That's not the point," said the girl.

"What's not the point? Look, I admit liability. Let's cut this short, here's my address." He held out a card.

She didn't take it. "Listen, you've got to understand." She took a deep breath. "This car," she gestured at the beat-up station wagon, "contains everything I own. It's not mine. In fact, I stole it. I had to, never mind why. I don't have an owning permit, a driving permit, a gasoline authorization. Anything. And now *you've* stranded me here with it."

They looked at each other for a moment. Gradually Michael assimilated her position. If the police came by and found her with the car, she'd face certain arrest.

"So what do you want?" he asked. "Are you expecting me to get you out of this somehow?"

"You got me into it." Her voice was still strong but he saw her hand nervously clutching the top of the car door. She was slim but athletic, her brown hair straight to her shoulders. Her face was attractive in a simple, unpretentious way. He guessed she was around twenty-five.

He hesitated, "Anything in your car that the police could use to trace or identify you?"

"No, I'm not that careless."

"Are you wanted for anything? Got a record?"

"No."

He made his decision. "Okay, get in. Quickly now." He opened the passenger door of his car. He saw her hesitate. "Come on, or do you want to be left here?"

"No. I just didn't think you'd do it, that's all." She strode across and sat down in the Toronado.

He glanced around at the scene once again. Probably making a mistake, he thought to himself, but what else could he do? He got in and slammed the driver's door, then accelerated forward, pushing between the people who had gathered in the street. He turned left, zigzagged through back streets, then hit a different avenue and sped up it, leaving the scene of the accident behind.

He glanced at her. She was sitting very tense, right up against the other side of the car, watching him apprehensively. "My name's Michael," he said, "and I'm not going to rape you."

She seemed to assess what he'd told her. "I'm Lisa. Is this your car?" She took in the customized instrumentation, the sterling silver bas reliefs, carved ivory door handles, alligator-skin door trim, yak-pelt carpeting, platinum-plated shift lever, and the mirrored underside of the roof where five gold disks were inlaid, like suns floating in a transparent sky.

"It's not really mine. Belongs to my partner." He took another look at her. Rich and poor classes seldom mingled, these days; he wasn't used to meeting women who looked like her—no makeup, no fashionable clothes, her skin hadn't been immaculated, her body hadn't been augmented. And yet she had presence; she was attractive.

"I'm not sure why you helped me back there," she said.

"The accident was my fault."

"But most people would have dumped me," she persisted.

"You're wondering what my ulterior motive is?"

"Naturally." She watched him, frankly and steadily.

He pulled the car over to the side of the street, set the brake, and removed his wallet. "Here." He held out a wad of cash.

She looked at it, then up at him. "Do you want sex, or what?"

"My partner's in the music business. I have no shortage of women to sleep with. No, this is partial compensation, for losing all your stuff back there. It's probably not enough, but it's all I have with me right now."

Slowly she took the money. "You've got to have some kind of angle."

"Put it this way. You can take my money, open that door, and run off home now. But I think I'd be interested in talking to you for a while, and if you stick around I can settle the rest of the debt for the accident. Up to you."

She looked at the cash in her hands. "I don't have a home to run off to."

"Why?"

"I was leaving town. That's why I stole that car. I had to get out of the city. I couldn't stand it here anymore. I've cut all my ties here." She pulled a crumpled color picture out of her back pocket and showed it to him. It was of a wide stretch of farmland, dotted with simple wooden houses. Young, healthy, happy people were working in the fields. "I was going to go there. It's in the South. They pay you, feed you, give you a place to sleep."

Michael handed the photograph back to her. "I'm sorry I fucked up your plans."

"Well, that's life." Her voice was weary. "So you see it doesn't really matter too much at the moment, what I do. Where are you going?"

"My partner has a concert starting in an hour. I have to get there soon."

She shrugged. "Okay. Why not."

"Good." He accelerated away from the curb and on along the avenue. He wondered if she could be the stimulus he'd been vaguely looking for. There *was* something about her. . . .

He turned on the radio. Music flowed out, filling the inside of the car like a giant pair of quad headphones.

"Bobby Black, people," the DJ cut in at the end of the song, "with his count-it third number-one suicide rock hit 'Take Me With You When You Go,' but people don't go, we got more music right here after this double-U rundown which says people things is peaceful in the city tonight, only reported urban unrest was coupla hours back when Riverside locals arsonized power company trucks and executed half a dozen of the employees. Reprisal for you remember that power shutdown they did last month on accounta the residents there wasn't paying their bills no more. It figures, I guess, ha-ha. Meanwhile, vigilante-wise. . . ."

Michael turned the radio down. "You heard of Bobby Black?"

"The one all those pre-teens have riots about?"

"Yeah. That's who my partner is. I wrote that song, on the radio. Write all his songs." As well as his interviews and his

"So this is *his* car. Now I understand." She laughed.

"What's funny?"

whole image, he added to himself.

"It just looks like it belongs to a pimp, that's all."

"You're certainly very direct."

"I'm sorry. I guess I should try to be more polite. Civilized. I mean, it seems you're trying to be nice to me."

He looked at her. There was something about the way she looked straight back at him that unsettled him. She would never bother to play any games, he realized. Social niceties were barely in her vocabulary. "Just keep on being the way you are," he told her. "I enjoy it."

"Just as well, 'cause that's the only way I know how to be." She smiled. She looked very charming, very kind, when she smiled. It erased the suspicion and aggression she'd shown toward him at first.

"There's a party before the concert. You can come along with me."

"A party? You mean a real-life, showbiz-type party?"

"Right."

"I'm not exactly dressed for it."

"It doesn't matter. Those people are all assholes, you don't have to worry about what they think."

"Will it be interesting?"

"Sure it will. Maybe take your mind off things a little."

The car moved on up the avenue, into the old city business district. Abandoned sixty-story monoliths stood dead and dark-windowed behind groves of ornamental trees and massive steel security barriers streaked with rust. There was some traffic on the avenue—motorcycles, mainly—and the streetlights still worked, but each cross-street they passed was as black and as uninviting as the mouth of a railroad tunnel, the asphalt littered with glass and garbage.

"You look like you're from a ghetto zone," Michael said, "but you don't talk like it."

"I grew up and was educated in a small town. The school system there still functioned. I only came to the city three years ago, seeking my fortune."

"You didn't find it?"

She laughed cynically. "What do you think?"

He guided the car up a ramp, out of the old city center, onto an unlit, empty, divided highway. It took them across a wide river, out into suburban areas where there were still pockets of high-income affluence amid the general middle-class decay. In the distance a big stadium came into view.

Michael pressed a switch and his window slid down. He slowed the car. "Listen." Faintly, from the distant stadium, came the sound of young girls screaming, a thin, ululating wail. "They're waiting to be let in, to see Bobby."

"Do I get to meet him, too? At the party?"

"Probably."

"This is all kind of unexpected."

"Yes." Once again he looked at her, and she looked back at him, open and direct.

TAKE ME WITH YOU WHEN YOU GO

You know
You must go
There's nothing left on earth
You find worth
Living for
You say
You can't stay
There isn't anywhere
You can bear
Anymore

    So if you're so dissatisfied
    You'll swallow your conscience and pride
    And go leap down some steep mountainside
    Or swim far out to sea on the tide
    Don't run from me, darling, don't hide
    I don't want to live when you've died
    Take me with you when you go
    Take me with you when you go—oh!

You need
To be freed
From everything you find
Hurts your mind
And your heart
Escape
From the hate
The tension and despair
All that tears
You apart

    So if you're so dissatisfied
    You can't take no more and decide
    To give up on all that you've tried
    And take that last automobile ride
    I want to be there by your side
    I don't want to live when you've died
    Take me with you when you go
    Take me with you when you go—oh!

PARTNERS

The walls of the large, long room were covered with giant holographic posters. Multi-hued lights shifted and flashed. The air was heavy with smoke and perfumes and the steady pounding of music. The bizarre, the rich, and the elegant stood posing for one another on the plush carpeting, dropping pills, drinking, getting wrecked in whichever way they chose.

Lisa stopped at the door. "You sure this isn't just going to be embarrassing? I mean here I am in my dirty jeans and old shirt, and there's, for instance, that women over there in a dress that must have cost . . ."

"No," said Michael, "these people are mostly ingrates. They'll be too polite to show they've noticed you, still less actually say anything. And anyway, I really don't give a shit about what they think." He showed a pass to the guard at the door, then guided Lisa in.

A waiter proffered a silver tray of drinks, pills, suppositories, smokables, sniffables, and injectables. Michael chose a glass of pale blue liquid for Lisa and took one for himself. The waiter moved on.

She tasted the drink. It was bitter-sweet. "Is your partner Bobby here?"

"I don't see him."

"The posters on the walls—they're of his face, aren't they?"

"Yes, they are." He looked slightly irritated. "You a fan of his or something?"

"No, just . . . interested. I don't know much about rock music. In fact, that bit of the song on your car radio was the first bit of Bobby Black I ever heard. Are they all like that, the songs you write? About death?"

"Yeah. It's a pre-teen thing, now. Suicide rock."

She started to ask another question but was interrupted. "Hey, Michael," said a large man, walking over.

Michael looked pleased to see him. "Laurence. How are things?" They shook hands.

"We're going to have a party in two days' time." He handed Michael a card. He had a friendly, open, innocent face, like a good-natured truck driver, with pale blue, dreamy eyes and long silky hair. He was wearing a hand-tailored vinyl jacket encrusted with thousands of rhinestones, glittering like an overloaded pin-ball machine. His pants were skin-tight red plastic. His feet were bare but immaculately clean.

He noticed Lisa. "This is your girl friend?" He spoke slowly, vaguely, like someone who has been smoking a lot of dope.

"We just met," said Michael. "Lisa, this is Laurence. He's an artist." He gave the word an almost imperceptible slur.

Laurence smiled amiably. He handed Lisa one of the cards. It was an expensively printed but amateurishly drawn picture of a little house in the woods. Hand-lettered above it was a date and time. "That's our farm. You can come too—it's going to be a big party. Here, this is my wife, Sheila."

He gestured to a small, intense woman who had quietly in-sinuated herself beside him. Like Laurence, she was clad in a jacket laden with glass gems. Hers depicted a gaudy island' sun-set, like bad color-TV out of control. Under it she wore a fancy pink gauze gown, and ballet slippers. "Pleased to *meet* you," she said, accenting the words oddly as if to imply something— sarcasm, cynicism, provocation, it was hard to tell. Her eyes were sharp and devious, and her face was pretty but hard and sus-picious. She stared at Lisa as if thoroughly weighing up her appearance, motives, personality, and finances, then seemed to lose interest.

Laurence moved closer to Lisa, quite unaware of his wife's subliminal broadcast. "Tell me," he said, "do you sew?"

"Do I what?"

"Sew. You see I was thinking, if you ever need some part-time work. These jackets are what I make for a living. It's my busi-ness. The rhinestones are all put in by hand. If the orders I'm expecting come in, I could use some help."

Everyone else in the room was showing manners enough to ignore the existence of Lisa's poverty, as Michael had predicted.

But Laurence was gauche enough not only to notice, but to offer to help her out financially. His friendly face showed simple concern for her obvious lack of money.

"That's really very kind," she told him.

"We have to *go* now," his wife interrupted.

"Why's that?" he asked innocently.

"Come *on*, Laurence." She steered him away, with one significant yet obscure glance back in Lisa's direction.

"He's been selling those jackets for a quarter of a million each," Michael said quietly to Lisa. "Ever since he did one for Bobby. Folk art gone Establishment. The only person who takes it seriously is him."

"He seems a nice guy."

"Yes, I like him myself."

"You do? But you seem to find him a joke."

"Not him. Just his so-called art."

She frowned. "Have you ever told him that? Or do you and your sophisticated friends just sneer at him behind his back?"

"It's not quite as simple as that."

"It isn't?"

"No. If you're trying to cast me as a socially dishonest rich man, unable to have a simple, honest friendship like you salt-of-the-earth poor folk . . . that doesn't really fit."

She squinted up at him, trying to read his expression. "You mean, most of the people in this room may act phony, but you're really not like them?"

"I hope not."

"Isn't this your crowd? Aren't you one of them?"

"Not really. They're mostly connected with my business—the music business—and I get on okay with Laurence, and, let's see, Jamieson, the one over there in the corner," he pointed out a pale, balding, emaciated man, "and Vickers, the tall one with the suntan talking to him. But that's about it."

"So your money hasn't bought you happiness, is that right? How corny."

"Look, I realize I've upset all your plans. But why are you going so far out of your way to be unpleasant?" He regarded her quietly, seriously.

She avoided his eyes. "I am? Maybe I am. I don't know. Frankly, I resent all this. These people. Their money. Your money, too, especially if you ever complain about it."

"I wasn't. I like being wealthy; I like what I do; but this," he gestured at the room, "doesn't interest me. So I'm biding my time, waiting for something else to come along. Eventually it will, one way or another." He looked carefully at her.

For a second she wondered if he was implying that she might be the something he was waiting for. No, that was ridiculous. Ah, but maybe he'd tried deliberately to create that impression, to see if she would pick up on it, and, if so, how she would respond. Was he that calculating? He'd seemed basically uncomplicated, though reserved. But that itself could be a contrived impression. She didn't know. She couldn't tell. "I'm not used to coping with anyone who has enough time and leisure to become sophisticated," she said. "I feel I'm like that man Laurence—people are probably sneering at me behind my back."

"But you manage to take care of yourself all right."

"How would you know?"

"I think I do know. And, incidentally, I'm not in any way sneering at you. The opposite, if anything." He glanced at the door. "Ah, now, here he comes. The star." His face changed for a moment, showing a flash of cynicism and distaste. Then, quickly, his bland, noncommittal expression reasserted itself. "We'd better get in there before the social vultures settle all over him."

Already the room was becoming polarized. People were glancing at the entrance and drifting discreetly in that direction. The focus of their attention was a short, stocky man of around twenty with untidy curly black hair, black eyes, and an aggressive, rough, but handsome face. He wore a skin-fitting suit covered in black sequins, with a blood-red splash over his heart.

A purple cape trailed from his shoulders. He walked on the balls of his feet, like a cocky young toreador, grinning, showing his teeth a lot.

Beside him was a young girl, soft skin draped in pastel silks and glitter, blond hair in long loose waves, a sensual adolescent face, pouting red lips. She was dressed in a pornographic edition of a 1950s-style movie star costume—the kind of thing Jayne Mansfield used to wear. Fashion wasn't in a fifties revival, or even a revival of the last fifties revival; rather, it was rediscovering the old taboo sex roles that had existed before Equal Rights. She fit it to perfection: the classic sullen nymphet.

Michael pushed through the mob, with Lisa following him, surrounded by the press of elegant clothes, remodeled faces and bodies. The scents and colognes were as rich as the air in a hothouse. The talk and laughter surged around her. She felt claustrophobic and alienated, suddenly plunged into this strange world, yet she was determined not to let her nervousness show.

"Hey, Bobby!" Michael called. The man in black looked up, disengaged himself from admirers, and came over, his girl with him.

"Michael, how ya doing?" He brushed aside a man in a dinner jacket who seemed to be angling for an autograph. "Let's get to the corner, talk a little. You got the car here?"

"Yeah, but I had a little accident. Big dent in the rear end."

Bobby's face screwed up. "What? Jesus Christ, you'd better have the name of who did it. I'll sue the shit out of 'em."

Michael gave him a sardonic smile. "Yeah, well, actually the accident was my fault."

"Well, maybe we can pin it on 'em anyway." Bobby grinned nastily, like a juvenile delinquent.

Michael shrugged. "If you like. The person concerned is right here. Meet Lisa."

Bobby turned to her and appraised her quickly, frowning. Then he took a second look. He turned back to Michael. "What is this? Some kind of joke?"

Michael explained the whole story. Bobby listened, then grimaced. "You're an asshole, involving us, helping her escape the law."

"The accident was my fault. *I* got *her* involved."

"She ripped off her car, she should take her chances. I'd have left her there, and tough shit."

"That's rotten, Bobby," said the nymphet-girl beside him.

"Come on, don't try to act naive with me," he snapped at her. He turned to Lisa. "So what's your name again?"

"Lisa."

"Ever been to one of my concerts?"

"Not at those prices."

"It figures. Well, I guess thanks to bleeding-heart Michael here, you got a front row seat tonight." He looked her over again, taking in her strong features, clear skin, high cheekbones. He grinned. "Maybe Michael ain't so dumb, after all. Maybe he's worked out a great new way to pick up girls." He studied her as if imagining what it would be like to fuck her. He dropped his hand on her shoulder, squeezing gently but firmly.

He had presence, and knew how to apply it. He was handsome, aggressive, sexy, and she wasn't immune to that. But something about him made her instinctively react against him. She took his hand off her shoulder.

He put his head on one side. "What's the matter? Don't you like being touched?" He grinned, his eyes still examining her.

She searched for a flip answer, but sensed that whatever she said, he'd somehow twist it around against her. She glanced hopefully at Michael.

"Lisa hasn't been introduced to Chris, yet," he said.

Bobby looked irritated. "Oh, yeah, Lisa, this is Christine, Chris this is Lisa. I'm sure you girls got lots in common." He turned to his companion. "Listen, Chris, honey, can you do me a favor? Check that those dumb females with the makeup are ready for me backstage. Last time was a fucking shambles."

She gave him a cynical look, then glanced at Lisa, then sauntered away across the room.

"That woman's been pissing me off with her princess act," Bobby muttered. "I don't have time for these rich bitches who think they're fucking prima donnas." He gave Lisa a meaning look as he said it.

"I know how you feel," she said, nerves making her belly go tight, but determined to face Bobby down. "Personally, I tend to be put off when *men* are impressed with their own glamor."

"Well, now, is that right?" he said, poker-faced.

"Yes."

"You know, when a chick like you has to go out of her way to insult me I just know I've made an impression." He squeezed her shoulder again. "Why are you trying to put me down? Do I make you nervous or something?"

"Actually, you do." She pulled free again. "That's why I'm being defensive. What's . . . what's *your* excuse?"

He laughed loudly and turned to Michael. "Christ, where did you find this little weasel?" Then back to her. "Listen, you know and I know, there's several thousand little girls out there who'd give all they've got to just suck my cock. Now you're going out of your way to tell me, *you're* not like *them*. Well, you've made it clear. So let's cut the shit and act like human beings. Or do you have to go on defending your pride by insulting me? I'm not going to rape you, baby, believe me."

His complacency was irritating her more and more. "*Have* you ever raped anyone?"

"Sweetheart, most times they rape *me*. Which is what I like about you, I feel my sacred flesh is safe, you're not about to rip my fly open, right? Isn't that what you're trying to tell me?"

She clenched her fists in frustration. She realized that all she really wanted was to puncture his ego. But she could never accomplish that here. It would take a carefully staged situation ever to inflict an injury.

"How about if you ditch your stony-faced escort," Bobby gestured at Michael, "and take a walk with me. I'll bet you never seen backstage of a TE theater before."

"Sorry, it doesn't really interest me." She gave him a cold, polite smile.

"You mean you prefer this robot's company to mine?" He pantomimed surprise. "Jeez, Mike, some time you got to tell me the secret of your success with women."

"Oh, come now, Bobby, you don't need *my* advice." His voice was quiet, cool, amused.

"Sharp. Sharp." Bobby tapped his forehead. "Listen, Lisa," he focused on her again, intently, catching her off-guard. "I'm going to be looking for you after the concert. Get off your uptight little female ego and grok that what I'm offering don't come every night."

His change of tactics was too quick for her. Before she could think of a reply, Bobby turned away from her, catching sight of a heavy-set, middle-aged man with a face like a veteran boxer, creased into a permanent frown. He was pushing through the crowd of elegant people. He grabbed Bobby's arm.

"All right, I hear you," said Bobby. "I'm performing in fifteen minutes and it's makeup time."

"Right," said the weary-faced man. "So let's get downstairs."

"See you later, kiddos," said Bobby, and left.

"That's Owen, his manager," said Michael. "Keeps him in line, holds it all together. Used to be a stockbroker before the second crash."

"Oh." She turned on Michael. "Why didn't you help me out, then, when he was coming on to me like that?"

"You were so hot to meet him, I thought you were enjoying yourself."

"Don't give me that shit. You could see what was happening."

"Well, you looked like you could handle it."

"Well, I couldn't. Don't you see I'm nervous enough here as it is? I could have used some reassurance, at least."

He paused, choosing his words carefully. "I'm sorry," he said, no longer flippant, "but I don't take sides against Bobby. We have an understanding. Our partnership hinges on it. He doesn't really like me—thinks I'm a moody, supercilious bastard. I don't really like him either—he's offensive, loud, and boring. But he needs me to write his material; he could never do it himself. And I need him to present it, on stage, through the media, because I could never do *that* no matter what I might like to pretend. So we cooperate with each other."

She was slightly unsettled by his candor. "I see. I didn't realize. You're being very frank with me."

"I suppose I am. Maybe too frank. I don't know. That's the trouble, when I do start talking to someone. . . ." He trailed off. She waited for him to go on, but he didn't.

"Why *was* he coming on to me like that, anyway?" she said, finally. "That girl with him, Chris, looks more like his type. And she's exactly opposite to me."

"Bobby comes on to anyone who puts him down," said Michael. "And he liked the idea of stealing a girl who was with me. Usually, I inherit cast-offs from him."

"Oh."

"But you probably interested him, as well."

"Because I'm dressed like a tramp? And I'm rude?"

"Yes. Precisely."

"And that's what interests *you*, isn't it?"

He looked wary, defensive. "Partly." He glanced at his watch. "If you want to catch his act from the good seats, we have to get them now, before the other freeloaders move in. There's only seventy seats reserved for friends of the performer."

"All right."

They walked across the room side by side. She half expected him to put his arm around her, or take her hand, or show some other token of affection. But he walked out with her without even looking at her, and without touching her.

The Total Experience

For the concert, one half of the oval stadium had been blocked off, leaving a horseshoe of tiered seats looking down onto a giant semicircular stage that filled most of the remaining floor area. "Ten, twenty years ago we could've filled the whole place," Michael told Lisa, as they walked down a long flight of steps past security guards to seats near the stage. "But not since the birth-rate falloff and middle-income austerity. So we reckon on a crowd of seven thousand, filling the lower two tiers. It's still good business."

He showed her to a seat facing the stage dead-center and sat beside her. She looked up at the high, wide, domed roof, then around at the pre-teen kids coming into the stadium like a deputation from some imaginary nation where psychosis had become the norm. Their fashions were postunisex. Male costumes were heavy on black leather and scarlet silk and vinyl with elevator shoes, tight pants, codpieces, shirts slashed to the waist and decorated with obscure symbols, military insignia, and ornamental chains. They wore peaked caps, and their faces were painted in pale gray and blue, like Hitler Youth at a fancy-dress death-camp ball. Some affected scarlet nail polish and artificial fingernails sculpted into claws. Others had had their teeth augmented into fangs.

The female costumes were frilly and frivolous. They were daringly cut, revealing mounds of artificial flesh—inflated breasts, exaggerated hips. Transparent panels in the girlish pink-and-lavender frocks revealed jeweled navels, rouged nipples, and bleached pubic hair. The girls postured and posed as they walked.

Despite the exaggerated differentiation between the sexes the kids were indiscriminately physical. The males touched each other as much as they touched the females. They had a distracted, distant look in their hollow eyes as they moved vaguely to their seats in the hall. They seemed excited, sitting restlessly, turning their faces expectantly toward the empty stage, but they hardly spoke beyond a few half-formed syllables and subdued cries, their hands moving at random over each others' bodies as if searching for something.

Lisa watched them uneasily. "I feel like an old lady at twenty-three."

"To them, you are." He handed her one of the publicity handouts that had been scattered throughout the stadium. "This'll give you some background. I'm going to check with the box office, see how big a take we've got."

The paper he'd given her had a lot of simple-minded slogans and pictures on one side of it. On the back was a reprint from a serious newspaper: SUICIDE ROCK—PRE-TEEN DEATH SPREE. The text began under a publicity photo of Bobby sitting with his legs apart, one hand dangling near an obscene bulge in the crotch of his pants, the other hand holding a dagger which was shown realistically slitting his own throat. Fake blood was spurting. He was leering evilly into the camera.

The text read:

Pre-teen idol Bobby Black tells fans "Only thing you're free to do is die." Total Experience technology in natl tour terminating here Aug mindhammers "subtle" message: Suicide the only real escape, since "drugs, sex, money, fast cars, spectator sports don't work no more" to distract from grim socioeconomic situation.

Spartans of America condemn suicide message. Says Rev Isaacs "Black is sick, antilife, antisurvival, stuck in materialist rampant consumerism habits of summertime economy born in defunct decades of greed and plenty. Confronted with New Austerity, Age of Scarcity, Black pushes suicide instead of rational unscrewedup Spartan response: prolife, pro-survival in frugality/simplicity."

Radicals charge govt backs suicide rock fad as antipopulation pop propaganda. But Michael Caidin, Black's songwriter/conceptualizer, says "could never be govt sanctioned because it's antigovt, protesting contemporary social chaos. If kids kill selves and/or each other after listening to Bobby sing my songs I take no responsibility. I'm saying only what people were sensing vaguely already—being alive is no longer a viable alternative to being dead."

There was more, but she had to stop reading. The house lights were dimming. Michael came back and slipped into his seat just as the curtains opened. She was blasted with sound.

It was a taped intro. A giant white Diacora screen backing the stage lit up with projected depth-images, fizzing and exploding in the air inches from her eyes. She lifted her hand as if to touch the 3-D shapes; the silhouette of her fingers intruded like holes in the pattern. All around her the kids had started chanting: "Black! Black! Black!" like an expression of hope, of negative wish-fulfillment.

Backstage, technicians at mixing consoles synchronized sound, color, and odor. Revolving dish antennae sprayed bursts of microwaves across the audience. Subsonics shook the spectators in their seats.

And then Bobby was onstage and the giant depth-effect screen behind him lit up with a live twenty-foot image of his face, moving as he moved, painted into a parody of sadistic lust. The clamor of the music increased, and the pre-teens rose up with hungry open mouths screaming, hands reaching out blindly. Bobby's face hovered in front of their eyes, shimmering, chroma-keyed through rainbows of color. Then he started singing, his voice picked up by a subvocal microphone implanted inside his throat, and death lyrics boomed through the stadium, broadcasting hate, lust, power, despair, sex, doom, greed, anger, revenge.

Dust rose in the thundering noise. Guards wearing earplugs, respirators, and infra-red goggles moved methodically down the aisles, clubbing crazed kids who tried to grope blindly out of their seats toward the stage.

The first song ended and the second began straight away. Death images flickered across the giant screen: blood, knives, nooses, guns, jaws, shackles, swords, and torture devices, interspersed with subliminal flashes of genitals and breasts.

The show went on, and on, building slowly toward some unimaginable climax. Smoke generators around the hall came to life, blowing white clouds over the audience till the stage and its 3-D backdrop seemed to float alone in billowing mist, like a platform in the fires of hell. Flickering red laser beams enhanced the illusion.

And then a giant chair rose in the center of the stage, fitted with flashing, sparking, sizzling lights, sinister wires coiling up to a black metal skull cap and iron wrist-clamps. Still shouting out his suicide songs, Bobby moved toward the chair as if dragged against his will. He sank into it, and the skull cap slowly lowered itself. The music started building to a crescendo. He started into a kind of free-form rock-litany:

> I'm going
> Where there's no more pain
> The skies will open into a pool of blood
> I'll fly free like an angel on batwings
> Shimmering into the death-dawn
> Stars exploding, rip my flesh
> Lobotomize me, disembowel me
> I'm going
> No one to hold me, no one to control me
> Atomize my entrails in a white-hot blast
> Rip me into harmony with cosmic vacuum
> Crystal corridors of eternity
> Ejaculate death rays in a fireball of lust
> I'm going! I'm going!
> I can feel it! Feel it rising in me!

He grabbed an enormous, phallic lever and started pulling it up between his legs.

> The orgasm of self-destruction
> The ultimate release
> I'm going!
> Take me!

The whole scene erupted in a sizzling, flashing explosion of fireworks and electric blasts, magnesium flares, and, spouting from where the chair had been, a thick fountain of gallons of pseudo-blood, swamping the stage, spattering the screen behind it, washing down across the floor, surging and bubbling and giving off steam.

The music died into intermittent rumbles like the aftermath of a thunderstorm. The screen segued to a midnight blue. The audience went berserk, screaming and stamping, little bodies writhing in ecstasy.

The smoke gradually dispersed. The music died to a single funereal tolling bell. The giant electric chair was gone from the stage. In its place were four guards all in scarlet, with black angel wings trailing from their shoulders and crows' heads covering their faces. Between them they carried Bobby's blackened, bloody corpse. They marched slowly with it around the stage, and the screen displayed the scene enlarged for all the audience to see.

Gradually the pre-teens' hysteria died down. The guards paused, their feet ankle-deep in the red goo that still coated the stage. A trapdoor opened. They slowly sank down into it, carrying Bobby with them, out of sight.

After a long pause, the house lights came on.

The whole show had lasted around an hour, but to Lisa it had felt eternal, as if natural laws of time and space had been suspended. She found she was sticky with perspiration. She felt mentally bruised. She looked at Michael and found him sitting there calm, and detached.

"Not bad," he said.

She pushed a strand of lank hair out of her face. "Not good, not bad, beyond good and bad."

"That's what Total Experience is all about."

"Did you devise all of that?"

"Yes."

"You have a perverse imagination."

He laughed. "No, I just enjoy theater." He stood up. "Let's go backstage."

She got to her feet, feeling shaky. Most of the kids were already jamming the exits but here and there young figures were lying unconscious in their seats, like insects sprayed with pesticide.

"OD cases," said Michael. "They're pilled-up when they come here, and we circulate a gray-legal amphetamine gas through the air conditioning, as well. Some of them get completely wiped out. Here comes the Red Cross." White-coated staff were moving down the aisles.

"I thought for a moment maybe those kids had taken your songs' advice."

"What? Oh, you mean killed themselves?" he laughed. "That hasn't happened yet."

"In that publicity handout you said you wouldn't be surprised if it did."

"That's just publicity. Did you read my quote: 'being alive is no longer a viable alternative to being dead'? Isn't that a great line? I planted it for the *Times* to pick up, people like that, social commentators. They loved it. Big piece in last week's Arts and Leisure section. 'New Nihilism in Rock.'"

"You're pretty cynical."

"No, I'm not. It's just a game, that's all. There'll be some completely different mania six months from now."

"There will? What can you do to follow death by suicide?"

"I've been thinking about it," he said, missing her irony. "It's a problem."

She felt queasy without quite knowing why. It wasn't his cynicism or disregard for the audience as human beings. It was more his coldness that disturbed her. His distance.

He led her through a side exit and along backstage corridors to a guarded doorway where a gang of blank-faced pre-teens were waiting like a pack of cowed wolves. The guards recognized Michael and admitted him with Lisa, while the pre-teens watched, envy mixed with malice in their eyes.

Bobby was just coming out of his dressing room, magically

resurrected after his act, traces of makeup still visible. There was a smug expression on his face, and he walked with a bounce in each step, still riding on the adrenaline high of his own performance.

"Like it?" he said to Lisa. "Wasn't it really something?"

"I guess it's not really my sort of thing," she said.

He didn't hear her. "Tell you what," he was saying, taking her arm, "there's a nice little place fifteen minutes from here. The Connection. They got the biggest choice of ups and downs around, legal and gray-legal, and in the back you can fuck your body as well as your mind. Sensie gadgets and movies, prosthetics, know what I mean?"

She rubbed her forehead wearily. "No, I don't know."

"Yeah, well, you'd really get off on it. What's the matter? Want Mike to come, too? That's cool. There's room for a threesome. Or a foursome. I'll get Chris . . ."

"No. No, thanks."

". . . or maybe we can pick up a coupla kids out there," he gestured at the stage door, "have us a *real* little party." He grinned evilly.

"No!" she said again, as forcefully as she could. And yet even as she said it she felt as if she were being a drag, conservative, unimaginative, cutting herself off from a decadent experience that perhaps she was afraid she might enjoy.

"So what the fuck is it with you?" said Bobby.

"This evening has been all so sudden, so weird," she said lamely. "Maybe . . . maybe some other time."

He studied her coolly for a moment. "Don't count on it," he snapped, then turned and walked away before she could answer. He slammed the door behind him. She realized he'd done it calculatedly, for effect, but she was left feeling she'd missed a never-to-be-repeated chance—exactly the way he'd wanted her to feel.

"You look tired," said Michael, beside her.

She felt empty. "Yes, I guess I am tired."

"There's a guest room back in my apartment if you want to use it, tonight."

She looked at him warily.

"You told me yourself you haven't got a home to go to," he pointed out. "Really, I'm not trying to involve you in anything."

"I guess you're not. Yes, okay, that'll be fine. Where do you live?"

"In one of the new havens, about ten miles from here. I'll call us a taxi."

"You don't have a car?"

"Not here. I was using Bobby's while he was on tour. He'll repossess it now. And I don't think it'd be tactful to ask him to give us a ride back to my place, do you?"

She smiled. Then she laughed. "No. It wouldn't be tactful." She looked at him. "Look, I want to thank you."

"What for?"

"For—I don't know. I'm kind of a suspicious person, you get that way in the city, but you've been a nice guy. You haven't given me a hard time."

"It wouldn't get me very far if I did," he said.

WE MIGHT AS WELL BE DEAD

We thought the door was open, tomorrow was here
But don't believe what you hear
There isn't a tomorrow and there isn't any door
So what are we living for?

> I say, hey, what happened to the future?
> They told us it was just ahead
> I say, hey, seems there isn't any future
> And nothing to look forward to instead
> I guess we might as well be dead
> Yeah, we might as well be dead

No way things can get better, the ship's going down
So man, if we're all gonna drown
What's the point of hanging on to the last?
Better get it over with fast

(chorus)

The more you go on living, the less they let you do
And this ain't just a phase we're going through
It's going to get worse, and that ain't no lie
The only thing you're free to do is die

(chorus)

I been around and seen about all there is to see
And this world is a depressing place to be
Now there's only one more journey that is left for me to take
A trip from which I'll never awake

(chorus)

THE HAVEN

Michael lived in a high-income development, a haven, one of several just outside city limits. It had an electric-fenced perimeter, a private police force making frequent internal patrols, and was completely covered with closed-circuit TV.

He let Lisa into his apartment and operated the complex locking mechanism on the door while she wandered into the living room, glancing at his furnishings and paintings, books and electronic equipment as if unimpressed.

He felt weird, as if he were watching her and himself from somewhere else rather than participating in reality. He had talked to her before the concert more than he had planned to—more than he usually talked to any woman. Something about her had gotten to him, and he had no idea how it had happened.

"Would you like something?" he asked her. "Coffee, pills, liquor?"

"You have real coffee?" She looked at him with sudden interest.

"Of course." What else would I have, he thought. "Come into the kitchen."

She followed him. Her presence made him uncomfortable. He wondered if she realized that. Probably not; he knew he didn't show much. And usually he was happy to seem unresponsive; it protected him from over-demanding situations. But she seemed so natural and spontaneous, he felt neurotically introverted by comparison. And he wasn't sure what she expected from him—if anything. It made him edgy.

"Why did you come back with me?" he said abruptly, turning and looking at her directly for the first time.

She seemed surprised. "I—thought you wanted me to. You invited me." No trace of artifice in her manner.

"You could have gone off for an interesting time with Bobby, instead."

"I'm sorry. I didn't know you wanted to be alone."

"I didn't mean to imply that. I'm glad you're here. I just don't quite understand. . . ."

"*You* don't understand." She laughed awkwardly. "Do you think *I* know what's going on? I can't make you out. You talk to me, but it's as if you're living on some other plane. You act like you're interested, and yet you don't. You invite me back, but then ask why I came and tell me I could have had a better time going out with your . . . your business partner." She paused. "I hardly know where I am, let alone who you are."

He didn't know what to say. He poured coffee for her clumsily, spilling a little. "Let's go and sit down."

They sat by the window. It overlooked a brightly lit, immaculate, tree-lined avenue beyond which other apartment buildings in the haven stood with windows glowing in the night. She studied the view for a moment, then looked away as if she had exhausted its interest value and wouldn't bother with it again. She turned toward him, sitting forward in her chair in a pose that was so unlike the studied boredom affected by most of the women who spent time with him and made inconsequential conversation that was just a polite ritual prefacing sex.

"Evidently you don't realize," he said, picking his way slowly and carefully, "that since I met you earlier, I've been very interested in you."

"Interested in me in what way? As a curiosity, or a way of broadening your outlook on life, or . . ."

"Interested in you as a person."

"Oh. I wasn't sure." She sounded skeptical.

"And I find you difficult to talk to because you're very different from the kind of woman I'm used to."

"I'm sorry," she said, defensively yet uncompromisingly, as if implying, there's nothing I can do about *that*. Then, as an afterthought: "I have the same problem with you."

"Well, I guess we've told each other where we stand." He wasn't used to talking personally and bluntly. It made him self-conscious. "Incidentally, I don't want you to think that I've forgotten my promise about replacing the things of yours that you lost. I'll give you cash enough to go shopping tomorrow, if you like. I don't fink out on my obligations."

"Fine. I mean, thank you."

There was an awkward silence. "I expect you'll head off out to that place in the country again, as soon as you have all you need."

"I suppose so," she said.

"You can certainly stay here a few extra days," he said, trying to sound casual, "if you want to."

"I'd feel kind of out of place."

"You'd be welcome here." He felt he was opening himself to her, much too much, and yet he didn't know how else to deal with her.

"Well, thanks," she said. "Let's see how it goes."

"Why exactly are you so set on getting out of the city, ultimately? Because you grew up in the country and you miss it?"

She sighed. "I don't think you understand how it is, living in town without much money. I've been here three years. I wanted to get a job as a graphic designer. There aren't any jobs, unless you have experience or know someone. So I've lived on state handouts. I've been robbed at least twenty times in the street, raped twice, my apartment . . ." She stopped, seeing that he was looking uncomfortable. "What's the matter?"

"Do you want me to feel guilty, because I'm wealthy and you're not?"

"No, I just want you to *understand.* People like you, with money, avoid the ghetto zones. And people like me are literally fenced out of places where you live. There's no communication between rich and poor. Even on TV, you don't see our street battles and demos because it's censored—too inflammatory. We don't see your lifestyle because it would be bad policy for the government to let poor people realize how well the rich have managed to continue living, despite the so-called New Austerity and Age of Scarcity."

"The news isn't censored. You're full of paranoid ideas. And it's still possible for people who aren't rich to get rich. I'm from a wealthy family, it's true, but Bobby came up from the bottom —a slum in the worst part of town."

"Bullshit! The old American dream, the old con—your pal Bobby, are you telling me he achieved success from his humble beginnings and achieved it *honestly?*"

"Well, he used to do some dope pushing, hustling, that's all."

"Sure he did. Because there isn't any other way to make it. You have to be mean enough and ruthless enough to get what you want by ripping off other people, till you've stolen enough from them to invest in something legitimate—like *suicide rock.* I'd rather stay poor than live like that."

"I see." He was expressionless.

"And if you don't believe the news is censored, you're a fool. Did you see on your screen," she gestured at the big silvered rectangle on the wall, "anything about the middle-income unemployment demonstration two nights ago? Right here in the city?"

"What demonstration?"

"What demonstration. Five city blocks were trashed and at least fifteen cops were killed. I know, because I was lucky enough to be living in the middle of it. And you wonder why I want to move out to a farm in the country."

He wondered if he could really believe everything she was saying. He'd assumed things were tough for ghetto dwellers, he'd assumed there was pressure on TV networks to play down material that might cause unrest, but. . . . Suddenly he realized she was crying, hiding her face from him.

Surprised and strangely moved by her tears, he found himself moving over to her, not quite knowing what to do. He touched her shoulder. She didn't respond. He put his arm around her. She felt strangely different from any other woman he could remember touching, and he realized it was because her shoulders were broader, she was not petite and ineffectual, she had muscles and hard firm flesh. "I'm sorry," he heard himself say. "Please don't cry."

She knuckled the tears away. It had been a brief spasm of self-pity. "It's not your fault, it's nothing to do with you." She sniffed, keeping her face turned away. "I'm not so simpleminded as to hate you just because you're rich and you've got all the things I never had. That's just the way things *are*, that's all."

He sat down beside her, close to her. "There's nothing I can say."

"I know; it's okay; I'm sorry I got upset. I'm very tired." Finally, she turned to look at him. Her face was weary and sad. For the first time, she seemed defenseless, all the barriers down. He stroked her tear-moist cheek with his finger, then slid his hand down to her neck and bent his head to kiss her. Their lips touched for perhaps ten seconds in a kiss that was tentative yet strong, intense, sharing half-felt, half-understood emotions. Then abruptly she pulled away.

"I think I'd better go to sleep," she said, avoiding his eyes. "Don't get mad at me. I'm not rejecting you. I like you, and I think you're very attractive but I'm feeling too shattered, too confused, I need a little time. You understand?" The words tumbled out quickly and mechanically, in a hurried attempt at politeness.

He realized he felt no resentment or anger at her retreat from him. "I'll show you where the bedroom is," he said.

She looked relieved, obviously having expected him to try to argue her into sleeping with him. She stood up. "The coffee was delicious," she said, gesturing at her empty cup. "I'm used to synthetic."

"There's more where that came from." His eyes met hers and she sensed what he was telling her. She smiled awkwardly, looking embarrassed.

He showed her his seldom-used guest room, with its private bathroom. Then he walked back into the living room and sat for a long time, staring out at the night.

Out there, he knew, were millions of people as poor as Lisa, most of them barely educated, stuck in conditions of poverty. He'd been brought up believing that if you stayed poor it was your own fault, and despite what Lisa had said, he still tended to think along those lines, even though he could see that it wasn't necessarily true anymore, now that the economy was so bad. The auto industry almost bankrupt, twenty percent unemployment in middle-income groups. . . . And yet, America was well off compared to some other countries. There was said to be starvation in places like Ireland, Denmark, and Italy. Some of the doom that everyone had predicted twenty years ago had come true in some parts of the world—resource shortages, especially, and famine resulting from overpopulation and crop failures.

In the USA many businesses had failed when productivity had been unable to keep pace with the cost of raw materials, leading to the now-familiar combination of unemployment, recession, and inflation. But the country was still strong; no one went hungry. It was government policy to avert social unrest by feeding people, and housing them if necessary. And some industries were actually doing well. Like the entertainment business. People needed a way to deal with life's bad news, to escape or at least reprocess it to make it more easily digestible. That was why suicide rock had worked. It was a camped-up way of turning the truth into a sick joke, so that you could enjoy it.

Michael stood up and walked through to his study, a small formal office in white and gray. He ran his fingers along the keyboard of his synthesizer, then picked up an old tape cartridge from his library and put it on the player.

"What You Get Is What You Take." His first song for Bobby. Their first small success. It sounded dated, now. And yet there was still some truth in it. Even Lisa would agree to that. Her question would be: is it right for the world to be that way?

He snapped the music off irritably, realizing he was miring himself in a sophomoric debate about social inequities. Certainly times were hard for many people right now. But where was it written that Americans had an inalienable right to eat meat every day and take annual vacations in Europe? Life had been more of a free ride in the decades of greed and plenty—the fifties, sixties, seventies. Who had ever believed that that was going to be permanent? Anyway, luxuries should be *earned;* they were rewards for people who were clever and worked hard enough and were lucky enough to deserve them.

Maybe there were a few unusual cases like Lisa—intelligent, even talented perhaps, but trapped in poverty because they were not aggressive enough to succeed. And maybe, as she said, things were intolerable in the ghetto zones. But that, definitely, was not his fault. He paid taxes—a hell of a lot of taxes—to local and national government agencies that had the responsibility to control crime, create jobs, and provide social services. Evidently government wasn't doing its job. Was he supposed to feel guilty about that?

He left his study and walked quietly to his bedroom, feeling that he'd resolved the questions she had raised. For a while he lay awake, examining in his imagination her serious, strong, yet gentle face. Then he slept, soundly, as he always did.

WHAT YOU GET IS WHAT YOU TAKE

People all around you
City air and sound, you
Have to fight for what you make
What you get is what you take

In this modern living
Businessmen ain't giving
Anyone an even break
What you get is what you take

> Statesmen, corporations
> Talk of conservation
> They know the score
> They're the ones who use it
> We're the ones who lose it
> Soon there's no more

Move while you still can, there
Ain't much longer than a
Couple of years before it breaks
What you get is what you take

> Saving for the future?
> Isn't any future
> Scrap all your plans
> Shortage of resources
> Brother your best course is
> Grab what you can

Do it now, if you don't
Do it now then you won't
Ever see your slice of cake
What you get is what you take

Satisfaction

A few hours earlier Bobby had taken Chris home with him from the concert. He was in a mean mood. Lisa had screwed up his evening. She'd damaged his car and she'd damaged his ego, though he'd never give her the satisfaction of knowing that. Little poor girl from the ghetto—she'd turned Bobby down as if he were nothing at all, and she'd gone off with Michael instead. That wasn't the way things were meant to work.

He didn't understand it. There were a million women like Lisa, with their hard-luck stories and shabby clothes and squalid lives, hanging around the city, leeching off the state. Bobby could pick up any one of them just by showing his face and his car, couldn't he? Well, couldn't he?

He drove the Toronado onto a divided highway that circled the urban center. Chris slouched in the passenger seat beside him, idly turning the pages of a magazine. He put his foot down hard and took the car up to a steady ninety-five, headlights sweeping, the blacktop blurring under the hood. Hardly any traffic these days, so anyone with enough clout or connections to get a private vehicle permit could drive as fast as he liked.

"They got an article here about that new operation, Bobby," said Chris.

He frowned, distracted. "What operation?"

"In the magazine here. To make girls smaller."

"Huh?"

"*You* know. They give the girl a kind of drug and do an operation to shrink the bones to like make her shorter, you end up like what they call petite, like a twelve-year-old."

"That's insane."

"Well, I'd like it."

"Ah, you're crazy."

"You'd appreciate it. I'd be real cute. And I could get that treatment, too, the one makes your what-you-call-them, hair roots, follicles go dead."

"You want your hair dropping out?"

"You're always complaining when there's fuzz under my arms or I haven't shaved my legs."

"Yeah, but what about the hair on your head?"

"I'd get a living wig."

Bobby paused. "Pubic hair—it kills that too?"

"They replace it with an implant. It's more hygienic."

Bobby rubbed his hand across his face. He wasn't in the mood for this. "What is it, you trying to gross me out or something?"

"No, Bobby."

"So what are you talking all this crap for?"

"I was just reading in the magazine. I could be like petite and smooth-skinned, it'd be nice for you that's all."

"Yeah? No shit."

"I want to be the way you want me."

He sighed. "Listen, Goddamn it, you're fine the way you are, okay? Just fine."

"Then how come you keep *ignoring* me? Are you thinking about that woman you saw with Michael? I mean is there any woman in the world you *don't* want to screw?"

"She's common as dirt, she don't interest me. Now just read your fucking magazine and get off of my back." He switched the radio on and the car interior filled instantly with loud music.

Chris slumped down moodily in her seat. She stared up at her own reflection in the mirror-paneled underside of the car roof. She looked synthetically good, she thought. But she was getting a little old for it all, pushing eighteen. . . .

The music ended. "Men, are you tired, rundown?" the DJ cut in. "Giving more than you got? Men, do you get so's you can't face another challenge you're afraid you can't meet? Another . . . failure to perform?" The voice dropped lower, becoming confidential. "Do women demand more than you can supply? Do you find it hard sometimes to satisfy, to . . . get up an interest . . . when you're alone together? Do you feel limp when you should be full of pep? Soft when you oughta be hard? Well, men," the voice suddenly perked up, becoming hearty, confident, "now there's a new product that really works to relieve those embarrassing bedroom scenes. . . ."

Bobby reached out and angrily turned the radio off. He glared at Chris. "Look, you don't *own* me, understand?"

Chris didn't look up. "I know. You always tell me."

"Yeah, so listen for once, and quit picking on me."

"I wasn't picking on you. I want to please you, that's all."

"Bullshit. You pretend you're jealous, you know that makes me mad. Makes *you* feel *good,* getting through to me."

"I don't feel good for having made you mad."

"Then why do you always do it?"

"I *don't.*" She sniffed, wriggled her shoulders, and slumped down still further in her seat, edging away from him.

"Jesus Christ, will you stop that? Your little routine over there."

"I can't help it if you make me unhappy." A little pause. "I guess I ought to know by now, you don't give a shit about what I want or how I feel."

"Like hell I don't."

She turned and stared at him. "Prove it."

Their eyes met. He put his foot hard on the brake. The car's speed dropped through the seventies, sixties, fifties. Tires squealing, it came to a stop on the shoulder of the highway. "All right," he said, "yeah, all right." He pressed a button and the armor-glass windows began to darken, shutting out the highway where garbage blew in the wind under smashed streetlights, decaying billboards, and route direction signs. He pressed a switch and the interior lights of the car segued from white to red. The seat reclined under them with a soft hum. She gave a little-girl scream of mock surprise as he grabbed her.

He tore roughly at her dress.

She was suddenly more self-possessed. "I'll do that." She took his hands away and released the three fasteners that held the garment together.

Soon the big luxury car was swaying on its springs as he had sex with her quickly and angrily, like a man spanking a child, while she watched him and made excited female noises, her face showing a quieter kind of satisfaction.

DIE WITH ME

You hate your folks, your school, your home
And long to be
Far far away and all alone
With only me
You hate the nowhere life you lead
The trap from which you can't be freed
But darling there's one answer to forever
Free both of us to always be together

First you'll lie with me
And feel me inside
And you'll fly with me
On a sensual ride
Then you'll sigh with me
After we come
And you'll cry with me
For what must be done
Is to die with me
To find our release
Die with me
Your troubles will cease
Die with me
Forever at peace
Die with me

You say I'm all you care about
To me you cling
The real world you could do without
I'm everything
You scheme and dream of an escape
From iron walls of life you hate
Well darling there's one way to be together
Alone in love, for you and me, forever

(chorus)

Our suicide
Will be forgiven
After we've died
We'll go to heaven!

(repeat verse one and chorus)

The Pleasure Palace

Lisa woke early. Sun streamed through the windows of the guest room. She had neglected to draw the drapes the previous night. For a while she lay in the wide bed, on the cool clean sheets, reliving the events of yesterday as if to make sure they had really happened. But this room, with its soft bed and carpet and faint hiss of air conditioning maintaining coolness like eternal springtime—it told her the events had been real.

She got out of bed, pulled on her shirt and jeans, and went to the kitchen, the carpets tickling the soles of her feet, the mellow colors of the comfortable living room glowing in morning sunlight. Michael was nowhere to be seen.

She looked in the refrigerator and found real orange juice, real milk, real bacon . . . nothing reconstituted, nothing powdered. For a moment she felt reluctant to touch the food, but then realized this reluctance was irrational, and part of her attitude generally. Ever since the car accident she'd been caught between resenting the wealth of the people she'd encountered and trying to let herself enjoy what they had to offer. She wasn't a poor person with so much pride she'd rather do without than eat at a rich man's table, was she?

She started cooking some bacon and drank a glass of orange juice. It tasted as good as a dream. Then she cooked toast, ate it with the bacon, and drank some milk. She felt a momentary twinge of anger, convinced that Michael didn't appreciate (and therefore didn't deserve) his fresh foods because he didn't know what it was like to live on substitutes all the time.

At that moment the phone rang. She hesitated, then decided to answer it. She picked it up before it could ring twice.

"Hello?"

"Is that Lisa?" a voice asked.

"Yes. Who's this?"

"Bobby."

"You want to speak to Michael? I think he's still asleep."

"I figured he would be. I wanted to speak to you."

She hesitated. "What about?"

"Come *on,* baby, you're still frozen up like I'm a door-to-door salesman, for Christ's sake. I ain't selling nothing."

She shook her head as if to clear it. "I'm sorry. I didn't expect the phone to ring. I was thinking . . ."

"Yeah, okay, so how about if you meet me downstairs in fifteen minutes from now? I mean, provided you have the *time,* I mean don't let me *bother* you, if you and Mike have *plans* . . ."

"No, I don't think we have any plans for today."

"Then I'll see you, let's see, around ten."

"For what? I don't . . ."

"Ever been to a pleasure palace?"

"No." She thought. "I remember reading something about it."

"Yeah, it was all over the media a couple of weeks back, when it opened. So how about it?"

She hadn't expected him to call. She had an idea that if she turned him down this time, he wouldn't try again. She remembered how she'd felt the previous night, wondering what she might have missed. "I don't know if a pleasure palace is my kind of thing," she told him, "but I'd like to try it."

If he was surprised that she was interested, he didn't show it. "Fine. Get your ass into some decent clothes, huh? You ought to be able to find a shirt and a pair of pants there that'll fit you."

"All right."

He hung up without saying anything more. She put the phone down. Then she looked up and gave a little jump, seeing Michael standing in the living room doorway in a robe, leaning against the wall, watching her.

"I thought you were asleep," she said.

"The phone woke me."

"Oh."

"It's okay, you know." He walked across the living room to the kitchen. "I kind of expected you to go out with Bobby sooner or later. It might as well be sooner." He opened the refrigerator.

"You expected me to?" she followed him into the kitchen.

"He *is* famous," Michael took out some eggs and broke one into a mixing bowl. "He *is* handsome," he broke another, "he *has* got charm," he broke another, throwing the shells away. "He's a big-mouth, of course, but the thing about big-mouths is, you're left suspecting maybe there's some truth behind all the hype. And once you start wondering about it, you have to find out, to satisfy your curiosity." He started beating the eggs, methodically and firmly.

"You act so detached all the time."

"What do you want, for me to be jealous of him?"

She sighed. "No, I guess I don't want anything from you." She started to turn away, but he dropped the fork he was using, and caught her arm. "Listen—you're the type who'll do what you want either way, regardless of anything I have to say."

"But what do *you* want me to do?"

"I invited you to stay here. I thought that that was clear."

"Yes, that's true, you did."

"Well, then."

"Perhaps I just wanted you to express more of an interest," she said. "I still don't understand you very well."

"Maybe you need more practice."

She forced a laugh. "Maybe you're right."

He went back to beating the eggs.

"Look, can I borrow some clothes? I'm sorry, but all I have is my jeans and shirt. You're not so different in size from me."

He looked at her and a momentary flash of frustration showed on his face. Then he turned and led her to the bedroom and gave her what she needed.

After she dressed she went straight down to the lobby of the building. She realized she'd felt uncomfortable with Michael ever since she'd met him. There was so much about him that was concealed. At least with a hustler like Bobby she knew what to expect.

And yet as she walked out from the cool lobby into the warm

morning she couldn't help glancing up behind her at Michael's windows, wondering if he were watching her.

She walked to the gently curving avenue, laid out so precise and neat between the trees and the other apartment blocks, as sterile as an architect's visualization. She sat on the curb in the sunlight, and waited.

A little later Bobby arrived in his Toronado, its rear fender still buckled where she'd rammed it the previous day in her stolen station wagon. It seemed a long time ago.

She stood up as he stopped the car beside her. The passenger door opened itself with a soft hum. "Hi," he said, chewing gum, dressed in an open jacket and shirt that exposed half of his chest, matted with hair. "Get in. It's kind of hot out there."

She got in. The car was cool.

"How ya doing?" he said, accelerating along the street.

"I'm fine."

A gate up ahead was opened for them by a guard watching impassively from his armored cubicle. They passed between the high electric fences disguised by foliage.

"Kind of a nice day," said Bobby.

"Yes. It is."

"So. You never been to the pleasure palace before."

She drew her legs up under her on the seat and turned her back to the passenger door, so that she faced him. "You don't need to make conversation," she told him.

He flashed her an irritated look. Then he shrugged and turned on the radio. A commercial came blasting through: "It's his eyes get ta me, those eyes of his, they make me like I don't know what I'm doin, I want him to like walk all over me, take me, tie me, do it ta me, rape me." The gushing female voice was garbled, inarticulate. "I'll be his slave how ever he wants on account of his eyes, the way they shine, that gleam he gets from Allure, ya know Allure eyeglo, gives that shine. Allure—medically certified, does not inhibit natural moisture in mucus membranes—Allure, makes me know what he wants, do what he

wants when I see it in his eyes *baby you can do it to me.*" The
track dissolved into grunting, gasping effects, smashing glass,
shouts, a cry.

"Do we have to listen to this?" she said over the noise.

Another irritated glance. "You want the music, you got to
take the plugs."

"So maybe we could do without." She turned the radio off.

"Shit, what is this?" He looked at her. "You *trying* already to
piss me off, or does it just come natural?"

"Natural, I guess." She smiled.

"Shit." He took the car onto the old expressway and boosted
their speed, gliding along under the morning sun. The city was
a haze-gray silhouette to the left. Suburbs lay ahead. They drove
in silence for a while.

"There's the palace, up ahead," he said eventually. He pointed
out a massive building, a mountain of giant slabs standing on
the edge of the river that divided city from suburbia. The rectangular concrete faces of the palace were windowless, bare, impassive. Giant neon signs on its roof flashed like an electric
crown.

"Is it open? It must still be early," said Lisa.

Bobby touched a silver button on the instrument console.
"Ten-nineteen and twenty-seven seconds," a soft electronic voice
murmured. He gave her a pleased look as if he'd somehow gen-
erated the operation of the gadget all by himself.

Suddenly she started laughing.

"Funny?" he said.

"You're just . . . just too much."

"Yeah, ain't I?" He grinned back at her.

They left the car in a cavernous basement garage and took an
escalator up to the entrance hall of the building. Bobby paid,
and they walked through into a maze of moving floors, shifting
light curtains, vibrating and pulsing walls, and music drifting

at random from above, below, and behind. Glowing signs on walls and ceiling listed routes to light rides, isolation tanks, cybernet, dream explorer, zero G baths.

Lisa held on to Bobby's arm, bewildered by the shifting 3-D effects and strobe lights calculated to sever reality referents right from the start. Mist rose out of the floor, which suddenly turned transparent so that she seemed to be walking a hundred feet above Niagara Falls. The floor tilted. Roaring and gushing noises filled the air. A floor section slid sideways, taking them with it, through a section of wall that opened in front of them.

They found themselves in a kind of mirror-maze, where the mirrors were liquid crystals, perpetually shifting from silver to transparent to opaque and back again. Lisa stepped forward, blundered into a transparent section, stepped sideways and found herself in a dead end.

"Over here," Bobby called. She looked around and saw multiple images of him, shifting and changing, fading like mirages, then reappearing in different areas altogether.

She started toward where she thought he was standing. A panel in front of her suddenly turned crimson and flashed a picture of a skeleton at her. Maniac laughter bellowed down from the ceiling. She stepped back, bumped into another panel.

"Hey, c'mon, Lisa." He sounded amused. "Where you at?"

She steadied herself, tried another path. Suddenly an image solidified in front of her—a man with a club, wild-eyed and vicious, running toward her. He opened his mouth and a blood-chilling yell came out.

Lisa stepped back. The image faded.

Hands gripped her from behind. She struggled, then looked around and saw it was Bobby.

"You'll spend the rest of your life in here if you go on like that," he told her.

"It was so realistic."

"Sure it is. Holograms. Project it right in front of you. But it ain't real. You got to face it down." He guided her forward.

The man with the club came to life again, running at them. Bobby kept on walking, right into the image. The man's scream became louder, enveloping them. Then suddenly they were through it, to the other side. "See? That's the only way you get to the top of this maze," he told her. "It's rigged that way, understand?"

She nodded blankly. He led her through the rest of the effects —locomotives charging at them, cars careening out of control with their horns blasting, Indians waving tomahawks, monsters dripping slime, soldiers firing machine guns.

Suddenly they were outside of the maze, in a plush, red hallway where canned music was playing.

"That was . . . an experience," she said.

"Nah, that's just for starters. Come on, in here." He led her down the hallway through another door.

Inside it was an inferno of noise: a synthesis of automobile horns, breaking glass, fingernails across a blackboard, screams of agony, roaring motorcycle engines, exploding bombs, jet engines, pounding jackhammers. Blinding flashes of white light swept down from the ceiling in tangible sheets. The floor jerked and trembled. Stomach-turning odors wafted through. Fans blasted freezing air, then a tornado of oven-hot wind that scorched the skin. Particles of steaming dry ice blasted out of the wall.

People were packed in the room, stumbling around, dazed and looking for a way out. Lisa and Bobby stood half-blinded by the effects. "Ain't this something?" he yelled to her.

"Out!" she shouted. "I want to get out!"

"Yeah, but it ain't that easy." He gestured behind them, where the entry door had closed and was now engulfed in a waterfall. Drops of water splashed onto them, showing it was real and not just another illusion.

Lisa went to the wall and touched it. The floor started giving way. She sank in up to her ankles. The wall gave her a sharp electric shock.

Bobby went over and took her hand, pausing to fend off other people blundering around, dazed but euphoric expressions on their faces.

He guided Lisa slowly around the perimeter of the room, through screeching, hollering noises and insanely flashing lights, billowing steam, and one odor after another. He kept testing the wall. Finally, he touched a spot that turned red-hot in response. He moved back a little, then pushed at the wall segment with his foot. There was a momentary smell of burning rubber as the wall singed the sole of his shoe. Then, abruptly, it gave way, and they found themselves blundering through soundproof doors, into another red passageway, where Muzak was still playing.

The doors swung shut behind them and cut off the furor of the chamber they had left. Lisa leaned against the wall to get her breath back. "What was that?" she gasped.

"Aggression chamber," he said. "It's programmed so it throws back at you anything that you throw at it. With a lot of people in it, it goes fucking berserk." He laughed. "And if you try to get out, it just gives you a harder time."

"You enjoy that kind of thing?"

"Sure. It gets you going."

"Isn't there somewhere in this place that's a bit, you know, *quieter*? I mean it is called a *pleasure* palace, isn't it?"

"Okay, I know just the thing."

"I'm serious, I don't want anything more like that," she gestured at the doors behind them.

"Yeah, I'm not bullshitting you, I know just what you want." He led her down the corridor, then up an escalator, through to the Love Garden.

Some citizens' groups had protested when the Love Garden had been opened in the palace, but they were a moralistic minority. Most people could see the need for a place where couples could go to feel alone in a romantic setting, now that the nearest open country was out of reach of many city dwellers because of soaring costs of leisure transportation.

Bobby led Lisa through two sets of doors, into semi-darkness. She found herself in an area as big as a movie auditorium. High above was a black sky of artificial stars and a replica of the full moon, shedding just enough light to see by. The floor stretched away in gentle undulating hills and hollows, matted with long plastic grass. Somewhere a nightingale warbled, and a soft breeze wafted through the man-made darkness.

Even at this time of the morning the place was crowded. Couples lay in the landscaped hollows, half naked, clothes tangled, bodies barely concealed from view. Behind the sound of the nightingale there was the laboring of giant fans, circulating deodorizer and disinfectant. Guards with infrared goggles stood unobtrusively in observation cubicles around the edges of the area.

"See, you can almost imagine like you're in a meadow some place," said Bobby.

She looked at him to see if he were being sarcastic, but it was too dark to read his expression. "It smells," she said.

"It's okay when you're out there lying down," he told her. "It's a real illusion. The way they've fixed it, you feel private, like you're alone outdoors. Except it's better—no insects, no damp grass, hard earth, cold wind, all that."

"But . . ."

A couple stood up nearby. They started walking toward the exit, the woman straightening her dress clumsily.

"C'mon," said Bobby, taking her hand and pulling her toward the freshly-vacated hollow.

"Couldn't we . . ."

"C'mon, try it."

She followed him reluctantly and sat down beside him in a dip in the "ground." The plastic grass was limp and slimy under her legs. The imitation soil was foam-lined; it sagged like a soft mattress. It was heated, reminding her of a recently vacated bed.

"Lie down so's all you can see is the sky," he said, putting his arm around her.

She did so.

Behind her she heard a couple coming to orgasm, grunting and gasping. To her left was the noise of a zipper opening. To her right, a muffled giggle. Her skin prickled.

She turned her head to Bobby to say something, but he quickly took her face between his hands and kissed her on the mouth.

Lisa hesitated between pulling back and responding. Finally she let herself be kissed, passively. She tried to concentrate only on Bobby's presence—his hard, aggressive body and his mouth on hers.

Then she pulled free. "Not here," she said.

"Oh, come on." He grabbed her again.

She brought her arms up between him and her and pressed the palms of her hands against his chest. "No." The word was flat and final.

He lay back on his elbow. "Shit, what *is* it with you? Why the fuck am I wasting my time here?"

"Listen," she said softly, "I'm not just trying to give you a hard time. Maybe I do want to make it with you, see how it feels with you. But not *here*. I don't like this place."

"You think you're some kind of special deal? I've brought women here who . . ."

"I don't care *who* you've screwed here," she said, her voice low but hard. "If I'm going to have sex with you I want to be able to enjoy it."

He grinned. "Oh, you'll enjoy it." His hand went out to her thigh.

She caught him by the wrist. "I *can't* enjoy it here, don't you see that? Will you *listen* to me?"

"Okay, okay, so what *do* you want?"

She brooded a moment. "Well, you're so rich and you've got a car, why don't we go out somewhere that's real? I mean real countryside. Why should we have to settle for this cheap imitation?"

"Jesus Christ. Come on." He took her hand and helped her

to her feet, then led her toward the exit. From the corner of her eye she saw another couple eagerly claiming the spot she'd vacated.

"Where are we going?" she asked him, as they walked out.

"I'm taking you home, that's where you're going."

For a moment she looked crushed. Then philosophical. "If that's what you want."

"No, it's not what I want, but I ain't going to be pushed around by . . ."

"Did you consider you might *enjoy* it? Going out of the city with me? I mean when was the last time you even saw the open countryside?"

They took an escalator down to ground level. "I only just come back from a tour all over the country," he said.

"I know you travel a lot. I mean when was the last time you took a break and went out somewhere where there aren't a lot of people and noise? Where there aren't any buildings?"

He shrugged irritably. "Fuck, I don't know."

"That's what I thought. It would do you good."

"Do me good?" he laughed. "Who are you, my doctor?"

"You don't know who I am."

"Ah, you're full of shit."

She put her hand on his arm. "Please, Bobby."

They paused opposite each other at the bottom of the escalator. He avoided her eyes. "Shit, all right, come on." He led her out of the building. "I got some friends. They have a farm about a couple hours from here." He still didn't look at her.

"Is it the people I met last night? A little woman called Sheila and an artist—what was his name?"

"Laurence and Sheila, yeah."

"Hey, that sounds great."

"Yeah, fantastic." He sounded pissed off. "You know you give me more of a pain than Chris, even? Jesus, I ought to dump you back at Michael's place, let *him* try to give you what you want. I don't know why I'm bothering."

Because you don't know how to stand up to me, she thought

to herself, suddenly feeling on top of the situation, and surprised at how easy it had been to influence him, despite his macho act.

They went to his automobile in the underground garage, among lines of motorcycles and bicycles and an occasional battered old sub-compact car. Some kids had gathered around the Toronado, staring at it. As Bobby walked up they transferred their attention to him.

"Bobby *Black!*" a girl screamed suddenly and threw herself at him, her arms around his neck.

Bobby grinned, fending her off half-heartedly as he unlocked the car. "Take it easy, honey," he said. "You're drooling on my new shirt."

She still clung to him. He finally managed to shake her off as he got in the car. She turned, zombie-eyed. "I touched him!" she said to her friends. "He spoke to me!"

Bobby slammed his door. Lisa got in the other side.

Bobby was still grinning and waved to the kids as he pulled away out of the garage into the sunlight. Then suddenly he turned to Lisa. "I'll take you out to this place," he said, hard and aggressive, "but you better not try to hold out on me no more."

She couldn't help flinching at the abrupt change in his voice and manner. "Well, you'd better not be a disappointment," she answered, trying to sound cool, but not quite making it.

He laughed, giving her a scornful look.

New Vista

Traveling together in the confines of the car, they inevitably ended up talking to each other. She found herself telling him about her upbringing on the farm with her parents and how the rural life had grown harder as costs of fuel, fertilizer, and all kinds of equipment and supplies had gone up and up. Crop yields had declined because of resistant insects, and taxes had increased, till eventually the business went into bankruptcy. And shortly after that her parents had been killed in a road accident.

She told him about her move to the city to try to make it as a graphic designer, and how she'd ended up in a tenement full of squatters in a part of town that everyone had given up on, including landlords, police, sanitation workers, and electric and telephone companies. She'd had a communal existence with the other penniless young people in the building, receiving a state handout from the local office every week, buying food from the state-run community food outlet, scraping along with just enough money to see a movie once a week. She told him about the street violence, interracial gang fights, the rats, the lack of heat in the winter, the leaking roof, the mound of garbage in the backyard that reached up to the second-floor windows. . . .

He wasn't too impressed. He could match all her hard-luck stories with ones of his own. Raised in a slum, beaten up by other kids at school, he'd learned the hard way how to defend himself, then how to get even, and then how to get more than even, pushing dope, working rackets. And in his spare time he'd started singing, and traveled locally with a band that played a couple of colleges where the kids from rich families went to get their education. At one of the college gigs he'd met a student named Michael who'd started managing the band, told Bobby to change his name from Bobby Schwartz to Bobby Black, and it had all gone from there, with a new image, new songs, no looking back.

"But in a way you're not so different from the street people who broke into my apartment and robbed me," she told him.

"We've all got to grab what we can," he said. "What you get is what you take. Right?"

"Yes, I don't blame you, you just did what everyone does, but why does it have to be that way?"

"Because there ain't enough for everyone. So some people got to do without."

"If people didn't want so much, though, there might be enough to go around."

He laughed. "Yeah, but the fact is, each of us wants all he can get. It's a fact of life."

She shook her head. "*I'd* be satisfied with less. Less than you have, for instance."

"You think so? Uh uh. You always want more than you got. Oh, sure, there's a limit—I mean after a while there ain't nothing left to spend money on. But then you start getting paranoid about *losing* any of what you've got. So you need more cash just to insure yourself against the future. Security. You always need more."

She was thoughtful. "I can't argue, because I've only ever had barely enough. I've always been poor. But I still can't help thinking, I'd be easily satisfied."

"Well, I guess if that's how you feel, that's how come you're still poor. You've got to have the hunger, for money, to get money."

"Well, at least you're honest about it."

"Sure I am."

"I think that's why I can talk to you. I may not like your attitudes, but at least you aren't a hypocrite."

"Is that right? So why were you such a bitch last night?"

"Because . . . because you were putting on such an act, you were so damned *pleased* with yourself."

He smiled cheerfully. "Well, I got a lot to be pleased about."

She shook her head. "You're hopeless." She looked out of the window, seeing he was decelerating, heading toward the next exit off the Interstate highway. "Are we almost there?" Suburbia had been gradually falling away, since they'd left the city. The land was beginning to look more open.

"The farm's a few miles further," he said. "I just want to detour through a construction project they got out here."

"A construction project?"

"Yeah. Did you meet a guy, Vickers, at the party last night? Tall, with a suntan. Works for the government. Says science is going to save us all, and like that."

"Michael pointed him out to me. I didn't speak to him."

"Well, he's one of the guys who planned the new city out here, the place they've named New Vista, you know?"

"New Vista? They actually called it that?"

"Uh huh. Thought we could take a look, see if it matches up to all Vickers' hype about it. It's kind of a showpiece. The government did it to inspire confidence." He swung the car through a tree-lined, winding back road. It suddenly led out onto a hillcrest overlooking a broad sweep of open land. "Yeah, will you look at that."

He stopped the car. Surrounded by man-made hills of brown earth churned by wheels of giant excavators, the city stood like a vast, grandiose, unified piece of modern sculpture. Hundreds of towers of shining white concrete, soaring ramps and pedestrian walkways, walls of glass, shopping precincts, rows and rows of apartment blocks.

"Now, you got to admit, that's impressive," he said.

She leaned forward with her elbows on the instrument panel. "They still building it?"

"Doing the interiors. Vickers was saying they moved a few people into part of it last month. They already got some stores open, even a couple supermarkets selling food, stuff that's irradiated so it keeps for years. Whole thing's going to be self-contained. But right near the Interstate."

"For people who still have cars," she said.

"Baby, who else is going to afford to live in a place like that?"

"I suppose you're right." The complex of buildings stretched away for miles. It was like looking at the towers of Manhattan from up on the New Jersey cliffs—a Manhattan that had been magically remade, all new and spotlessly clean, transplanted into the open, green country.

"That's the future, so Vickers says. Like if the government just got organized, got the new power—the fusion thing, whatever it's called—they could re-make cities all over the country like that."

"It's a nice dream," she said.

"Yeah, ain't it?"

"Do you think it'll ever happen?"

Bobby shrugged. "I ain't got a proper education, I don't know nothing. If Vickers says so, why not?"

"We're supposed to be so short of resources."

"Ain't no shortage of sand and cement to make concrete, and glass for the windows. And according to him, if you plan it right, a new city like that costs less to run than an old one."

"I suppose. And yet, the economy is so bad, and there are so many people unemployed, and you know yourself what it's like in the ghettos."

"Yeah, well, if they get this cheap power he keeps talking about, and if those guys in Washington stop pissing tax money away giving pay raises to each other and their secretaries and their cousins, I mean, who knows?" Bobby started the car again, spun the steering, turned across the road, backed up, and completed the turn, heading back the way they'd come. Lisa looked over her shoulder; she caught a last glimpse of New Vista receding behind them, like a mirage.

THE FUNNY FARM

They drove back to the Interstate and up it a little further, then turned off again. Bobby followed some narrow back roads, finally taking a rough graveled track. The countryside was lush, dense with rich vegetation. Insects darted to and fro through beams of summer sun.

A gate came into view. "Shall I get out and open it?" Lisa asked.

He shook his head, stopping the car. "They got a gadget, in the plastic bush there, sees us here, rings a bell in the house."

"Who is it?" said an amplified voice from a concealed loudspeaker.

He lowered the window. "Sheila, it's Bobby," he shouted.

"Oh, come *in*." As she spoke the fake-wood gate, complete with moss, smoothly folded up and out of the way.

Lisa started laughing. "Some cute little old farm you brought me to."

Bobby looked pained. "Now come on, don't start shitting on everything again."

They rounded a bend in the track. A fake-carved-wood sign with a floodlight for night illumination stood to one side. THE FUNNY FARM, it read. "Sheila's joke," Bobby explained.

"She's got a weird sense of humor."

The house came into view. At first glance it was a charming old colonial residence. Then she realized that it was mostly made out of aluminum. It overlooked a lawn so perfect it had to be Astroturf, with beds of flowers that looked distinctly plastic. "Back to the roots," she murmured.

"They got a real field and all out the back," said Bobby. "The garden at the front they made up to look good for visitors."

"Hmmm."

Bobby parked his Toronado in a wide graveled space beside the house, where a Cadillac and a brand new pickup truck were already standing. He opened his door.

A twelve-year-old boy came running out from the house, screaming inarticulately. He was dressed like a guerrilla, with two ammunition belts around his shoulders, mud daubed on his face, and weeds in his long, tangled hair. He pointed a machine gun at Bobby and pulled the trigger. It hammered away realistically. Plastic bullets zipped through the air. "Take that, ya fucking Commie cocksucker!" the kid screamed.

Bobby put his hands in front of his face, fending off the stinging missiles. "Cut it out, Sheldon!"

The kid bit the pin from a hand grenade and threw it. Bobby ducked. The grenade hit the Toronado and exploded realistically, scattering plastic shrapnel and leaving a burn mark on the car's paint.

"All right, you little bastard!" Bobby advanced on the kid.

"Sheldon, maybe you better go *play* out the *back*," said Sheila, coming out onto the porch.

The kid wheeled and fired his gun at her, making her flinch from the spray of bullets. Then he ran around the house and away, still yelling.

"He fucked up my car's paint job," said Bobby.

Sheila seemed uninterested. "I think he missed a dose of medication this morning. He gets very manic."

"Do you realize how much it costs to get a customized paint job like that with the aluminum flake finish?"

"Mmm. It's *nice* of you to come and *visit*," said Sheila. "Who's that in the car?"

Lisa got out into the sunlight, now that it seemed safe to do so. "I met you last night. At the party. I'm Lisa."

"Oh yeah, of *course*."

"Let's go inside," said Bobby. "Hot out here."

"It's hot inside too," said Sheila, as they followed her in.

"Thought you had that solar-heat-exchange gadget in the roof," said Bobby. "Ecologically designed like it's warm in the winter and cool in the summer."

"Yeah, but something's *wrong* with it," said Sheila. "Seems like it's warm in the summer and cool in the winter now. Laurence is up in the attic trying to *fix* it, but he just screws it up."

The interior of the house was infernally hot. It was also chaotic. There were tracks of ingrained dirt and mud all over the white plastic floors. Chrome and aluminum modernistic furniture lay scattered around as if there'd been a brawl. An armchair was turned over on its side. Every surface was covered in a litter of magazines, books, video cassettes, records, tapes, Sheldon's toys, discarded clothing. Music was blasting from six enormous units. "We were *playing* your *album*," said Sheila to Bobby, giving him a cynical smile, as if sharing an obscure joke.

If there was a joke, Bobby missed it. "Can you turn it down?" he shouted above the blaring music.

She picked her way over old newspapers and soiled under-

wear, to a control panel in the wall. "Why, don't you *like* it?"
she said meaningly, turning the sound off altogether. "Oh, sorry
about the *mess* in here, by the way." She sounded almost pleased
about the mess.

Laurence walked in from the other room. His hands and arms
were black with grease. He saw Bobby and Lisa and stopped.
Slowly he smiled, with obvious simple pleasure. "Oh, hi," he
said. "What a surprise."

"Yes, *isn't* it," said Sheila.

"I've been trying to fix the system," said Laurence, "up in the
roof. But the trouble is, I really don't understand how it works."

"I told you we should call the repair people," said Sheila.
She picked a wad of gum out of her mouth and wrapped it in a
tissue, which she threw in the vague direction of a waste bin.

Laurence went over, apparently without thinking about it,
picked up the wadded tissue, and dumped it in the bin. "I
wanted to fix the system myself to save us some money," he said.

Sheila shrugged. She sat down on a surreal piece of modern
furniture, slouching back. "It certainly is *hot* in here," she said,
and turned on the TV by her elbow. Instantly the room was
full of bellowing sounds of a soap opera.

"I've got to go to the kitchen and wash," said Laurence.

"Bobby and I will come with you," Lisa said firmly.

"Oh. Okay," said Laurence.

Lisa and Bobby followed him out of the room. "You people
staying for lunch?" Sheila called, when they were almost, but
not quite, out of earshot.

Bobby went back into the room. "If you got it."

"Put it in the oven for them Laurence," she shouted, still
slouched in her chair watching the TV.

"All right, I'll do it." He led the way through to the kitchen.
The back door was open. So was its screen. The place was
crawling with insects. "I don't understand why she has to do
that," said Laurence, as if genuinely puzzled by irrational be-

havior. He shut the screen door with a firm but gentle touch. Then he went to the sink and started washing. "You know it's really nice to see you, we don't get many visitors here." Grease and detergent from his arms ran down over stacks of unwashed dishes.

"What are you growing at the back?" asked Lisa, looking out of the window at a ploughed field stretching away behind the house.

"Wheat," said Laurence. "Sheila wants to make bread." He finished washing, took three packages out of the freezer, and dumped them in the oven.

"You have a way to grind the grain into flour?" she asked.

"I expect we'll buy something to do that when the time comes," he said vaguely. "Frankly, I'm waiting to see if anything actually grows out there. We haven't had much luck."

"You still got the animals?" asked Bobby.

"No, I'm afraid not. Sheldon fed the chickens and the pig rat poison and strangled the goat with his Young Commando equipment. Anyway, the barn fell down." He gestured to a great mound of timber that Lisa had assumed was firewood.

"That's sad," she said.

"Not really, the animals were a pain in the ass. Do you know anything about farming?"

"I grew up on a farm."

"Oh, *really?* Gee, you could explain some things to us. Do you know how to fix a tractor?" He pointed at a vehicle at the far end of the land, resting with two wheels bogged deep in mud.

"What sort is it?"

"I don't know. It's supposed to be remote-controlled from that panel there." He showed her some levers and dials.

"We didn't have anything as fancy as that."

"You know I think that's the trouble," he told her, absolutely serious. "Sheila buys all these gadgets, and they're too *complicated.* Like the geothermal power generator, for our electricity. It's never worked. It cost us a hundred thousand, can you be-

lieve that?" He opened the oven. "I think the food's ready, if
you want to eat."

"That was quick."

"It's an X-ray oven." He peeled back the foil lids of what
turned out to be TV dinners. He cleared a space on the kitchen
table by sweeping his arm along it, piling up old magazines,
unanswered correspondence, dirty dishes, and jars of vitamin
pills at one end. "We could eat in the dining room," he said,
"but the dining room's a bit of a mess right now."

The screen door smashed open and Sheldon ran in, still
screaming. Laurence reached out with surprising speed, grabbed
him by the arm, then got him by the neck with casual ease,
applying a disabling wrestling hold. "*You* didn't take your medication this morning," he said to the kid.

Sheldon bared his teeth like a young ape. He made growling
noises.

Still holding the kid with one hand, Laurence reached for a
big jar, removed the lid with his other hand, and took out two
green capsules. "Open," he said.

The kid opened his mouth wide and rolled his eyes.

Laurence threw the pills down his throat. "Swallow."

The kid did nothing.

Laurence's hold on his neck tightened.

The kid gulped.

Laurence released him. He ran out of the room. His pounding footsteps receded into the house. "He has to be sedated,"
Laurence said vaguely.

They ate the packaged food. "One day," said Laurence, "I
know you'll laugh at me for saying this, but one day we're really
going to eat food that we grow ourselves."

"It does take time to get a farm going," said Lisa.

"Well, I guess that's true. We've only been here a year."

"I'm going to take a *nap*," shouted Sheila, from the other
room. "I seem to have some kind of migraine. I think it's because
of the *heat*."

"All right," said Laurence.

"Don't forget the repairman. And put the dishes in the washer."

"I will." He turned to his guests. "I seem to end up doing most of the chores around here," he said, sounding mystified.

After they ate, Bobby suggested that Laurence should show Lisa his handmade jackets. Laurence was glad to do so. He then went further and showed her some of his collection of antique electronic gadgets—digital watches and calculators from the late nineteen-sixties. "Some of the older ones, the first of their kind, are really quite valuable now," he told her.

She got through it as quickly as she could. "Maybe Bobby and I should go out for a walk," she said.

Laurence seemed mildly surprised. "I suppose you could. There's some real nice country around here."

Bobby was reluctant. "I don't know."

"Come on," she told him, "it's been years since I've been out of town. And you too, you told me yourself."

"Okay, okay. For a short walk."

Laurence went down with them to the back porch. Lisa paused outside the house. It was almost unnaturally quiet. Then she realized what was missing. "You don't seem to have any birds around here."

Laurence laughed, looking embarrassed. "Well, I'll tell you, you may think I'm weird, but I had them exterminated."

"Exterminated?"

"You've no idea how much noise they made in the mornings at sunrise. It was driving me crazy. So we bought some kind of sterility virus that wiped out most of the ones that had nests around here. And now there's a big antenna thing on the roof that sends out ultrasonic sound. That keeps the rest of them away. They hate it."

"You know, that's why you have such an insect problem."

Laurence's brow furrowed. "Why?"

"Birds eat insects. They keep them under control."

He looked doubtful. "Really?"

"Sure do," she said. "That's basic ecology. Come on, Bobby. Thanks for the lunch, Laurence."

"Oh, you're really very welcome." He stood on the back porch, looking vaguely up at the empty trees and sky, as if mulling over what she'd just suggested to him.

BY THE RIVER

From the end of the field the land sloped down, covered with long grass, dotted with bushes and trees. Faintly, Lisa heard the sound of a stream flowing. "They own all of this?"

"Yeah, they got a couple hundred acres." Bobby was squinting against the glare of the sun. "Jesus, it's hot."

"Well, take your jacket off."

"Oh. Yeah, I suppose I could."

"I hear a stream down there. Have you ever seen it?"

"No. Listen, Lisa, I don't get off on this back-to-nature thing, you know?"

She realized he was trying hard to be polite. She took hold of his arm. Getting out of the city had put her into a totally carefree mood. "I know, Bobby, but just for a half hour or so—look, we'll find the stream down there under the trees. It'll be cooler in the shade."

"I'm gonna get my clothes messed up out here."

"You're a rich man, you can afford to have them cleaned." He couldn't argue that.

She led him down the sloping land, following the sounds of water, under some tall birches. "There, look—it's beautiful—and there's a pool." The water was tumbling down over rocks, under the canopy of green. Someone, years ago, had made a dam, forming a little lake about twenty feet across.

"It's probably polluted," said Bobby.

"With what? See any factories or sewers around here?" she started unbuttoning her shirt.

"What you doing? You going to swim in that? You're crazy."

"Can't you swim?"

"Yeah, of course, but not in that, all that mud and stuff."

She cast off her clothes, and jumped straight in. "Come on, try it." She ducked under and resurfaced. "It's great."

"Ain't nothing going to get me in there." He found a clean slab of stone on the bank and sat down deliberately, glancing around with distaste. He wiped his forehead and waved irritably at a couple of flies buzzing around him.

"You're stuffy, you know that?" She swam around for a few minutes, then climbed out and sat beside him on the bank. "You don't know a good thing when you see it."

He looked at her. She was naked, beaded with water that gleamed in the sun. Her body was compact but strong, the breasts high and firm.

"I don't, huh?" he said.

"No, you don't." She looked frankly into his eyes. Then she reached out and touched him gently on the cheek.

"You got wet hands," he said, not making a move toward her.

She sighed. "You've never done it with someone outdoors, have you?"

"Done what?"

"Oh, come on, who do you think you're fooling?"

He kept his expression blank and controlled. "I think we better get back to town."

"Why, because you don't like it here? Or because you don't like me telling you how sexually repressed you are?"

"Me, *repressed?* You're full of shit."

"No, I think you are."

"Look, stop trying to get me mad, will you?" He ran his hand through his hair. "Or how'd you like to walk home?"

"Is that the only way you can deal with a woman, by threatening her?"

He shifted his shoulders uncomfortably, hot and sticky under his shirt, and getting angrier every moment. "You know, you better watch your mouth."

"Or else what?" She was getting angry too—angry with him for disappointing her, here by the river.

He instinctively half-raised his hand, forming a fist.

"Go on," she said, "do it. Prove how tough you are."

He slowly forced his hand back down by his side. "Ahh, you ain't worth it."

"What's the matter, scared I'll hit you back?" She smiled maliciously. Without warning she flicked water off her wet hand, into his face.

"Bitch!" His cheeks flushed. He lashed out to deal her an open-handed slap.

She caught his wrist before he could touch her. She was strong, not like the fashionably thin, glamorous women he was accustomed to. It was a stand-off in physical strength.

Suddenly he wrenched his arm free and pulled back from her. He was breathing hard. "God damned bitch."

"That was dumb. Even for you." She was trembling but she stared him down.

He avoided her eyes. "You got me all screwed up."

"I did? All I wanted was for us to make it out here on the grass."

"Then how come you're getting at me, trying to make me mad all the time?"

"I didn't. I didn't mean—oh, damn it."

He looked at her and saw a mixture of frustration, openness, helplessness. He looked away again. "I didn't mean to hit you. But Jesus, you was asking for it."

She shifted closer to him, moving her face into his line of sight. "Bobby?"

"Look," he said, still avoiding her eyes. "I'm sorry, okay? I apologize. How's that?"

She brought her mouth down over his. He started to pull away, then thought better of it, as if he didn't know what he ought to do.

She started unbuttoning his shirt, watching his face.

"I just don't want us to make it out *here*," he said. "Can't you understand that?"

She slid her hands inside his shirt and ran them over his skin. "No, I can't." She started undoing his pants.

He shifted uncertainly, made as if to stop her, but then changed his mind again. Somehow he'd lost control of the situation. She'd taken the initiative, and that hardly ever happened to him, so he was left feeling dumb, feeling he'd already acted like a jerk by trying to hit her, and now he didn't know what to do to get back on top of the situation.

"Listen," he said. "Lisa, cut it out."

"Lie back," she said, pushing gently on his chest.

"This ain't gonna work."

"Lie back!" She went on pushing. Gradually he yielded, till he was flat out on the ground.

She lay down over him, covering him with her wet skin. She kissed him hard. He responded woodenly. She slid her hand down to his penis, pulled it gently out of the fly of his pants, and went on touching it.

"Lisa," he said, "I'm telling you . . ."

She placed her finger across his lips. "You talk too much. We both do. That's the trouble."

"You're weird, you know that? Weirdest bitch I ever met."

She smiled, still fondling him. "I'm going to go down on you."

"It ain't no good telling you 'no,' is it?"

"That's right. I'm even more stubborn than you are."

Quickly, before he could resist, she shifted her head down and took him in her mouth. He started to object, then shook his head confusedly and lay back, watching her do it to him. For a few minutes it was silent, there on the river bank, under the trees. The only noise was the stream flowing over the rocks and trickling into the pool.

Finally she raised her head and looked down at him. "You're half way there."

He looked embarrassed. "How about if you and me go back to my car. The front seat folds over, it's like a big bed."

"No, you're just beginning to get into it out here." Her hand went on touching him, busily, insistently.

"Yeah? How would you know?"

She laughed. "I can feel your interest in me growing bigger all the time." With her other hand she started tugging his pants off. His skin had an even, mellow tan—sunlamp tan.

"Weird," he said. "You are *weird.*" He sounded nervous.

She got his pants off and lay beside him, very close. Her hand still held his penis. It was getting hard in her grip. She kissed him. After a moment he started responding, getting up on one elbow. She yielded, and they rolled so that they faced each other side by side.

She saw he was breathing a little faster. He looked as if he wanted her. But he was on edge. He touched her breasts tentatively, then reached between her legs. She opened her thighs. She was moist inside—she'd started feeling aroused several minutes ago.

"Fuck me," she whispered to him.

It turned him on, as it was meant to. He pushed her onto her back and lay over her, kissing her again. His legs shifted between hers.

She started to guide his penis into her. He took her hand away to do it himself. He thrust in, and she smiled up at him, wrapping her arms around him and holding him close. But he was still tense, clumsy, uncomfortable.

He started making love to her very quickly, as if he wanted to get it over with, or was afraid that if he didn't hurry he'd lose his erection.

"Easy, take it easy," she whispered.

He paused, breathing hard. "Yeah, you can say that. Meanwhile, I'm skinning my knees on the rock here."

"Then let me get on top."

He didn't look as if he liked that idea either. She pushed him over before he could think up an excuse. He came out of her; quickly she straddled him and put him back inside. She bore down hard, taking him deep, clenching her muscles. He gave a little involuntary gasp.

She braced herself with her arms on his shoulders. Her legs were strong and her body was lithe. She started a steady, insistent rhythm, and felt him gradually start to respond. She watched perspiration break out on his skin and watched his expression change as he became more aroused. His hands moved up and closed over her breasts.

"Want me to get back on top now?" he said, when he was really turned on, his breath coming in short gasps.

She shook her head. "I can keep this up for a long time."

"Yeah?" he looked dazed.

She started moving faster on him and felt his hands clench and his body stiffen. He pushed his hips up under her.

She sensed he was getting near orgasm. She put all her energy into a final burst of activity. She saw his jaw clench. He groaned, through his teeth.

Then he came. She let herself fall forward on him as it happened to him. She took his head between her hands and kissed him hard and deep, till it was all over and he relaxed under her. Then she just lay there on him, keeping his penis in her. His breathing slowed. Clumsily he embraced her.

"I got rocks sticking in my back," he said apologetically after a few minutes.

She rolled off him and lay down beside him, close to him.

"So that's how it happens, out here on the farm." His voice sounded strange. It didn't have the usual edge to it. He seemed confused.

"I shouldn't have gotten you mad like that," she said. "But to me, you know, you were rejecting me."

He didn't answer for a moment. "I didn't see it from that point of view. But I guess, yeah, I understand. I'm, uh, sorry

you didn't come, just then. Wasn't much I could do underneath
you like that."

You could have thought of touching me with your fingers,
she thought to herself, but didn't say it. "I don't come easily,"
she told him, "and it doesn't matter that much to me. Really."
She smiled. "I just wanted to make it with you, that's all."

"And now you have."

"That's right, I suppose I have." Putting it in the past tense
like that suddenly made the event seem trivial. She'd been so
worked up—wanting to get the better of him, wanting him to
want her, wanting to prove something to him, and wanting to
be able to say to herself that she'd fucked a wealthy rock star.
Now she'd done it, and there was nothing left to do next.

"Look, uh, Lisa." He still sounded confused. "I'm sorry if I
gave you a hard time just now. I mean, you're right, I never did
it outdoors like this before."

"It's okay. You don't have to apologize for anything."

"Damn it, I ain't apologizing!" That was more his old style.
But then she saw him bite back on his anger and hold it down,
till he looked almost meek. "Yeah, well, it was good, you know.
I mean I really got off on it."

"Me too."

"You did? I mean, you're not bullshitting me."

She felt uncomfortable. "No, I wouldn't lie."

He touched her body. "That's good. I never known anyone
quite like you, you realize that? You cut through all the crap,
you know what I mean?"

"You'd better start insulting me again, else I'm going to
wonder what's happened to you."

He grinned self-consciously. "Ain't nothing wrong with me.
Nothing in the world. Uh, you going to come see my concert
tonight?"

"You have another performance?"

"Yeah."

"I . . . don't know. You see, it isn't really my kind of thing. It's loud, and heavy. It knocked me over, last night."

He shrugged. "Okay. Maybe see you afterward. You could come over to my apartment, or I'll take you out to dinner, something like that."

"Well, why don't you see how you feel after the concert, and call me then?"

"You'll be at Michael's?"

"I don't have anywhere else to go, do I?"

He started to say something, then decided not to. "We better get back," he said, instead. "I got to prepare for the show and all that kind of shit." He scrambled up onto his feet, looking around at the afternoon sun, the river, the grass, the trees. "You know, I still say it makes better sense to screw in bed." He grinned. "Back at my place I got a whole room that's a bed. And all kinds of things to go with it."

"Really?" She couldn't help sounding a little distant. She pulled her pants on.

He watched her dress. "You got a nice body."

"I should have thought you'd prefer someone more glamorous."

"Makes a change to look at someone who's natural. You ain't never had cosmetic surgery."

She buttoned her shirt. "No."

He stepped close and kissed her on the mouth. She found herself feeling awkward, wanting to back off. "Mustn't be late for your concert," she told him, forcing a smile, at the same time thinking, what had happened? Why was she acting like this?

"Okay kid, let's go." But it didn't sound like him, and he had a funny look in his eyes.

He dressed, and they walked back toward Laurence and Sheila's house. When they were almost at the back door, it opened in front of them, and Sheila stepped out. She paused, looking from Lisa to Bobby and back again. "Well, hi," she said. "Did you two have a *nice time?*"

"Yeah, fine," said Bobby. "Look, we got to get back, else I'll be late, so I'll see you. . . ." He trailed off, noticing someone coming out of the house after Sheila. He recognized the person as she came into the light. It was Chris, "Shit," he muttered.

Chris came out, saw Bobby, and stopped. "What the fuck are you doing here?" she said.

He shrugged uncomfortably. "Just visiting, I guess."

She gave him a searching, skeptical glance, then turned her attention to Lisa, looking her over. "Bobby, you told me you had to be in the recording studio all today."

"Yeah, well, the plans got changed, and when I tried to call you, you was out. So don't go making a big deal out of this, all right?"

"You're a fucking liar. Where've you been with her?" She gestured at Lisa, without looking at her again.

"We went for a walk," said Bobby. It sounded unconvincing, even to him.

Chris glared at him, then turned and started back into the house, without saying anything more.

"You coming to my concert?" he shouted after her. She didn't reply. Bobby shook his head, muttering something. "See you around, I guess, Sheila."

"I'm sorry about the *embarrassing scene*," she answered, with enjoyment.

"Yeah, well, you know Chris, she gets jealous easy. Even when there ain't nothing to be jealous about. Come on, Lisa."

She went with him around the side of the house, to the Toronado. He unlocked it and they got in. "I guess you and Chris must have been together for quite a while," she said.

He sat in the driver's seat, staring abstractedly through the windshield, not bothering to start the car. "Yeah, but Christ knows why. She's always bitching, the whole time."

"What brings her out here? She asked you why you were here, but you didn't ask her."

"I don't give a shit why she's here, that's why I didn't ask.

She comes visiting sometimes, Sheila's kind of a friend of hers."

"Chris has a car?"

"I gave her that Honda." He pointed to a two-seater sedan that had been parked beside Laurence's pickup. "Look, Lisa, you got to understand, Chris don't mean nothing." He put the ignition key in the lock, and started the motor.

Lisa blinked. "She doesn't?"

"No, she's just an easy fuck." He backed the car and turned it. "She hangs around, know what I mean?" He started down the drive, away from the house. "Like I keep her around, 'cause there hasn't been anybody better, see?"

She wondered if he was trying to imply anything. It was hard to tell what was going through his mind. "I see," she said. "But Chris is pretty hung up on you, isn't she?"

"Ah, who can tell? She squawks about it a lot. All I know is, she gets a lot of groupie status being my woman." He drove along the back roads, looking preoccupied. Then he reached the Interstate and accelerated hard, quickly hitting 110, the empty highway flashing under the car, the air hissing past. "Hey, you know I feel good," he said. "Yeah, real good. You know maybe I ought to buy some land myself, get a little place out here. What do you think?"

"I don't think you're the type."

"How come you say that? I think you convinced me, it's good, out here, the green trees and all that."

She shook her head. "You'd get bored inside an hour. Or you'd be like Laurence and Sheila and make an ass of yourself, treating it like a fad, moving half the city out here with you."

"What you mean?"

"Those gadgets and stuff. That isn't country life."

He shook his head. "I still don't understand you."

"I guess we're a bit of a ridiculous mis-match, Bobby."

"Ah, come on, you shouldn't say that, not after the good time we just had. Don't start putting things down again."

She looked at her hands in her lap, feeling stupid for feeling afraid of hurting his feelings. "I'm sorry."

"You could be wrong about me," he told her. "In fact I may just prove you wrong and get a little farm myself somewhere. Except I wouldn't try to handle it all on my own, like Laurence. No, I'd get someone like a caretaker. Someone like you who knows about that stuff."

"Someone like me?" she asked innocently.

He glanced at her quickly. "What is this, you trying to tell me you want the job yourself?"

"Maybe I'll apply for the position if it ever exists."

"Yeah, well, I'll consider your application." He grinned. "You sure you ain't coming to my concert?"

"I'm sure."

He reached out and touched her thigh. She remembered back to that morning, when he'd done the same thing, in the love garden at the pleasure palace. It felt a long time ago.

VICKERS AND JAMIESON

"Did you have a good time?" Michael held open his apartment door for her. She walked past him into the living room.

"It was . . . interesting."

He shut the door and followed her. "Somehow I didn't expect you back here."

She sat down in a chair. They looked at each other. It felt odd to be back indoors again, in Michael's apartment, after being in the country with Bobby. "So what did you do, today?" she asked him.

He sat down opposite her. "Tried to work."

"New songs?"

"New concept. Except I didn't really get anywhere. Actually, I don't really like talking about my work."

"Oh. All right."

They looked at each other again. Michael was so quiet, so oblique, after Bobby. She wondered if either man would be interested in her, if the other wasn't. "Don't let me get in the way if you want to do anymore work now," she said.

"I don't want to. I'm pleased to see you." He seemed tense. "There's a restaurant I know, if you'd like to go out."

She paused, remembering Bobby's similar invitation, and his promise to call her after his concert. But that wouldn't be for at least another two hours, and she wasn't sure she wanted to see him that night anyway. "This restaurant, is it a fancy place?"

"I wouldn't take you there if it was."

"Why—afraid I'd use the wrong fork or something?"

"No, I just assumed you wouldn't enjoy a fancy place."

She smiled. "You try hard to please."

"No, I just assume that if we go somewhere that one of us doesn't enjoy, it won't be a good evening for either of us."

"That sounds very reasonable." Almost too reasonable, she thought—he *was* trying to please, whatever he said. "Well, yes, I would like to eat out."

"Fine. Shall we leave now, or do you want to sit a while, to shift gears?"

"Shift gears?"

"Isn't it kind of different switching over from being in Bobby's company, to being in mine?"

"I think I can handle it," she said dryly. "Can you?"

He paused a moment. "Please stop sparring. It shouldn't have to be like that."

Their eyes met. She realized she was still feeling competitive and defensive, from dealing with Bobby early on. "I'm sorry," she said. "I guess you're right."

It was a small, quiet restaurant with rather mediocre oil paintings on the walls, checked tablecloths, and a plain wooden floor. There was only one waiter, and he seemed also to be the proprietor. A decade earlier, the place would have been full of artists, writers, people in the media, but these days artists and writers weren't doing so well, like many people in service industries, and the once-fashionable neighborhood had slid downhill. Most other restaurants on the street had gone out of business.

"Are you going to ask me where I went with Bobby today?" she said.

"No."

"Are you interested?"

"Yes, naturally."

"Well, he took me to the pleasure palace, which he liked and I hated. Then we went out into the country."

"You mean actually walking around outside? Or did you just drive?"

"We went on a walk."

"I'm impressed. You must have been persuasive."

"I was." She slowly ate a mouthful of steak, savoring it. "You seem to understand Bobby pretty well."

"Of course I do," he said.

"You know, I think I'd be more at ease with you if you didn't seem to know so much and be so much in control."

He shook his head. "I don't know why you think that. I'm not in control of anything. I'm . . . inept, socially."

"No, you confess too easily. It comes out so smoothly."

"Well, I suppose I have made that particular confession before."

"That's what I mean. If you were really socially inept, you wouldn't know how to confess. You'd be tongue-tied, you'd blunder around and blurt things out."

He laughed. "I didn't say I was socially *spastic*."

"All right, all right. But I do get the feeling you're the kind who covers himself—keeps a lot buried underneath."

"Caution," he said. "Self-interest, maybe."

"And instant candor like that just makes me more suspicious."

"Then I can't win, can I?"

"You do your share of winning."

"I mean I can't win your trust."

"Trust isn't really won," she said. "It grows, when the conditions are right."

He thought about that. "I guess I wouldn't know. Most of my life, it hasn't been an issue. Mutual distrust is taken for granted in business deals. And on a personal level most of my relationships have been casual."

"Why casual?"

"That's what I wanted."

"Want*ed*? What do you want now?"

"I told you last night, at that party. I have no idea." He shifted uncomfortably in his chair. "This conversation is too heavy. I always end up feeling as if I don't have a sense of humor when I'm talking to you. Why do we get so bogged down?"

She shrugged. "Defensiveness. Or self-consciousness."

"I suppose that's it. When two people are both self-conscious together, it's hard for things to get off the ground." He smiled. "Especially when one of the people is socially inept."

After the meal, it was still early. "There's a bar near here where some friends of mine sometimes hang out," Michael said. "Want to try it?"

She felt good, with the real food inside her. "Sure. Who are the friends?"

They started walking along the street. It was one of the few reasonably safe areas left in the urban center—a nucleus of home owners with enough money and loyalty to persist in living in the heart of the city, despite urban decay.

"I pointed them out to you last night," Michael said. "Jamieson and Vickers."

"Vickers—he was involved in designing a new city?"

"Yes, New Vista, they're calling it."

"We went past it today."

"Oh." He seemed momentarily irritated by her mentioning something she'd done with Bobby. "Well, Vickers is a generalist, government technical advisor. Started as an architect, writes books about the future environment, he's a futurologist, a part-time consultant to a committee in Washington on power sources, all kinds of stuff like that. Self-made man, expansionist type. Jamieson's just the opposite. From a rich family. He dropped out, inherited wealth, gave most of it away. Kind of a latter-day Ralph Nader. Lonely man. Him and Vickers do nothing but argue. Vickers says it's because he enjoys the intellectual stimulation, but I think all he really wants is to *convert* Jamieson. He's a missionary at heart." He stopped outside a fake-late-American bar. "This is the place."

An imitation old-fashioned air conditioner hung over the door, complete in every detail, down to the rusty edges and water dripping from one corner. There was a genuine antique neon beer sign in the window. The facade was of bricks, cunningly laid to simulate the fake-brick facades popular in the seventies.

She walked in with him. Inside there were authentic bar stools covered in expensive vinyl. Wood had artfully been used to simulate plastic in the decor, and in the corner a beautiful, old 1960s stereo jukebox was all lit up. Behind the bar were rows of bottles—brands she'd seen as a child, driven out of business when the pharmaceutical industry moved into the leisure-stimulants field. Looking more closely she saw that most of the old bottles had been converted into pill dispensers.

In the back was a space where there were tables. Jamieson and Vickers were sitting there. Michael introduced Lisa to each of them.

"Good evening!" said Vickers, with enough enthusiasm and vigor to convert the evening to being good, whether it was or not. He gave her a wide smile and a strong handshake.

"Pleased to meet you," Jamieson said, restrained and formal, as if irritated by the interruption. "Excuse me if I don't shake hands. Thalidomide."

She glanced down and saw he had prosthetic arms. "Oh, I'm sorry," she said, stupidly.

"What are you popping?" said Vickers, thrusting the embarrassing moment out of the way.

"Maybe a little Ritalin, for me," said Michael. He looked at Lisa. "You too?"

She shrugged. "Okay."

Vickers went to the bar to get it.

"Did you see this, this morning?" said Jamieson. With his prosthetic hand he pushed a long news sheet across the table. It was the standard summary dispensed overnight from the domestic telefax units installed in most private apartments.

"Only glanced at it," said Michael.

Lisa scanned the sheet. The main item described a government reshuffle and a forthcoming presidential announcement.

"This new man Winchester," Jamieson began, pointing to a name at the top of the list of new appointees in the Cabinet. "So-called advisor. He's from the Pentagon. Replaces a liberal that they finally managed to kick out. Now, go down the list of other names. All military backgrounds. And their job titles are next to meaningless. Now, look at these people who've been retained or promoted. Five ex-presidents of major corporations. Steel, food, construction, transportation, power—all the major areas are represented." He sat back as if he'd made a conclusive point.

"What are you getting at?" said Lisa.

He turned his face toward her. He was pale, looked undernourished. "Why do you think these reshuffles of non-elected officials have been going on, just recently?"

"I don't follow politics much."

"Then I'll tell you. We have a president who sold out to the military and industry years ago and has now been stripped of what little authority he had to begin with. He's been feebly trying to arbitrate a power struggle, but now, finally, it's settled.

He's totally surrounded by ex-military men on one side, and on the other side, corrupt persons representing the interests of monarchic business families. You think this is healthy?"

Vickers had come back from the bar carrying a couple of glasses of amber liquid, each glass standing in a saucer with a pill beside it.

"Jamieson's been predicting a dictatorship and/or a para-military takeover for some time now," Vickers explained with a grin, as if inviting Michael and Lisa to share a joke.

She accepted the glass and washed the pill down with some of the amber liquid. It tasted like old-style scotch whiskey.

"You know about these men, Vickers," said Jamieson, gesturing at the news sheet. "You can't tell me you're happy about an old fool like Winchester being so close to the president. First thing he'll do is start pushing for financial cutbacks on half of your pet research projects."

"Winchester's a fool, I agree. That's why he's unimportant."

"But he's been given power!"

Vickers sat down and leaned back in his chair. He waved his hand airily. "He doesn't have real power."

"Aha! Maybe that's true now, but don't you see, if there's a successful alliance between the military and big business, in cooperation with politicians. . . ."

"If, if, if," said Vickers. "I don't admit the possibility. There are constitutional safeguards . . ."

"Which are constantly being eroded by wealthy people taking steps to *protect* their wealth." He turned suddenly to Lisa. "You, you're evidently from one of the poorer areas, by your appearance. So you're not insulated from reality. Don't you sense the truth of what I'm saying?"

She wanted to be polite, but at the same time she felt she had to be truthful. "Politics has been corrupt through all my lifetime," she said. "When I was born, in the seventies, when they got rid of Nixon, they thought they'd uncovered everything and it could never happen again. But it seems to me, all it meant was that the people who didn't get caught realized they had to be more careful in the future, to go on getting away with it."

"Yes, yes, that's true, but there's a qualitative difference between a malfunctioning democracy of the seventies and a plutocracy in alliance with the Pentagon in the nineties."

"I'm sorry, I don't really understand. I mean, what do you expect me to do?" she shrugged. "Voting doesn't influence anything. You need money or connections."

"If you really feel that your vote is useless," said Jamieson, "why aren't you organizing and demonstrating? You don't need to be rich to pose a revolutionary threat to the status quo."

"There are street protests in the poor areas," said Lisa. "But they don't do anything."

"Because they aren't organized widely enough."

"The point is," said Vickers, interrupting with a friendly but slightly bored voice, like a father dealing with squabbling children, "the point is that, basically, everyone these days is cared for. Even in the New Austerity, no one starves. There are state handouts. So why *should* we expect widely organized demonstrations? Especially when there are such good prospects for a return to affluence. Fusion power . . ."

"Power won't solve the problem of lack of resources. Here we are running out of tin, lead, nickel, platinum, zinc, silver . . ."

Vickers erased the objection with a wave of his arm. "Still being mined in deposits that will be viable for years to come."

"But at what *cost*? How many gallons of gasoline are needed to end up with a couple of ounces of refined nickel?"

"You always under-estimate the powers of technology, Jamieson. You see what's possible now, and you assume that it's as far as we're ever going to get."

"The curves have all turned downward. Admit it."

"Not all of them," interrupted Michael.

Jamieson turned to him. "Name an exception. Real wealth, productivity, business indices, national income . . ."

"The entertainment business is okay."

Jamieson sighed. "Yes, of course, the purveyors of simple escapism. I suppose there's no harm in it. But don't you see," the proselytizing fervor came back into his voice, "you could be *using* this power you have over those kids out there. Instead of your . . . your suicide-rock music—you could be injecting positive messages, making people aware, making them think."

"They wouldn't buy it," said Michael.

Jamieson slouched forward, looking morose. "No doubt you're right. And yet I still believe, if people were really *aware*, we'd still have a chance. . . . Although I wonder, after tomorrow's special presidential announcement, things may look different."

"What presidential announcement?" said Lisa.

"Explaining policy changes after the Cabinet reshuffle," said Vickers, his thumbs hooked in his belt, his ankles crossed, a bored expression on his face.

Jamieson shook his head. "I have a feeling it's going to be more important than that."

"Well, we'll see, won't we?" said Vickers. "You going to that party, out in the country? The one they were giving out the invitations for last night? It's tomorrow, isn't it?"

"I may," said Jamieson.

"Then we can all watch the TV there," said Vickers. "Give us a chance, just for once, to actually test one of your predictions of doom." He smiled at Jamieson as if making a friendly joke. But Jamieson just stared at the table, at the reflection of his own lined face and receding hairline.

"The trouble with being a predicter of doom," he said, finally, "is that there's no satisfaction if and when one is proven right. Really, Vickers, all I ever want is to believe in your comforting philosophy of unlimited expansion and growth. I wish I could."

Vickers laughed. He was a big man, aggressively healthy, the kind you expect to have a collection of hunting stories and anecdotes about adventures everywhere from Asia to the corridors of power in Washington. "You wouldn't be happy if there wasn't anything to feel miserable about," he told Jamieson.

Michael finished his drink and looked at Lisa. "Shall we move on?"

She shrugged. "Okay."

"Maybe see you both at the party," said Michael, to the two men. Vickers waved cheerfully in response; Jamieson just sat there in his poorly fitting suit, like a marionette with half the strings broken.

After the Concert

Usually it was good, usually he was high for hours afterward, but this evening the performance had been crummy and he knew it. Worse, he guessed that other people knew it. Even the audience. Usually the kids had about as much sensitivity as a crowd of lobotomized rats, but they seemed less enthusiastic, less convinced by his act tonight. He just hadn't been able to get involved in the music and project himself.

Owen came into the dressing room. "It looked good," he said.

Bobby shook his head. "You don't have to come in here trying to put my ego back together, man."

Owen pulled up a chair, turned it and sat astride it with his elbows on its back. "What's the problem?"

"It was rucking terrible. Don't bullshit me."

"We sold out the house."

"Sure, sure."

"All right, tell me." The man's wrinkled, weathered face regarded Bobby with equanimity. It was the kind of face you could talk to easily.

Bobby shrugged. He started peeling off the makeup. "I don't exactly know." He wadded the plastic into a ball, tossed it aside. "Got something to do with the woman I saw today."

Do I know her?"

"Michael picked her up last night. Name's Lisa. From one of the ghetto zones."

"I saw her last night at the party. Didn't look like much."

"She isn't. But. . . . We went out of town this afternoon, because *she* wanted to, then we had kind of a fight, she pissed me off, and then . . ." He trailed off.

Owen laughed. "She sounds like a pain in the ass."

"Yeah, she is."

"So forget about her."

"It ain't that easy. She got me confused."

"About what?"

"About the way things are. I mean she acts like all the things I am, things I got, don't mean anything."

"Yeah? What's she got instead that's so great?"

"Nothing! But that ain't how she acts."

"So she's a con artist."

"Uh-uh. She's honest, I'll say that."

Owen scratched his head. "Listen, we're not getting to the point here. You've told me what you don't like about this woman. So what *do* you like about her?"

Bobby thought hard. "Well, first she was a challenge, 'cause she acted like she didn't need me." He thought some more. "She talked straight, didn't play games, didn't try to get money out of me, didn't act dumb about my image—you know how some of these women are, they drool all over me? She ain't that way. Talked to me like I was a person. I guess sometimes it's like, you know, you kind of want to impress a woman, and it fucks you up if you don't make it."

Owen raised his eyebrows. "You mean you *didn't* impress her? A kid like that from the ghetto?"

"I don't know. I just don't know. I don't have a handle on it. I don't understand her, but—and this is the worst part—I feel like she understands *me*. It's creepy."

Owen yawned. He rubbed the stubble on his jaw. "Sounds to me like the mystery's going to wear off, if you just see this woman a couple more times."

"But I don't know as how I will see her."

"Why not?"

"She's staying at Michael's."

"Ah, come on, Bobby, you steal Mike's women, he don't steal yours."

"Sure, but, I don't know. I said I'd call her after the concert . . ."

"So call her. She's probably waiting for it."

"Okay, okay." He went over to a phone on the wall and dialed the number. He waited, then put the receiver back on its hook. "No answer. See what I mean? I tell her I'll call her, and she goes out somewhere." He sat back down.

Owen sighed. "Look, what does this woman want most of all?"

"What does she want? Well, she was saying how she can't stand the city, and she wants to get out of it somewhere."

"Right. Easy. You get some place in the country and tell her she can stay in it." Owen spread his hands. "She can't refuse, if that's what she really wants. Then you got all the time you want with her, whenever you like. And if it don't work out with her, you can still tell her to leave."

Bobby gave him a funny look. "I kind of figured that angle myself," he said slowly. "Seemed a lot of trouble to take, for a dumb situation like this."

"Well, maybe. But I been thinking anyway, you ought to invest some of your cash. You know six months back I bought myself a piece. Farm in Nebraska. You can't go wrong with farm land, the way the food situation's going. It's an investment. You don't have to do anything with it—just wait while it gets more valuable. You ought to own some, whether this woman's in on the scene or not."

"You think so?"

"I've already taken my own advice. You take it, too."

"Farms and countryside, it ain't my thing."

"Making money's your thing, isn't it?"

"True."

"Then what you do is, tomorrow, you go to a real estate office upstate somewhere and make a purchase. There's easy pickings—a lot of people selling, and not many with the cash to buy. I'll come with you, even. See you don't get burned."

Bobby grinned. "Hey thanks, Owen."

"What I'm here for."

"Yeah, but thanks, anyhow." He stripped off his stage costume. "You're right, it's what I ought to do." His energy suddenly started coming back. "I was getting myself screwed up there, in circles."

Owen clapped him on the shoulder. "Happens to everyone, now and then. Look, this woman Lisa ain't home, but you still got Chris, right?"

"Right."

"So why don't you go over to her place now? Wouldn't do no harm."

"You trying to tell me something?"

"Kind of. She was here an hour back, stopped off to watch a bit of the concert . . ."

Bobby's expression clouded. "She saw my act?"

"Only a couple minutes. Said she was hungry, was going to eat, you could find her at home later if you wanted her. She, uh, seemed kind of pissed about something."

"Yeah, I know."

"Well, I don't think it'd do any harm to go see her and smooth it over. Cover yourself both ways, know what I mean? Mend your fences."

He nodded thoughtfully. "Yeah. I see what you mean. Yeah, I'll do that."

Michael put some music on—some old tunes from the mellow period of the seventies—and made himself comfortable beside Lisa on the couch. The pills they'd taken at the bar were working and they both felt more relaxed.

"Makes me feel good to eat real food," she said.

"Good food, good drugs."

"Which one of those two men do you believe?" she asked him. "Vickers or Jamieson?"

"Me? I don't believe either of 'em. The truth's in the middle somewhere. People were predicting doom twenty years ago—back when this music was recorded. Things did get harder, since then, but not impossible. There's never an ultimate crisis. Life goes on." He looked at her. "What about you? How do you think the future's going to be?"

"Bad, I guess. I'm a pessimist. But it doesn't really worry me; all I'll ever want is a little space where I can live in peace and do what I want."

"That's all?"

"Yes, that's all."

He shook his head. "It's not enough."

She smiled faintly. "You and Bobby Black."

"Me and him? What do you mean?" He was suddenly alert.

She poked him gently in the ribs, refusing to lose her relaxed mood. "You're just a little bit greedy. Although, actually, that's not fair—you don't have the same real hunger for money that he does."

"I enjoy what I have. I enjoy earning more. I can't deny that."

"Yes, I know, and I've been enjoying all the little luxuries myself, tonight. But the real question is, could you still be happy without them? Bobby couldn't—he could never be happy with less. But I could, and so could you, if you had to. If the future turned out really bad."

"Well, we'll never find out who's right till it happens, if it happens." He touched her shoulder. His fingers moved delicately, caressing the side of her neck. When she looked at him she found his face was close to hers.

They didn't say anything. They watched each other for a moment. Then he kissed her. His lips touched hers very softly, tentatively, and she let herself respond, putting one arm lightly around his neck. His hand ran slowly down over her body, as if learning its outlines. He was unhurried and relaxed.

"You know," he said, looking down at her, "some of our conversations have been awkward, and you aren't synthetically beautiful in the way I'm used to, but I like you a hell of a lot."

She looked uncertain. "Thank you," she said.

He kissed her again, still very restrained and gentle. His arms went around her, holding her as if afraid of hurting her—or making her feel trapped. The kiss lasted a long time.

Then: "Let's go in the bedroom," he said, still holding her close.

She looked up into his eyes, then away; then at him again. She shook her head quickly.

His face changed. Surprise, then frustration, then the emotions were erased as he reasserted his self-control. He let go of her. "I guess you don't like having sex with more than one guy per day."

"You don't know that I had sex with him."

"I think I do know."

She sighed. "Don't you see sometimes it's easier with someone who's simple to understand? I mean, I feel in control when I'm with Bobby. It's easy—he's predictable. But I don't know what the hell is going on when I'm with you."

"It doesn't have to be so complicated," he said. "We just go in there and fuck and enjoy ourselves."

"No. That would be wrong, with you. It'd be a waste. I don't want it to be casual. But . . . but at the same time I don't understand you enough for it to be deep or mutual or whatever you want to call it. And I don't like talking about it, because

I end up sounding corny or repressed or dumb, and anyway talking never helps, it just makes it even more awkward."

She avoided his eyes. He watched her, sizing up what she'd said. "I guess I understand," he said. "You don't want to fuck, because you don't trust me." He sounded scornful. Then, surprising her, he quickly grabbed her face between his palms and kissed her savagely, with none of the tenderness he'd shown before. His mouth forced hers open and pressed hard. His hands shifted, grabbing her shoulders, his fingers digging in. Then, just as she started resisting, he released her completely.

She looked at him in surprise. He stood breathing hard, hands hanging by his sides. "You don't believe anything I tell you, so I thought I'd *show* you how I feel."

She felt shaken. She didn't know what to say.

He turned and walked away. "I'm going to bed," he said, over his shoulder.

"Please, Michael," she called to him.

"Please what?" He paused.

"Don't fight with me."

"I'm not. I'm going to bed."

"You're all messed up with your pride and your jealousy of Bobby—damn it, you . . . you mean more than he does, you know. Don't you realize?"

He paused a moment longer. "Thanks."

"Don't rush it, that's all. I'm a conservative person."

He nodded. "All right."

"See you tomorrow?"

"Sure." He sighed. "This is all very juvenile. Good night, Lisa." He went into his bedroom, shutting the door behind him.

Chris' Apartment

Like Michael, Chris lived in a haven. Bobby had to stop and show a pass at the gate. Then he drove along the wide street to her building, peering up at her windows on the top floor—

the apartment that he'd chosen and rented for her himself.

Her lights were on. He grunted with satisfaction, parked the car, and walked into the building lobby.

The lobby guard recognized Bobby and greeted him with a professional smile. "Evening, sir. Good concert tonight?"

"Yeah, just fine, thanks."

"Shall I announce you, sir?" The man picked up a phone.

"No, I think she's kind of expecting that I might drop in."

"I don't think she is, sir."

Bobby stopped by the guard's desk. His eyes narrowed. "What do you mean?" He felt in his pocket and pulled out a few bills.

"She came in with another gentleman, sir." The money disappeared discreetly. "They went up about a half-hour ago."

"Bitch," Bobby muttered. "Just because, this afternoon. . . ."

"*Shall* I announce you, sir?"

"No. I've got to get something from my car." He strode out. He returned a second later and went straight to the elevators. "I'll announce myself, thanks."

Up on her floor, he took out a bunch of keys and found the one to her door. He opened it, tense with anger but keeping very quiet. He crept into the apartment, stopped, and listened.

Voices from her bedroom. Sounds of movement.

He went quickly through the apartment and kicked open the bedroom door. "Surprise," he said.

She was naked with a man he'd never seen before. They both looked up at him, frozen in attitudes of surprise, tangled up together in the bed that filled most of the mirrored room.

The strange man scrambled up clumsily onto his knees. "What—who the hell are you?"

Bobby half-smiled, half-sneered. "Her husband. What's your story?"

"Bobby, you got no right coming in here," said Chris. "Go on, why don't you go and . . ."

"Get this bum out," he told her.

"Maybe he don't want to go," said Chris. "Or maybe I don't want him to." She sounded cowardly behind her bravado.

Bobby reached in his pocket and pulled out the knife with a quick motion he'd never forgotten since his days on the street. He bent his knees slightly. The knife blade snapped out, gleaming, pointing at the man's face. "You got half a minute to put your clothes on," he said quietly, savoring the scene. Pretty-boy rich kid, he thought to himself. Watch him run.

The guy backed off across the big bed. "All right," he said suddenly. "All right, all right, I'm going." He looked at Chris. "Hell, you didn't tell me you were married."

"He's not my husband, you asshole." She pulled a blanket over herself, retreating into the corner. She glared sullenly at Bobby.

The naked man took only a few seconds to locate his clothes and get into them. Bobby advanced on him and chased him from the apartment like a scared cat. Then he slammed the apartment door, locked it, and returned to the bedroom.

"You think you can do what you like," Chris shouted at him, launching into a speech he guessed she'd been preparing. "You lie to me and go off with other women and treat me any way you want and then you expect me to do anything and always be here when you want me, like I'm some kind of service you don't even have to pay for."

"Oh, I'll pay. Here." He emptied some bills onto the bed. Then he started unbuttoning his shirt, looking at her body.

"No sale!" She clutched her knees up to her breasts. "Go away. Get out of my apartment."

"You ain't fooling anyone with your little routine." He stepped out of his pants. "I know what you want and so do you. And I got it right here."

"You're disgusting."

"Oh, sure."

"Do you think I'm your slave?" Her voice was shrill.

He got onto the bed and advanced on her.

"Leave me alone!"

"You're making too much noise." He grabbed her by her

shoulders and pulled her up against him, forcing his mouth onto hers. She struggled against him, but it was feeble and unconvincing. His hand went down, to her breast, to her thighs, feeling her crudely. For a moment he remembered how Lisa had felt, outdoors on the river bank, so strange and yet so good; quickly he thrust the memory away.

"You bastard," she said weakly, when he took his mouth from hers.

"Yeah, I'm a bastard, you know that." He twisted his fingers in her hair and tugged, watching her wince. "In fact, sometimes sweetheart I think that's what you like about me." He kissed her hard again. Then he pushed her over face-down on the bed, held her there, and entered her. "In fact I think you love it," he added, half to himself, looking down at her.

He remembered Lisa again, and suddenly found himself feeling detached, uninterested in Chris, despising her for being so easy.

USE ME

I said, Hey excuse me
Baby why don't we go somewhere?
You couldn't refuse me
You thought I looked sexy standing there
And you thought you could use me
To get you some action
Hurt and abuse me
For your satisfaction

> You were just cruisin'
> Pilled-up and boozin'
> Ready to grab all you could get
> Selfish and mean the night we met
> It soon got confusin'
> Who was doing the usin'
> When you discovered I was more
> Than you had ever bargained for

And now you accuse me
Of stealing your heart and hurting you
You know you amuse me
I only did what you'd tried to do
You thought you could use me
Like some little boy
Hurt and abuse me
Make me your toy

Coda:

You never thought
Your plans would fall through
But now you're caught
And I'm using you
Oh yes it's true
I'm using you

TRANSACTIONS

"The answer to our problems does not lie within these glass doors." The amplified voice echoed across the parking lot, shrill and insistent. "The answer is not in consumer goods, it is not in wealth, it is not in luxuries. The answer is inside each and every one of you. Self-denial! Self-sufficiency! The decades of greed and plenty are gone. Trying to pretend that this is not so can only lead to *emotional torment!* You!" The speaker at the microphone pointed to Michael and Lisa, walking toward the entry doors of the giant suburban shopping center. "Yes, you! Stop and think. Can true happiness ever come from gratifying your senses with materialistic self-indulgence?" The speaker was a tall, white-haired, red-faced man in a clerical collar and an old denim suit. He stood on a simple dais under a utilitarian sign: WESTBURGH SPARTANS WELCOME REVEREND ISAACS. A dozen disciples dressed in rags were handing out literature to anyone who would accept it.

"I'm convinced those people have to be government-supported," Michael said, walking into the store with Lisa, out of range of the loudspeaker.

"It was the Reverend Isaacs that they quoted against you in that publicity release about suicide rock, wasn't it?"

"Probably. I don't remember. I try not to take any notice of the Spartans. I'm not necessarily against living frugally, but the way they self-righteously try to ram it down people's throats. . . ." He trailed off. He was feeling depressed. Both of them sensed her rejection of him the previous night still hanging over them, as something unresolved but unmentioned.

They wandered through the vast store, guiding a king-size electric shopping cart and pausing in front of the hundreds of automatic goods dispensers, using his magnetic ID to order everything from clothes to a camping stove and cooking utensils. Canned music drifted through the shining corridors.

They didn't say much to each other. Lisa finally dropped the pretense of enjoying the expedition when the cart was three-quarters full. "I can get the rest some other time," she told Michael.

"That'll mean a separate trip. We might as well finish now."

"I don't want to. Let's go."

"Didn't you want to come here? I was just trying to do what you wanted, Lisa."

She shook her head, feeling mixed-up and irritable. "No you weren't. You were . . . you were trying to get back at me."

"I don't understand."

"Yes you do. You insisted on bringing me here this morning. I didn't suggest it. You wanted to rub my nose in it—my plans to leave town on my own. You wanted to make me feel guilty. Either that or you're testing me, and my feelings. I don't like those kinds of games."

He stared moodily at the mound of purchases. "You're very acute."

"I'm not dumb, certainly." She took his arm. "You're acting sullen and it doesn't suit you. Let's go out somewhere. Laurence and Sheila's party is tonight, isn't it? There's the whole afternoon till then. You rented that station wagon this morning; we might as well use it and drive somewhere."

"What about all this stuff we've bought?"

"What about it? We'll take it with us. I still want it, if that's what you mean. I'll need it when I—I still *want* to get out of town. Eventually. I don't enjoy ghetto life, you know."

"Who says you have to go back to a ghetto if you remain in the city?"

"It's either that or accept favors from someone who supports me, which I wouldn't like."

He shook his head. "Not necessarily. I could probably find you some work as a designer, if that's what you're good at."

She looked dubious. "Of course, there's another possibility."

"What's that?"

"You could leave everything in the city and come away with me."

He laughed. "Oh, sure. Sure I could."

They left the store. Outside, the Spartans had been joined by a picket line of suburban dwellers holding placards reading FOOD FOR OUR KIDS and WE WANT JOBS. Michael avoided looking at them as he wheeled the giant cart of purchases across the lot and started loading them into the station wagon.

"A thousand acres, and all of them arable," the salesman shouted above the noise of the helicopter engine. He swept his arm in a grand gesture encompassing the rich green fields a few hundred feet below. "Three springwater sources, one yielding at least two hundred gallons per minute. Artesian well. Low soil acidity. Certified agricultural analysis and surveyors' reports from two independent agencies. Farmhouse with eight outbuildings. Well-maintained equipment—four tractors, one seed drill. . . ." The spiel went on.

"Looks good," said Owen.

Bobby shrugged. "If you say so. But it's a hell of a lot of cash."

"Well, it's a hell of a lot of land."

"It'll half-way clean me out, Owen."

"But you aren't spending the money, you're investing it."

"I'll try and remember that." Bobby tapped the salesman on the shoulder. "Let's get back to your office and talk terms," he shouted above the noise.

"Fine!" He gestured to the pilot, and the helicopter wheeled around and headed back to the small town where the real estate office was located.

By late afternoon the deal was closed. Bobby signed the contract and Owen witnessed it. Then Bobby gave his universal credit number and watched the salesman punch it into the computer terminal, followed by Bobby's name and a dozen other statistics. Finally, Bobby wrote his signature on a sensor plate and pressed his fingerprints beside it.

There was a minute's pause while electronic equipment several hundred miles away verified the transaction and the identities of the parties involved. Then the line printer clattered out the news that most of Bobby's assets had been instantly converted from bonds, savings accounts, and small investments into cash, then equally magically transferred from his account to the agent's, whence it would pass, less a percentage, to the account of the vendor of the land.

"Do you remember when it all had to be done on paper? Used to take days." The salesman chuckled cheerfully. He handed the deed to the land across his desk. "Signed, sealed, and delivered, as they used to say. It's all yours. Going to move onto the property right away?"

Bobby looked at the document, feeling slightly queasy. He couldn't shake the impression that he'd just been electronically robbed. "I'll get a caretaker out there in a day or two," he said. "Right now I think maybe I'll go back to town."

"Well, your farm's out there whenever you want it, young fella." The salesman shook hands vigorously and gave a cheerful wave as Owen and Bobby left the office.

"You know, even if you have second thoughts," Owen told him, "you can always sell that land. Probably at a profit."

"Yeah, I guess so." Bobby looked thoughtful.

"So why don't we head over to Laurence and Sheila's? It's a couple hours' drive from here. Be just in time for their party. You can celebrate."

Bobby grinned. He stuffed the deed inside his jacket. "Yeah, that's right. Celebrate."

A Time of Crisis

Michael and Lisa drove up the track to Laurence's house. It was eight o'clock and the warm summer evening was alive with the sound of crickets. The car engine murmured; the tires scuffed the gravel; insects flashed across the headlight beams.

Coming closer to the house, they heard music on the night air. They turned a corner and found the driveway full of parked automobiles. Floodlights had been erected over the front lawn, going through kaleidoscopic changes of hue in rhythm with sounds playing through loudspeakers at the corners of the garden. A big table had been set up outside the house, dispensing pills and liquor. Fifty or sixty guests were out on the Astroturf under the lights and the soft black sky.

Laurence was standing by the table handing out ups and downs. He was wearing one of his jackets, its gems flashing through cascades of color. "Would you like something to drink?" He saw Michael and Lisa walking over to him. "Hi, I'm glad you could come. Have you had a nice day?" He was talking strangely, vaguely, as if not quite aware of what he was saying.

"We've been driving around. We revisited the place where I grew up as a child," said Lisa.

"Oh, that's nice."

"Yes. Although it's all changed now—it's owned by a big farming combine. How are you? Did you sort out your problems?"

Laurence's brow creased. "Problems? Well, Sheila and me have been . . . oh, you mean problems with the farm and the solar heating and everything." He shook his head. "There's a man supposed to be coming tomorrow." He paused uncertainly. "I hope this is going to be a good party, I had to do most of the preparations myself. She wanted to cancel it, but. . . ." He trailed off vaguely.

"Where's Sheldon?" said Michael.

"We fed him a whole lot of Seconal. Excuse me." He went to meet two new guests.

The music boomed across the garden. Elegant people in elegant clothes struck poses and exchanged smalltalk on the lawn. A barbecue turned a cut of soysteak in front of infrared burners. An olfactory unit plugged in with the music broadcast heady odors on the summer air. And yet there was a strange sense of ennui, as if the party were just ending, rather than just beginning.

"It isn't working," said Lisa. "There's something missing."

"Give it time. Once people get stoned . . ."

"Well, hi there," said a voice. Bobby's voice. "Mike, Lisa." He came up to them, looking pleased with himself, immaculate in a costume of black silk interwoven with streamers of vivid yellow and red, licking up from his ankles to his waist as though he were being devoured by flames. "Hey, Mike, do you mind if I talk to Lisa for just a moment?"

"Go ahead," said Michael. He didn't move.

"Yeah, it's kind of personal, understand?"

The two men looked at each other. "All right," said Michael, cool and quiet. "I'll be in the living room. It's almost time for the presidential speech, and I don't want to miss it after what Jamieson said last night."

"I'll join you there in a minute," Lisa said to him. Then, as he left, "What do you want, Bobby?"

He seemed not to notice the reserve and hostility in her voice. He took her arm and walked her across the plastic grass. "Got some news for you. Wanted you to be the first to know. I went and bought myself a thousand acres today, upstate."

"You bought land?"

"Sure did." He grinned. "I'm telling you, Lisa, I decided, after what we talked about, I wanted a place in the country. When I want something, I go get it. You should see it. Kind of a quaint old farmhouse, maybe a hundred years old, but in good shape. It's got its own well out back, pure water, not like the piss they pipe in back in town." He was watching her face, as if playing a game with her, waiting for her response. "I figure I'll get some cows, for fresh milk, cheese, you know? Chickens for fresh eggs, and maybe hire labor to plant crops. Yeah, I done it, the whole bit."

"You're very lucky," she said stiffly, "to be able to go out and get that, so easily."

"Well, I guess that's true. But I ain't going to hog it, know what I mean? If you wanted to stay out there any time . . . in fact, you know how I was joking about needing a caretaker?"

Well, I guess it ain't a joke anymore, 'cause I certainly need *someone* to look after the place, who knows about farming."

"I see."

"What's the matter? You don't sound like it grabs you. I'm telling you, Lisa, you'd love it out there. There's birds singing and there's trees and a little river, everything."

She sighed. "I didn't think you'd actually go this far."

"Well, baby, when I do something, I do it all the way. So what do you say?" He took her shoulder, turning her toward him. Then he saw her face. "Hey, for Christ's sake, what is this?"

She wiped her tears away with an angry gesture of her arm. "Nothing. I think you'd better leave me alone."

But he kept hold of her. "What is it? Hey, is it Mike, has he been upsetting you?"

"*No!*"

"Then what—shit, I thought you'd be pleased, to have a place you could go to out of town."

"Yes, yes, it's just exactly what I wanted."

"So?"

"So I can't accept your kind offer, do you understand?"

He stood and stared at her, trying to figure her out. "You can't accept? Why not?"

"Your money won't buy you everything. There are people who don't take bribes." She pulled free from him and turned and ran away across the lawn, pushing between the other guests, disappearing into the house.

Bobby scowled. He muttered something under his breath, then went striding after her, grabbing a handful of pills from the table as he passed and throwing them in his mouth.

Lisa found Michael in the living room, with ten or fifteen other guests sitting around the television. Jamieson was there, and Vickers, and Chris, Laurence, and others whom she didn't know. She went and sat beside Michael, trying to keep her expression and emotions under control. On the TV screen there was a picture of the White House.

"And now, live from the Oval Office, the President of the United States."

Bobby strode into the room. He scanned the faces, "Hey, Lisa?"

The president's face came on the TV screen: weary, pale beneath layers of makeup, pouches under his eyes. "My fellow Americans," he began. "Good evening to you all."

Bobby started around the room. "Lisa, for Christ's sake, I ain't trying to bribe you."

"Shhh!" said someone.

"Hey, come on, Lisa." He took her arm.

"Leave me alone."

"The news I have tonight is not good news," the president was saying in a leaden voice. "But in this time of crisis, I and my advisors have determined that there is only one course open to us, to rebuild this great nation and finally *end* the so-called Age of Scarcity."

"I just want to talk to you, that's all," Bobby persisted.

"She said to leave her *alone*," Michael put in, deliberate and firm.

"You keep out of it!" Bobby glared at him.

"Hey, come on, we want to listen to the speech," someone shouted across the room.

". . . the worst year ever, for agriculture, for manufacturing industries, for employment, for our cities. . . ."

"Lisa, there *ain't no strings*. I'm offering you what you said you always wanted."

"I know what you're offering, and the answer is *no!*"

". . . measures to halt the slide of our economy once and for all, protect our resources from any further unscrupulous exploitation, and preserve law and order at a time when chaos threatens the very fabric of society. . . ."

Bobby swore. He glanced around the room. For the first time, he realized Chris was there, sitting watching him, looking pale and grim.

". . . a special committee including representatives from the Congress, determine that there is no alternative but to impose controls on resources strategic for national survival. These resources include mineral deposits, fossil fuels, isotopes of uranium, arable farmland. . . ."

Bobby moved across the room, ignoring the people he stepped over and in front of. He made Chris move up, and sat down beside her, grabbing her to him with his arm around her shoulders. He glared across at Michael and Lisa.

". . . also subject to controls including privately owned reserves of oil, gasoline, timber, and metals such as gold, silver, nickel, aluminum, platinum, zinc, tin . . ."

Chris was looking at Bobby as if she wanted to pull away from him but was scared to do so. He tilted her face back, then kissed her roughly on the mouth.

". . . and ammunition, firearms, armored vehicles, and individually held stocks of food in quantities exceeding that necessary for the sustenance of one individual for seven days."

"In other words, no hoarding," said a voice. It was Jamieson, sitting in one corner. His attention was focused on the TV screen. He had hardly noticed Bobby's presence in the room.

"That ain't so bad," someone else said.

The president leaned forward confidentially. "What does this mean, to you, the average American? How are these controls going to be enforced? Well, first of all, there will be penalties for the acquisition or the storage of the resources I have just mentioned. These penalties take effect *as of now;* due to the state of national emergency, the Congress has agreed to waive the usual procedure of formal discussion and enactment of legislation. We must stop the stockpiling of survival resources by selfish private individuals, and stop it now, before it has any chance to get out of hand."

"Unconstitutional," said Vickers.

"Yes," said Jamieson, with no surprise.

"Secondly," said the president, "strategic commodities, in-

cluding food, are to be rationed. The disastrous harvests this
summer; the pressure from abroad to export food to our allies,
suffering far more than we here in America; the decimation of
crops by resistant insects; the pollution and depletion of fish
stocks in our oceans—all of these factors have combined to
create a food shortage far worse than any we have experienced
before. Ration coupons will be issued by the Internal Revenue
Service, to *all* taxpayers and their families."

The room was stunned into silence. Even Bobby started paying attention to the speech.

"Lastly and most importantly," the president paused, as if
finding difficulty in continuing, "with greatest reluctance—
especially, my fellow Americans, on the part of myself, your
president . . ." he paused again, "at a time when our survival
depends on our resources, we cannot any longer allow these
resources to be exploited by selfish individuals in an unregulated
economy. Prices *must* be stabilized, commodities *must* be con-
served, and the only way to assure this is by federal control.
Henceforth, as of now, by special consent of the Congress, the
Senate, and the Supreme Court of the United States, the federal
government will exercise temporary powers wherever necessary
to effect compulsory purchase and control of privately owned
land containing mineral deposits, fossil fuels, uranium isotopes,
and of course farmland, so vital for our nation's diminishing
supplies of food. In no other way can we protect the people of
this nation from unscrupulous speculators who would wish to
control these resources for their own selfish ends."

Bobby stared at the screen. Slowly he began to understand
what the man was saying.

"The compulsory purchase of such land, at a figure determined by the federal government, will of course *only be temporary*, during this limited state of emergency. Once these controls
have achieved the dramatic turnaround in our economy that we
anticipate, hopefully within six months, definitely within one
year, it will be possible to return to the system of private owner-

ship and free enterprise in which I, as you, so wholeheartedly believe."

"Totalitarianism," said Vickers, looking stunned.

"It has not been an easy task, my fellow Americans, to bring you the news of these emergency measures." The president seemed to want to avoid looking into the TV camera focused on his face. "I trust you will understand the gravity of the situation, and do all you can to cooperate in this time of crisis. Limited deployment of the National Guard will be authorized wherever necessary to ensure that everyone *does* cooperate with these measures. No one will be allowed to evade the law—to hoard, control, or consume more than his fair share."

"With the exception of those who are *above* the law," said Jamieson, quietly.

The president paused, as if knowing that he still had more to say, but lacking the energy to say it. Where was the obligatory closing note of guarded optimism and hope? Abruptly he seemed to abandon the task. "Goodnight, my fellow Americans."

And the picture went dark; then cut back to the exterior shot of the White House. "Ladies and gentlemen, you have just heard a special broadcast from the President of the United States. For a commentary on the speech, we return now to our studio where guests Paul Friedman, the noted economist; a representative from the Spartans religious organization; and . . ."

"Turn it off!" someone shouted. "Off, turn it off!"

Someone turned it off.

It was very quiet in the living room. Then, as if on cue, Sheila wandered in. "What are all you people *doing* in here?" she said, into the aching, gloomy silence. "I mean this is supposed to be a *party*, isn't it?"

Laurence had been sitting watching the speech with everyone else. He stood up and walked toward her.

"Why aren't you out in the garden with the *guests?*" she complained at him. "This party was *your idea*, wasn't it?"

He grabbed her arm, unexpectedly roughly. "Outside," he told her, pulling her after him.

As they left, people started talking.

"Well?" said Jamieson, to Vickers.

"They've made a mistake. A very big mistake. They don't have the power that they think they have."

"This country still commands a large army," said Jamieson. "Now that the line seems to be being drawn between the haves and the have-nots, the army personnel are all on the haves' side. Like civil servants in general." He gave Vickers a twisted, ironic smile.

Vickers scowled. He stared at the blank TV screen. "Those stupid, senile sons of bitches; they don't know what the fuck they're doing." Suddenly he stood up. He strode out of the room.

"Back to Washington, I suppose," murmured Jamieson.

Lisa leaned across to him. She put her hand on his arm. "Mr. Jamieson?"

"Yes? Oh, it's . . . Lisa, isn't it?"

"Yes. Did the speech—the things he described—mean that the government can literally *take away* farmland? For a token price?"

"That was the implication."

"Will they actually do it?"

"They wouldn't have said so, if they don't intend to."

"I see. Thank you." She sat back beside Michael, with a strained smile on her face. She looked across at Bobby.

"It don't mean shit," he said suddenly. He stood up. "There'll be a demonstration, a fucking revolution."

Jamieson turned and looked at him. "You're fooling yourself. The American people allowed their democratic powers to be taken away years ago."

"People won't stand for it!" He turned and grabbed Chris' arm, pulling her up on her feet. "Come on," he told her, "we got to go find Owen."

"What's the matter with you?" she was saying as he hustled her out of the room. "Why are you acting so weird?"

Gradually the room emptied out, till Jamieson, Michael, and Lisa were the only people left.

"Bobby bought land today," Lisa said. "Farmland."

"Ah," said Jamieson. "Now I understand."

"Was that what he had to tell you out there on the lawn?" asked Michael.

"Yes. He wanted me to go and—to live on it—it was a bribe, he wanted to have me where he—it doesn't matter. You heard what I told him."

"Yes, I did. I didn't realize he wanted you that badly."

She looked at the floor. "He doesn't, really. He just thinks he does."

There was a short silence.

Michael turned to Jamieson. "So what happens next?"

"Next?" Jamieson laughed dryly. "Well, these supposedly temporary emergency measures were described as being to protect people from being exploited. But of course they'll have just the opposite effect. This country has grown steadily poorer in the last fifteen years, as resources grew scarcer and the economic system failed. The lower-income groups suffered first, then unemployment eroded the middle-income groups. Finally the people who still control the really big concentrations of wealth and power decided to do something to stop the erosion of wealth rising any higher through the system."

"How do you mean?"

"Well, this anti-hoarding law. It restricts you and I from stockpiling food, say, or gasoline. In that sense it keeps us poor. But you don't imagine the people with real influence will be limited, do you? They'll have ways around it. Likewise the compulsory purchase idea; small and medium-sized holdings of land and resources can now be bought up by the government, but you can bet that won't happen to any of the big holdings, controlled by the major corporations. No, all of this is an attempt to grab what's left of the resources in America, keep them for the wealthy classes, and leave everyone else on a subsistence level."

"I thought I was part of the 'wealthy classes' myself," said Michael, with a faint smile, "but I don't see that any of this is going to help *me* at all."

"No, because you're nouveau riche. Do you have friends in government? Relatives in any of the big business families? Connections who could get you into one of the armored superhavens in the Midwest, where the super-rich are beginning to retreat now? No, your position is not that good."

"Well, I can live off my savings. . . ."

"You have the money invested?"

"Very little of it. The market was so bad."

"Then I assume it's held by banks?"

"A lot of it."

Jamieson sighed. "You have to realize that the banking system is controlled by some of the most powerful, least scrupulous people of all. It wouldn't surprise me, now, if first of all the banks were closed, to avoid a run on them in the initial panic that these new measures will cause. And then it's quite possible for many of the banks to default, or pretend to. Perhaps depositors could be paid a small percentage of what they had in their accounts—like stockholders when a corporation goes bankrupt."

"But you're just guessing."

Jamieson shrugged. "Naturally. But even if you keep your money, inflation is going to be something no one has ever experienced before in America. And what will you spend your money on, when large supplies of all the real necessities are either controlled or rationed?"

Michael frowned. He massaged his forehead. "There'll still be an entertainment business. People will always need entertainment."

"Maybe. But for how long will they be able to pay for it, as their wealth is eroded? Will they be able to pay for concerts, tapes, record albums? There'll still be radio and TV, but you can expect the government to take over more and more of that, as stations go bankrupt when their advertising revenues disappear, as they will, when the masses can no longer afford to buy anything that's made commercially."

"You think I should go into another line of business?"

"I think you should forget the notion of 'business.' The only businessmen who are going to stay rich are the ones who sell to the government, directly or indirectly."

"What? Then what's the answer?"

Jamieson coughed apologetically. "You may just have to accept a lower standard of living."

"Less and less, right? Till there's nothing at all?" He shook his head. "No, no, that's no way." He frowned. "There has to be a way around this. They can't . . ."

"They can. Or at least, they think they can. Oh, there's going to be a furor, naturally. I'm sure that Congress as a whole didn't consent to these panic measures, and in effect the government has been subjected to a kind of a coup. But the erosion of constitutional safeguards has gone so far, I doubt that people like Vickers, or anyone else, can reverse things at this stage."

"You're convinced of that, aren't you?"

"I'm afraid I am."

Michael stood up. "I have to think this through." He looked down at Lisa. "Will you wait for me here? I'm just going for a short walk, to try to clear my head."

"I'll wait, yes."

"I won't be long."

He went out of the room, through the house. The party had fallen apart as news of the speech spread and its implications sank in. Half the guests were leaving, and the other half were swallowing downers with an air of grim self-destructiveness. Someone had put a Bobby Black album on the stereo, and the song of death and doom wasn't a joke anymore.

Laurence and Sheila were standing in the hall. "But there must be *something* you can do!" she was shouting at him.

Laurence spread his hands. "Tell me what."

"Well, you've got friends, haven't you? People with some kind of influence? I mean you're not telling me you're just going to let us be *thrown out* of this place."

"No one says we're going to be thrown out."

"But we haven't got *security* anymore, have we? You just said, they can buy this place from under us for ten cents whenever they feel like it!"

"So what do you expect me to do? Picket the White House?"

"I don't expect you to be so damned *useless!*" Her voice was a shrill screech. She seemed hysterical.

Laurence was growing angry. It was surfacing, under his normally abstracted, slow disposition. "Let me tell you something," he said. "If we *did* lose this farm it wouldn't mean anything."

Her mouth fell open. "Wouldn't *mean* anything? Jesus Christ you schmuck, it's all we've got!"

"We've been poor before."

"What are you *saying?*"

"I'm saying it wouldn't hurt to be poor again. You're behaving like it's the end of the world. But we don't need this place, all these gadgets, all this dumb, worthless *shit.*"

She had turned quite pale. She was looking at him blankly. "But you're my *husband,* I always thought I could *trust* you!"

"Yeah? Trust me to do what? Earn a living *and* do the housework *and* make a farm out there as well, while you watch TV and mess the place up the whole time? Well, I may be a schmuck, but I'm not a fucking *moron.*"

She reached for him. "Why are you talking like this?"

He shook her hand off. "Because I've had enough. Your insecurity and your demands and your shitting on me. I'll tell you, if we got rid of all this crap," he swung his arm around, encompassing the house, "you know it wouldn't bother me. It wouldn't matter a damn." He turned his back on her and walked away.

Sheila stood looking shaken. Slowly she wandered through to the front garden. Michael followed her. "He's right, you know," he said quietly, touching her shoulder.

She looked up at him sharply. She seemed bewildered, like an abandoned child. "This farm is all we've got," she said blankly.

"You lived okay before you had it."

"You don't understand. I was *relying* on Laurence." She turned away from Michael and wandered across the floodlit garden. Chris was sitting on her own on one of the ornamental benches. Sheila walked over to the girl and joined her. Feeling he ought to be able to help in some way, Michael followed.

". . . still got each other," he heard Chris saying dully. Michael saw that the women were holding each others' hands.

"But it's all fallen apart," said Sheila.

"I know. Bobby told me, he put most of his money into that land. All of it. With an instant credit transfer. Oh, Christ, what are we going to do?" Chris started crying.

"I don't know."

"I don't have anything saved. Bobby's been supporting me. Now he's saying he can't afford to. I don't know if he's being straight with me, or what."

Sheila stood up. She helped Chris to her feet. "Let's take a walk."

The record was still playing through the outdoor sound system. "So if you're dissatisfied, you'll swallow your conscience and pride, and go leap down some steep mountainside . . . take me with you, when you go. . . ."

Not knowing quite why, Michael started following the two women, far enough behind them to be unnoticed. They climbed over an old wooden fence in shrubbery at the end of the garden. When he next caught sight of them they were walking up an incline of moonlit grassy land dotted with bushes and trees.

They stopped at the crest of the hill. The noise of the party seemed far away.

"... interested in that other woman," Chris was saying. "Says he isn't but I know he is. I don't understand it. It's all so fucked up."

"Laurence and I have been fighting a lot, too."

"Yeah?"

"I always *relied* on him." Sheila sat down on the grass.

"There's an old fifties song I used to sing," said Chris. Her speech was a little slurred, as if she'd been taking a lot of pills. "Back when I first met him, you know? I used to get real romantic." She laughed, a forced, miserable sound. "It goes, 'Each night I sit at home, hoping that he will phone, but I know he has somebody else, still in my heart I pray, that there will come a day, when I will have him all to myself. I want to be Bobby's girl, I want to be Bobby's girl, that's the most important thing to me, and if I were Bobby's girl, what a thankful, faithful girl I'd be.' Christ, can you believe that?" She stood up unsteadily. "Fuck you, Bobby Black!" she shouted, as loud as she could. "You bastard! You miserable bastard!" She started crying again.

Sheila pulled her back down beside her and embraced her. The two women kissed. They lay down together on the ground.

Feeling embarrassed in the role of voyeur, Michael turned and crept away from them. Discovering that Chris and Sheila had a lesbian relationship hadn't surprised him, he realized; too much else had already happened that evening for him to be capable of being surprised. It was as if he had blinked and the world had fragmented. Nothing was the same, now. Except maybe Lisa. Although that was uncertain, too; a tenuous beginning which could lead to something good or fall apart like everything else. He felt a sudden need to get back to the house and try to resolve something out of all the intangibles.

He walked back. When he reached the front lawn he found couples and groups sprawled on the ground half-naked over each other, groping around in drugged stupors. The suicide rock songs were still playing, and Michael felt a sudden wave of anger at the music, at himself, at the whole mess. He strode into the house. "Turn that fucking noise off!" he shouted.

No one paid any attention. He pushed between people zonked out on downers, found the control console and stopped the music himself. But then the silence was almost worse. He found some more upbeat material and put that on instead.

"Why'd you kill my songs, man?" It was Bobby, lurching into the room, stoned out of his head.

"They weren't helping any," said Michael.

Bobby swayed. "You killed my music, you motherfucker."

"Talk to me when you're straight." Michael tried to push past him.

Bobby grabbed his arm. "We got something to settle first."

"Come on, Bobby, cut it out. What's the matter with you?"

Bobby laughed without any humor. "What's the matter with me? Are you kidding? Are you dumb or something?"

"We're all in the same situation. You're no worse off than Laurence or me or anyone."

"I'm in the *shit*, man. That fucking bitch . . ."

"Chris?"

"No, you asshole. Lisa. Lisa the cockteaser. I'd still have some bread left if it wasn't for that bitch."

Michael wasn't in any mood to try to humor Bobby. "You don't have anything to curse her about. You had your chance at her, didn't you? Wasn't that what you wanted?"

"I buy the fucking land, I piss away my money, now she tells me to screw off." Bobby kicked out suddenly. His foot thudded into a piece of wooden sculpture. The wood split with a crunch; Bobby's shoe ruptured open. "She tells that to *me*."

"If you thought you could buy her by buying the land, you were making a dumb mistake."

Bobby rounded on him. "Don't tell me what to do, motherfucker. You smug bastard. You came off all right, didn't you? Nice, very nice. I make an asshole out of myself over that bitch, and you wind up with your hooks in her."

"Go and sleep it off," said Michael. Again, he tried to push past Bobby.

Bobby grabbed him and stopped him. "You don't walk out on me, man."

"I'll do what I please."

Bobby laughed nastily. "Oh no, we got a partnership, remember? A beautiful little partnership. I put up with your shit, you put up with mine. Right?"

Michael shook his head slowly. Suddenly, he realized what he had to do, the only way to go. "We don't have a partnership. Not anymore."

Bobby absorbed the news slowly. It penetrated his fuzzy, drugged senses. It reached his brain. "What you telling me?"

"We don't work together anymore. You're on your own."

Bobby shook his head. "Oh no. No, we got a contract, you bastard, and you'll stick to it."

"You're going to *force* me to think up new songs for you? Good ones?" Michael grimaced. "You can try."

Bobby looked incredulous. "You son of a bitch."

"What are you going to do about it, Bobby?" Michael felt a little intoxicated, high on the confrontation. "Going to sue me? Or beat me up?"

"You ain't running out on me and dumping me in it, that's for sure." Bobby lunged at him.

Michael side-stepped. His mind was clear; Bobby's was fogged. It was easy to avoid him. He blundered, slammed into the wall where Michael had been standing. "I'll get you," he promised. "I swear to God."

A big hand landed on Bobby's shoulder. "Time to go," said a voice.

Michael saw it was Owen, weary and looking old, but resolute.

Bobby turned slowly and focused on his manager, then grunted. "You fucking me over like the rest of 'em?"

Owen shook his head. "All I know is we got to get back to town. There'll be some business to attend to tomorrow, first thing. We've got to come out on top of this situation."

"Tell that to *him*." Bobby jerked his thumb at Michael.

"He'll come around, tomorrow or the next day," said Owen. "Tonight's not the time to settle anything."

"I'm *not* coming around, tomorrow or next week or next month," Michael said deliberately. "I'm through."

Owen looked at him. "You're a fool if you mean it."

"I'm not a fool. I'm being realistic."

"Since when is giving up being realistic?"

"Since tonight. I'm just leaving the ship before it sinks, that's all."

Owen shook his head. "There'll always be a way to make a buck in the city if you're smart enough. That ain't going to change."

Michael shrugged. "I wish you luck."

Bobby turned and spat at him. "That's what I wish you, you cocksucker."

Their eyes met. Michael felt himself clenching his fist. He started trembling. Finally, his control broke. He moved suddenly, erratically, swinging his arm. He bashed Bobby in the mouth.

Bobby reeled back. His lip started bleeding. He looked as if he couldn't believe it. He touched his face and looked at the blood on his fingers. Then he looked up at Michael. "I'll fucking kill you," he said.

Michael stood breathing fast, his mouth dry, his head ringing. "I should have done that a long time ago. God knows I wanted to often enough."

"If you try it again you'll find me in your way," said Owen.

Michael shook his head. "Once was enough." He collected

himself. "I'm sorry I hit him in the face. Wouldn't want to spoil those looks of his." He wiped his hand across his forehead and found he was sweating. "Go on, Owen, take him away. I don't want to see him again. Ever."

"You're making a mistake, kid." Owen took Bobby's arm. "Come on, can you make it to the car?"

Bobby staggered. He shook Owen off. "I'm not a fucking cripple." He lurched to the door, turned and looked once again at Michael. "You'll get yours," he shouted. Then he went out into the hall and was gone, Owen following him.

Michael found a chair and sank down on it. He was still shaking. He took slow, deep breaths, looking at his feet on the thick-pile carpet, trying to shut out the party, trying not to think about what he had just done.

"Michael?"

He looked up. It was Lisa. He tried to gather his thoughts. "I didn't realize you were around," he said.

"I saw the whole incident."

"With Bobby?"

"Yes."

"I acted badly," he said. "He was drunk and I took advantage of it. I lost my temper. It doesn't happen often."

Her eyes were steady on his face. "You didn't take advantage of him. You'd have done the same if he'd been sober. You're not a coward."

He shrugged awkwardly. "Maybe. I guess. I didn't realize you were here."

"I'm glad I was."

"What? Why?"

"It gave me a chance to watch you expressing yourself."

He laughed ironically. "You mean, making an asshole out of myself."

"Don't be dumb. Bobby's the one who made an asshole of himself. As always. Come on." She took his hand.

"Come where?"

"Jamieson's in the other room. We've been talking."

He followed her, feeling dazed. The walls of the house moved around him like an illusion. "I don't understand, Lisa."

She turned to face him, pausing in the hall. "You committed yourself just then, didn't you?"

He laughed, feeling crazy. "Committed myself, yeah, the way you commit yourself to an asylum."

"No. You gave up on it all. Your partnership, your business, all of it."

He gestured hopelessly. "Because it's not going to work anymore. Jamieson's right. Maybe things'll drag on, for months or years, but I just see it, now. The whole thing is collapsing." He looked at her. "I don't *want* to give up on anything. I want to stay rich. But . . ."

"I don't care *why* you decided it," she said. "I just wanted you to do it. See where you were going and say to hell with that way of life." Suddenly she hugged him close to her. "Michael I'm so happy."

"Happy!" He laughed crazily again. "How can anyone be happy tonight?"

"What have *I* ever had to lose? Tell me that."

He thought. "I . . . I don't know."

"I've got nothing to lose, everything to gain. So have you. We're free now, don't you see?"

"No."

"If there isn't a future anymore, there's nothing to plan for, worry about, guard against. We just live for each individual moment. Because that's all there is. Come on, come and talk to Jamieson."

Dazed yet euphoric, touched by her warmth, her craziness, he went after her. They found Jamieson sitting alone in the kitchen.

"Michael's just quit from Bobby," said Lisa.

Michael shook his head. "I don't know, it was an impulsive thing, I mean, maybe tomorrow I'll feel different."

"No," said Lisa, firmly. "You won't go back."

"But I don't make decisions this way. I don't just suddenly turn around on a whim and abandon everything."

She hugged him again. He felt her body against him. "Michael, do you still want me?"

"I—yes."

"Then you haven't abandoned *everything*." She turned to Jamieson. "Will you tell him what you told me?"

Jamieson coughed. He gestured to a crumpled photograph lying on the kitchen table. "It all began just now, when Lisa showed me this."

Michael looked at it. It was the picture she'd shown him, on the night he'd met her. The photograph of the smiling people in the open fields. The place she'd originally been heading for. "Yeah, I've seen it," he said.

"I had to warn her," said Jamieson. "The whole thing is a fraud, almost without doubt. The superhavens they're building out in the Midwest and the South are using pictures like this to lure people out there as menial farm labor. It's a medieval setup, as I understand it. You work twelve hours a day in the fields for a small wage. You buy food from the company store. You live in a hut. Once you're there, you're trapped. Unfortunately, a lot of people in city ghettos are easily taken by the idea of simple, honest, country living. There's a plentiful supply of manual labor, as a result. Cheaper than using machines, these days. I told Lisa, if she wants to get out of the city, this," he gestured at the photograph, "is the last place to choose."

Michael spread his hands. "So it doesn't matter what you do, everything's a con, there's no way out at all. Is that what you're saying?"

"No." Jamieson stood up. "I took the precaution a year or two ago of setting up a little hideaway for myself. A place I could retreat to, when I needed solitude. It's of special importance now, because I think there's going to be a lot of urban unrest. Not in the ghetto zones—they have nothing left to lose—but in the middle-income areas. Demonstrations, which the National Guard will subdue. A lot of robbery, stealing the resources that people aren't allowed to buy in bulk anymore. It's going to be dangerous, in the city, for a while."

Michael shook his head. "It all sounds so abstract."

"Violence in the streets isn't abstract. You *might* be safe in your haven; on the other hand, can you trust the police who are supposed to be there guarding it? It's every man for himself, or at least, that's how people will be feeling, once they realize how much has been taken away from them."

"So what are you suggesting?"

"I offered Lisa the chance to stay at my retreat for a while. She asked me if I'd offer the same thing to you. I will. I have food and necessities for several months, and she tells me that you happened to stock up on a lot of possessions today yourself, by chance."

"But, all my work's back in my apartment. My recordings."

Jamieson shrugged. "It's up to you, of course, but Lisa and I will be leaving here tonight."

"Tonight!" He paused. "Well, I guess I could go into town in a couple days' time if things seem okay and collect my stuff then."

Jamieson shook his head. "There'll be no way to tell if things are 'okay,' because the media will be playing down any incidents that occur."

Michael sighed. He rubbed his hands over his face. "I can't deal with all this. It's too much."

Lisa put her arm around him. "Come with us."

She felt good, close to him. That was the one fact, the only fact that he was sure of at that moment. He looked down at her. "Do you—*trust* me, now?"

"Yes. You've shown how you feel."

He sighed. "I don't know. Where is this hideaway?"

"Not too far. Some wasteland to the west. Too stony for

farming, no use to anyone, really, which is why I chose it. I have a two-room cabin beside a small stream. The water's been tested for purity. It's nothing fancy, but it's enough."

"It's just that everything seems to have fallen apart so *suddenly*."

"Not really, this has been building up for a long time, though people preferred not to recognize it. The politicians and the businessmen were forever mortgaging the future, to maintain a semblance of normalcy. But now, now the debt has been called due." Jamieson smiled faintly. "What you get *is* what you take."

INTERIM: THE CABIN

Michael and Lisa stayed with Jamieson for almost a month. It was primitive and cramped in the little cabin, and he found it hard to get used to the lack of air conditioning, instant hot water, and all the other conveniences of the apartment where he used to live.

At the same time he discovered, as Lisa had predicted, that he could do without luxury more easily than he had expected. He was a self-contained, self-sufficient person.

During the daytime they often went for walks in the land around Jamieson's place—rock-strewn hillsides of no potential for developers, farmers, or speculators. They found out more about each other. His defenses yielded to her; her trust in him grew deeper; they achieved a quiet, intense closeness.

If Jamieson felt too much an outsider to their relationship, he concealed it. Accustomed to long periods of work and solitude, he was writing a book that he had titled *The Rise and Fall of Technocracy*. He freely admitted that by the time he finished it there might not be any publisher left in business to print and distribute it. But he felt that someone, somewhere should be chronicling what was happening.

News from town was not good. They watched a small TV

every night, powered by a little gasoline generator that produced enough current for the set and a couple of light bulbs. The bulletins were grim for the first two days, full of stories of riots, demonstrations, street violence, and arrests. But then, overnight, the reports changed. Faces of familiar newscasters disappeared and were replaced by new men and women, hearty and complacent, projecting warm reassurance. It was like watching a glossy, cosmeticized version of Orwell's 1984. The world was a good place and getting better, and any hardships were purely temporary. At the same time, commercial advertising disappeared from TV, and it became obvious that rationing of food and resources had been instituted.

"But still I don't really understand why it *had* to happen," Lisa said one night, sitting with the others around a small log fire in the total quiet and coolness of the night up in the hills. The little cabin was shadowy and primitive around them, yet reassuring.

"Purely a matter of resources," said Jamieson. "Things started getting tight at the end of the sixties. Raw materials were being used up; as they grew scarcer, mostly they became more expensive. There were exceptions—the price of gasoline was held artificially low for years, because allowing it to rise was so politically unpopular. And for a while, manufacturers could buy time by shifting operations to poorer countries where low labor costs compensated for costlier raw materials.

"But in the end the prices of resources rose so much that inflation became uncontrollable, and businesses went bankrupt because no one could afford to buy their products anymore. The government juggled with the variables as always—unemployment was allowed to rise, federal spending was cut back. A recession was the result, making everything worse. And prices *still* kept going up, because nothing was getting any cheaper, from energy to steel to plastics.

"Well, they then tried to reflate the economy by switching tactics and spending money on projects to generate employment

The government started a number of things I consider follies—
that city of Vickers' for instance, New Vista. This too made
everything worse in the long run, because it consumed still more
of the non-renewable resources whose scarcity was causing
trouble in the first place—energy, steel, electric equipment,
plastics.

"You see, there was only one rational course of action, given
that the cost of materials was rising faster than productivity and
efficiency: Get everyone to use less. And recycle as much as
possible. But the back-to-the-land idealism of the seventies was
long since passé, and the recycling thing was never made profit-
able. A company that exploited the land could get all kinds of
tax shelters and government concessions, but a company dedi-
cated to recycling metals, for instance, didn't get any breaks at
all—*and* had to deal with the apathy of a public that had been
brought up preferring to throw things away. There were too
many old, bad assumptions—that the future would always be
brighter, you got richer as you got older, you could always make
a buck in business if you were smart, and so on.

"Now, maybe a charismatic new-thinking politician could
have turned it around before the crisis point. But no one *wanted*
a new-thinker. They wanted reassurance as times got tougher,
not someone telling them to make sacrifices and give up on
consumerism. So, tired old men with old ideas got themselves
reelected. There was one other hope for survival, of course, and
that was technology; real advances, in fusion power and mining
asteroids out in space, far-fetched stuff like that, could have
sustained us. But the old politicians axed those kinds of research
projects before anything else, because they seemed so irrelevant
to the immediate crises.

"In the end, businessmen saw where everything was leading.
For decades the big corporations had exploited the American
consumer; as soon as it was clear that the exploitation was bringing in diminishing returns, the corporation men began pulling
⸱t. We had that fatal alliance between them and the politicians,

then with leaders of the armed forces as well. Now you know the end result. The rich and the powerful are literally abdicating to their superhavens, where they have their own hydro-electric power, their own stockpiles of resources, and peasant-level labor tilling the surrounding fields to supply them with all the food they need. The rest of the country will be more-or-less kept under control for a while with the new laws that were passed. But as far as I can see, once the socio-economic system is thoroughly wrecked, our ex-rulers will have no further interest in their ex-subjects, and large parts of the country will be left to revert to a relatively primitive state."

It was a long speech and he stopped abruptly, as if he were embarrassed to find himself expounding.

"You sound philosophical about it all," said Michael. "But I still find it hard to accept."

"It doesn't matter," said Lisa, putting her arm inside his. "If we're really sliding toward a predictable situation, what good does it do to wish you had the chance to live well for another couple of years? We might as well start living in the way we're eventually going to have to live."

"I know, I understand that intellectually," he said. "I just don't *feel* it. I keep expecting to wake up and get back to work on Bobby's new album. It feels so idle, here, like a vacation I hadn't planned to take."

"There've been compensations," she said.

He looked at her. Their affair was still new enough for him to feel desire for her almost every time he studied her face or her body. He put his arm around her and kissed her. "Don't misunderstand me," he said quietly. "In many ways, coming out here with you is the best thing that's ever happened to me. I just need something to replace what's been taken away."

Jamieson coughed. He stood up. "Well, I think I've got time to work on the end of the third chapter, before going to bed." He started toward the other room of the cabin, which he used as his study and bedroom.

"We're going to have to buy more supplies soon, aren't we?" Lisa asked him.

Jamieson looked thoughtful. "Yes. There *is* a small town not far from here, but of course you won't be able to buy in bulk—maybe not at all, since we don't have ration coupons. You know, I never intended this cabin to be a *permanent* retreat."

There was an uneasy silence. "Fair enough," said Michael, "and we're grateful to you for letting us stay here this long. But what are you implying? We should go somewhere, Lisa and me, and start a farm on our own to feed ourselves?"

"Of course not. Even if you were allowed to—or if you squatted on some land and evaded detection somehow—it would take months before the land started yielding any food for you. Nor do I suggest you go back to town and live off handouts with all the other people. No, I've been thinking, perhaps that new city, that folly of poor Vickers, could have a use after all."

"New Vista? In what way?"

"Well, some families had moved into a small group of buildings at the north end of it, as a kind of showpiece for the media. They even stocked some of the stores with processed-irradiated food that keeps for years. But most of the city's empty, and will stay that way. No more construction work now—the government will have given up on its grand gestures."

"But if we went there, what would we *do* there, in a place like that?"

"Survive," said Jamieson. He smiled. "Goodnight."

PART TWO

WINTER

1999

The tiny, white-walled kitchen was dusty, cold, and damp. Its gray, plastic floor drained the warmth from Reid's bare feet. He stood holding his hands over the little camping stove where breakfast was cooking, and he wished it were spring instead of winter.

He rubbed grime off the window and peered down into the shadowy street. Thirty stories below, the asphalt was a dark strip walled in by the somber faces of apartment blocks planted on either side in neat, close-spaced lines. But above, where the buildings caught the morning sun, their concrete became a mosaic of sunrise colors crowding up into a vivid blue sky.

Reid's breath misted the little window and blurred the color patterns as if shifting them out of focus. He traced a path through the condensation with his fingertip. Tiny water droplets united into glittering rivulets, refracting the golden light from outside and running down to the bottom of the pane where the glass was encased in crystal patterns of ice. New Vista was empty and it was dead, but it could be beautiful.

Reid turned from the window, took food packs out of the boiling water and slit their plastic seals, emptying the food into three plastic bowls that were dull and worn from frequent use. Then he used the water left in the pan to make instant coffee and carried the breakfast through to the other room where he had slept with Lisa and Michael.

He set the food and coffee down quietly. Diffuse light was filtering through the single dust-patterned window, touching Lisa's face where she lay asleep with Michael, huddled under overcoats and a couple of old blankets. Reid looked at her features with a mixture of emotions—tenderness, wistfulness, detachment. She seemed very much at peace.

Then the smell of the food woke her and she rolled over, sitting up on the air mattress, revealing her browned, compact body. She brushed her hair out of her face and smiled, still sleepy, while Michael slept on undisturbed beside her.

Reid sat down on the floor next to Lisa. He put his arm around her, feeling the warmth of her skin, and she kissed him gently on the lips. Then, still sitting close to one another, they began eating. Neither of them spoke; the room was almost totally silent. From somewhere very far away came a fragment of bird song; then it, too, disappeared into the stillness.

The room was unfurnished. A built-in closet stood with its door open; it was empty. The plastic floor of the room was filmed with dust and there was no bulb in the overhead light fixture. The walls were flat white. The space felt as if life had never touched it. The other apartments, in that block and most other blocks in New Vista, were the same—sealed containers of slow time, as empty and bare as monastic cells.

Reid had first met Lisa and Michael when he had wandered through the city the previous winter. For a while, another woman had also been with them; before her, two men who had left when it became so cold that it was hard to sleep in the unheated apartments. People in the zone wandered freely; sometimes one little group would encounter another and would pause to trade what news there was, but most of the time was spent within one's own nomadic party, in isolation. Little was said, nothing was planned.

Lisa finished her food. She turned and shook Michael awake. He opened his eyes, smiled at her, and pulled her down to him, firm but gentle. He held her and they kissed unhurriedly, her breasts naked against his chest. They broke apart after a moment and he ran his finger down her bare back as she turned and swung her legs out from under the covers. At the other end of the room, Reid had begun dressing.

Michael's hair was long, now, and bleached lighter by the sun. He had gained muscular weight around his shoulders, arms, and thighs. His face was tanned and looked younger and relaxed, suggesting more equanimity than before. Yet his eyes were still restless, and there was a contained tension behind his movements.

He stood and walked to the window, his breath steaming in the cold air. He rubbed a circle in the dirt on the glass. Beyond the nearby buildings, in the distance, he saw a flash of sunlight on steel, and a flicker of movement. It was the morning train moving slowly down the track that had been laid hastily a year ago along the empty strip of the Interstate highway, sweeping around New Vista a mile away, linking the older cities to the north and south. In the old urban centers some kind of social structure was still functioning, though Michael had little idea of what it might be and was not concerned by it. The daily trains never stopped by New Vista; evidently their passengers had better things to do than pause to inspect a vast piece of apparently uninhabited, incomplete urban planning.

Michael turned from the window. "The shopping center near here has a stocked warehouse."

"That's right," said Lisa.

"We need more blankets. And food." He picked up the last bowl of breakfast paste and started eating.

Lisa was stowing her possessions methodically into one of the group's backpacks, sewn from blanket pieces and old clothes. She picked up a school composition book, filled with tiny, precise handwriting. The book was growing into a novel; she read chapters of it to the others, as she wrote it. Each member of the group had a spare-time occupation—Michael was slowly producing some miniature woodcarvings and adding to a notebook of songs he doubted would ever be performed. Reid was teaching himself to paint; the blank walls of a hundred thousand empty apartments were his canvases.

When they were ready, with all their belongings stowed and nothing left behind, the three wanderers shouldered their packs and walked unhurriedly out of the apartment. Ignoring the elevators, they walked down thirty flights of emergency stairs to street level, following a trail of footprints that they had laid themselves in the dust the previous night.

Outside, the apartment blocks stood like gigantic uninscribed tombstones, thin slices of yellow morning sunlight slanting between them. The topmost windows shone in a blaze of silver and gold, like beacons in the cold, shadowy, silent wilderness of concrete.

Dwarfed by the landscape, the three human figures walked down the center of the wide street. They were the only specks of life or movement in the barren panorama.

Michael paused where the street intersected a broader avenue that curved away to the left, lined with more large apartment blocks. "Up there." He pointed along the avenue. Just visible at the end of its gradual curve was the beginning of the shopping center—a complex of soaring ramps, intersecting walkways, and vast signs hanging like faded heraldic banners in the stillness.

They walked toward the center. Dead electric signposts pointed to eating houses and fallout shelters, public toilets and play zones, amusement arcades and movie houses.

They walked up a slanting ramp, through strips of sun and shadow, sometimes pausing to survey the scene around them. The city seemed forever frozen in the frigid air. The wide, blue sky hung over them like an ice-cold pool, so tangibly vivid that it seemed possible to reach out and plunge one's hand into it.

Like several other shopping centers in New Vista, this one had been completed ahead of schedule, as a showplace for potential residents. Some of the storefronts were empty behind their dusty display windows. Others showed faded signs advertising forthcoming attractions. And just a few were stocked with merchandise, waiting for the residents who had never arrived.

Michael, Reid, and Lisa headed down a narrow passageway between two buildings, leading through to a warehouse at the back. But before they reached the end of the alley, they found the body.

It was sprawled on the concrete, under a ramp that bridged the alley twenty feet above. A torn overcoat lay across the head and shoulders. A hand stuck out at an odd angle, white skin flaked with dried blood from a small cut.

They gathered around it slowly, without saying anything. Then Lisa bent down and touched the figure. It seemed lifeless. She turned the body over, noticing that the clothes under the coat were crisp and neat, tailored like a military uniform. She pulled a strip of the overcoat away, to expose the face.

For a moment she stared at the features. Then, uneasily, she glanced up at Michael. There was a long pause.

"So what the hell is *he* doing here," Michael murmured.

"It is him, isn't it," said Lisa.

"Is who?" asked Reid. "You know this guy?"

"Yes," said Michael, "we know him."

At that moment the figure on the ground stirred. He opened his eyes and muttered something, then winced in pain. Lisa pulled back from him quickly. "He was only unconscious."

The man squinted up, blinked, and managed to focus. Then he broke into a painful, cynical smile. He coughed and winced again. "Hey, that you, Michael?"

"Yes, it is, Bobby."

"He must have fallen from up there," said Lisa, gesturing at the bridge overhead.

Bobby closed his eyes for a moment, obviously still in pain. "Yeah. I fell. Remember slipping. Help me sit up, huh, Lisa? It's Lisa, ain't it?"

"Yes, it's Lisa," she said, making no move toward him.

"Well, gimme a hand, will you?"

She extended her arm and he took it, pulling himself up.

He clutched at the back of his skull. "Jesus. Hit my head." He slowly felt down over his body, testing gingerly. "Boy, do I have bruises. Hope to hell nothing's broken."

Michael watched him. "So what are you doing out here," he said quietly.

Bobby looked up. He licked his dry lips. "Doing? Shit. I come out here, I got to . . . to warn you, is what. . . ."

"Warn us?"

"Yeah." He coughed. "Look, can I get some water somewhere?"

Reid opened his pack and took out a flask, handing it over.

"Hey, thanks. Who're you?"

"Name's Reid."

"Yeah? I'm Bobby. Used to know these two." He gestured at Michael and Lisa. "Long time back." He drank thirstily.

"You're from one of the old cities," said Reid.

Bobby put the bottle down. His eyes narrowed. "How'd you guess?"

"Your uniform. I was there myself, before I came out here. You're with the peace force."

"I was. Split from those guys."

"But what are you talking about, coming here to warn us?" said Lisa. "You haven't seen me or Michael in two years. You had no idea where we might be."

Bobby paused. "Yeah, I didn't know *you* was here. I meant I got to warn anyone here. About the peace forcers, what they're planning. I'm running from those bastards."

Michael sighed. "This isn't making any sense. Do you need food? We were going to the warehouse."

"Man, if you got food, I can use it," said Bobby. "There ain't much at the center. Rationing." He struggled up onto his feet. He was thin under his uniform, and his face was very pale. He tested first one leg, then the other, and took a couple of deep breaths. "This is a real break, meeting you this way.

Small world, huh?" He grinned.

"Isn't it," said Michael.

"Last time I saw you was at that party, right?" said Bobby. He was eating from a plastic pack of food and sipping water from another flask, in a shadowy, cavernous warehouse filled to the ceiling with giant cardboard cases. "Yeah, that was when you hit me, on the jaw." He laughed. "We was all of us fucked up that night. I mean, I don't hold a grudge, know what I mean?"

"It was a long time ago," said Michael. His face showed nothing, but his eyes were intent. "Where have you been, since then? Is there still a rock scene?"

"Nah, the music business don't exist. Me and Owen kept trying for a while. But the guys with the real money and real power got out of town fast, to the armored superhavens in the South and Midwest, and took their kids with 'em. Services started fucking up. Food distribution went to hell. Even the National Guard pulled out after a few weeks, when the feds gave up on the East Coast on account of there wasn't enough farmland and resources here to make it worth their while. Without no one running things in town, it was a shambles. Then there was a half-assed people's revolution, but that wasn't any better.

"So me and Owen looked at the mess and decided it was like back to the urban jungle. So, three months after I last saw you, I was back on the streets, working a black-market drinking water racket."

"Typical," murmured Lisa.

Bobby laughed. "Yeah, and looks like you ain't changed none either, sweetheart. I can see that. So anyway, a few more months went by, and then these middle-class people, ex-vigilantes from the old neighborhood crime-fighter days, they got together and set up a temporary local government. They reopened factories, imposed law and order. They was stamping out the rackets, so I figured I'd quit while I was ahead. I joined up with them, their peace force, and right away I was supervising a ten-block neighborhood."

"You mean you were a kind of a cop?" Lisa looked amused.

"No, not a cop. Administrator."

"Who carried a gun," said Reid.

"A gun?" said Michael. "Where is it now?"

"It was taken off me. Well, anyway, a year after the collapse, we had things organized good. There wasn't no gasoline to speak of, but we had a power station burning wood and coal, set up trade with the local farms, got people working in the fields. We laid that railroad up the Interstate to encourage trade with other centers. Used salvaged track and subway cars."

"What happened to Owen?" Michael asked.

"He got wiped out in an epidemic. For a while we had scarlet fever, cholera, typhoid. One in five died."

"But not you," said Lisa.

"No, because people in the peace force got immunized. So, the last ten-twelve months I worked my way up the ladder, you know? Headed for a seat on the urban council. Then, couple of weeks back, just when things was looking real good for me, some creep who didn't like my name or my face or something, rigged a fake hoarding charge against me. Carries the death penalty if you're found guilty—it's rough justice, dog-eat-dog, understand? And this guy has relatives on the council. So they put me in custody and took my gun. But I bribed a guard and got out. Hid on the train out of town yesterday and jumped off when it passed here."

"Why here?" said Reid.

"Because it's outside of the system. Not too many people knew about it, and those that did wrote it off 'cause it was never finished. But I remembered it and figured maybe there'd be people here, squatters or whatever, and even some food."

"You were correct," said Michael.

Bobby glanced around at the stacks of supplies. He grinned. "Yeah, my luck held up real good, didn't it?"

"So what's this crap about *warning* us?" said Reid. Something about Bobby seemed to have instinctively made him hostile and suspicious.

Bobby finished eating from a pack of food and wiped his mouth on the back of his hand. "Early this morning I was wandering around, all alone. Didn't know where I was, where to go. Then suddenly some guy starts shooting at me. A bullet knocked a piece out of a wall right beside me. I caught a glimpse of him, dressed like a peace force regular. I thought, Christ, they followed me out here. So I ran. I shook them, but I slipped, took a dive, where you found me. Must've been unconscious an hour or two. The thing is, if these peace force guys ever see a storehouse like this," he gestured with his thumb at the piles of cases all around, "they'll clean it out. It and the whole city—every last pack of food back to the old center, on the railroad. And anyone who gets in the way . . . understand?"

There was a long silence in the big warehouse, while they digested Bobby's story.

"You're full of shit," said Reid, at last.

"What you mean?"

"You weren't shot at—we didn't hear any gunshots. And how would the peace force know you'd gone here? And hell, why'd they *bother* to come looking for you? Haven't they got enough to do keeping order back in town?"

Bobby sighed. "Look, I'm being straight with you. The shots were at dawn—maybe you were sleeping then. And it's a matter of prestige for them to get me. I was high-ranking back in town, they don't want to lose face, by losing me. I figure someone on the train yesterday saw me jump and reported it. That's how they followed me here."

Reid shook his head. "It's still not right. You're still one of them."

Bobby looked puzzled. "What you mean? Hey, why're you coming on so hostile?"

"He means that people in the old city live in an old way," Lisa explained. "Government, law and order, work, control, the old traditions."

"That's right," said Reid.

"But you just told me yourself," he said to Reid, "you was from there originally."

"Yes," said Reid, "but I was never part of its system."

Bobby sighed. "Look, I don't pretend I understand any of this. All I need is for you to show me how things work here, who does what, where the supplies are, how you survive. Then I'll leave you guys alone. Or I'll work *with* you. I mean, whatever you want." He turned to Michael. "Come on, you owe me that much, man."

Michael nodded. "We could do that, yes."

"I disagree," said Reid.

Lisa put her hand on his arm. "You're over-reacting. We lose nothing by keeping Bobby with us for the time being."

"Do you believe what he's told us?"

"Perhaps."

Reid turned to Michael. "Do you?"

"I've known Bobby for a long time," Michael said vaguely.

Reid shrugged.

"I won't be no trouble to nobody," said Bobby. "You'll see."

Michael stood up. "If there really are people from the urban center out here looking for you, we should take what we need and move out of this neighborhood."

Bobby nodded. "Right. I was thinking, if we could go to wherever you got your organization set up here, and put the word around New Vista, we could warn people about the situation, maybe hide your supplies or defend 'em if it came to it."

Michael paused. "Yes, of course, you're right. We have to get *organized*, don't we?" He smiled faintly.

"Now you're talking."

"Gather yourself enough food for four days," Lisa told Bobby.

"Okay. What about water? Where do you get that?"

"Some buildings have water pressure," said Michael. "There's a big reservoir in the hills outside the city. It still comes through." He gestured toward the back of the warehouse. "There are clothes back there. Get yourself a new coat. Yours is ruined."

Bobby started exploring down the aisles of cartons. "Hey, there's all *kinds* of shit here for the taking."

"Make yourself some kind of sling to carry everything in," Lisa called to him. She turned and looked at Michael. Her eyes were questioning.

Michael looked back at her. Without saying anything, he nodded slowly.

A little later they walked out of the warehouse, carefully closed its doors behind them, and entered an adjoining department store. Mannequins on the ground floor stood fashionably dressed, coated with dust. Incomplete displays and fittings lay around. Cables dangled from the ceiling where closed-circuit TV had been being installed, at the time New Vista was abandoned.

Michael led the way up an escalator that was shiny and new under a thin film of dirt. On the top floor he went to an emergency exit door and leaned on it. It creaked open, letting in gray light from above.

"Where you taking us?" said Bobby. He was breathing hard from the swift climb.

"The roof. See if we can see anything. Or anyone." Michael climbed the emergency stairs, and the others followed him.

It was cold and desolate on the roof. Beyond a crude parapet of rough concrete, the shopping center stretched away in a confusion of rectangular glass and concrete patterns. The sun shone from low in the sky, picking out the taller buildings, hiding lower areas in shadow, creating vast mosaics of light and shade. Looking down at the grid of intersecting streets and pedestrian paths, there was no movement, no sign of life anywhere.

The light suddenly dimmed, and they glanced up as a shadow

spread over the city, from a high white cloud creeping across the sun. Lisa shivered. "There's snow coming. I can feel it."

Michael walked on around the roof. He scanned the view from the other side. "Look down there," he said quietly.

They joined him. For a moment they saw nothing; then the sunlight returned and there was a flash of reflected light from the barrel of a gun in the hands of a man in a dark uniform, walking cautiously down the edge of a street five blocks distant. He was a tiny figure, dwarfed by the landscape and diminished by distance, yet his presence in the silent, sleeping city was somehow menacing.

"If you had a rifle we could pick him off right now," Bobby murmured.

They watched the intruder, their breathing the only sound on the rooftop. Wisps of exhaled air rose frost-white around them.

"Let's get away from this area," said Lisa.

Michael nodded. "There's a bridge from the second floor that links with one of the powerpaths. Remember it?"

"Yeah," said Reid. "That way we won't be too exposed."

They started quickly for the emergency exit, off the roof, and back into the department store.

Pragmatists

The four of them went back down the escalators to the second floor, then through a series of doors and shadowy passages, and over a glass-walled bridge to an adjacent building. A wide, dusty pedestrian concourse opened onto an enclosed shopping mall. On one side were turnstiles under a sign that read POWERPATH.

They vaulted the defunct turnstiles and went out through doors onto a ramp that led into the open air. The powerpath had been built to carry pedestrians in and out of the shopping center, from and to the residential areas. It was an elevated walkway with concrete walls five feet high, snaking around and between buildings, climbing several stories above street level.

They hurried along it, hunched forward between the protecting walls, the interleaved steel plates thrumming gently underfoot. All around, the towers of the silent city stood in the pale sunlight, looking down on the four figures moving quickly, furtively, away from the shopping center.

After twenty minutes they paused to rest. Bobby sat down with his back against the concrete wall. "I ain't used to this kind of exercise," he said, with a weak grin. "Ain't been eating well, you got to remember." He fished a pack of food out of his improvised sack. He ate the paste from the plastic bag with nervous, hungry movements. "Didn't realize this place was so big, neither."

"New Vista? It's ten miles long, five wide," said Michael. "They built on a grandiose scale in those days."

"What you mean, 'those days'? Wasn't more than two years ago."

Michael ignored him. He squinted at the sun. "It gets dark so early, this time of year, but I think we can make the north end by sunset."

"You got your headquarters, your center, up in that part of town?" asked Bobby.

"That's right."

"Good. I feel kind of weird out on our own like this. With all these empty buildings." He looked from Michael to Lisa and Reid, standing around watching him. "So ain't you people going to eat?"

"While we're walking," said Michael.

"Oh, okay. Well, don't let me hold up the party." Bobby folded over the top of the food pack and stood up.

Without a word, they continued along the path. They walked steadily, through the clear winter afternoon, the sun touching the landscape yet hardly seeming to warm it at all.

Hours passed. Gradually clouds began accumulating in broad furrows across the sky, darkening to a purple-gray overhead and becoming edged with pink and crimson where the sun sank below them toward the horizon. The sides of the endless apartment buildings turned chrome-yellow and ochre where they faced west, and the ground far below became shadowy and indistinct in the grayness of evening, till the powerpath began to seem isolated from the rest of the world like a magic ribbon of steel floating on volumes of soft, dark space between the impassive blocks.

When the last colors of sunset had died and it was quite dark, they descended a service ladder to the ground. A dim yellow half-moon had risen, shedding faint light between shifting clouds.

"Where we going?" said Bobby.

"Small supermarket near here," said Michael.

"We already got supplies."

"Yes. But some permanent residents moved into this area before the collapse, and the ones that stayed are paranoid about strangers. The isolation drives them crazy. So in this neighborhood we don't walk into apartment blocks after dark. Best to stay the night in the supermarket."

"Yeah, but I thought . . ."

"We'll make contact with our other, friends, tomorrow. They're still quite a walk from here."

"Feels like we already came at least ten miles to me."

"The powerpath doesn't take the most direct route."

Bobby shrugged. He walked with Michael, Lisa, and Reid down a cross-street, leaving the powerpath, a black silhouette across the moonlit sky.

The supermarket occupied the ground floor of one of the apartment buildings. Michael paused just inside the doors, listening. "I think we have the place to ourselves." He took a flashlight from his pack and used it sparingly, flicking the beam up each aisle, catching images of piles of detergent boxes, canned food, bottled drinks, dehydrated vegetables, and packaged meals that had collapsed off shelves onto the floor.

"Great place for a picnic." Bobby sat down on a heap of plastic-wrapped paper towels. "Although I could do with something better than this crappy irradiated junk food. Christ, don't you guys get tired of eating it all the time?"

"Yes, but you also get used to it," said Lisa. "And it's vitaminized. Who's healthier, us or you?"

Bobby shifted irritably, trying to make himself comfortable. "If you'd been through what I've been through the last couple of years back in the old urban center, you wouldn't look so good, neither. At least I can say I didn't cop out."

"What do you mean?" she asked.

"A lot of people from town talk that way," said Reid. "He means he didn't run off to a farm in the country or go and work as slave labor for one of the superhavens. He stuck things out, trying to put civilization back together again. Right?"

"Yeah, that's right," said Bobby. "I didn't give up."

"Give up what?" said Lisa.

"Come on, cut the crap, you know what I mean. Didn't give up trying, give up hope."

"I *don't* know what you mean. Hope for what?"

"For the future, for Christ's sake! You want us all to end up like peasants eating nuts and berries?"

There was a short silence. "Hope for the future sounds a bit out of date to me," said Michael. "We're more pragmatic."

"What do you mean, pragmatic?"

"We live in whatever way works best, in the present moment, wherever we find ourselves. We just do whatever is practical and satisfying. Abstract ideas about rebuilding society and planning the future are irrelevant."

"That's it?"

"It's enough. In fact it suits me very nicely."

"Well, shit, I don't know, Mike." Bobby munched another portion of mushy processed-irradiated food from its plastic pack.

It tasted of synthetic eggs and cheese. "I mean, hell, we been doing pretty good back at the old center, putting things back together the way they used to be before it all went to pieces. Seems to me that that's worth trying for."

Lisa seemed suddenly to grow bored with the conversation. In faint moonlight filtering through the glass storefront Bobby saw her move closer to Michael and whisper something to him, putting her arm around him. But he shook his head, murmuring to her; she nodded and went from him over to Reid, nearer the back of the store.

At first Reid seemed uninterested, but Lisa talked to him softly and took his hand, and he stood up and followed her through the almost total darkness, away out of sight behind one of the aisle dividers. In the silence Bobby heard the rustle of clothes, more whispered words, then heavier breathing, and sounds leading up to lovemaking.

Bobby kicked at the paper-towel packages, making a rough mattress of them across the floor. He stretched out on them, wrapped his coat tightly around himself and tried to find a position that he could lie in without his bruises hurting him. He saw that Michael was still watching him, silhouetted against the supermarket windows. "You waiting for something?"

"Just looking at you," said Michael. "Remembering a whole lot of things."

Bobby sighed. "I don't understand you, man. You're not the same anymore. You used to be full of ideas and things you wanted to do, and you went out and did 'em. But now, you don't seem interested in anything."

"Well, things are very comfortable."

Bobby grabbed a package of towels and threw it across the aisle. "Shit, this is *comfortable?* It ain't more than twenty degrees in here."

Michael studied him for a moment, as if puzzling something out. "When it gets cold," he said, "I pick up a couple of extra blankets next time I'm near a warehouse. Do you understand?"

"No, man, because someday there ain't going to be no more blankets or food or anything else. You're living off the past and it's going to get used up. Don't you see that?"

"Of course."

"Then why don't you do something about it?"

"Well, when the time comes, I'll move on somewhere else." He was smiling faintly, as if playing with Bobby, and yet everything he said sounded sincere enough.

"That ain't no way to live," said Bobby. "That's the way a bum lives. A caveman. A scavenger."

"And I should be dissatisfied, is that right?"

"Yeah, damn right!"

Michael stood up. He walked closer to Bobby. "Well, you listen to this." His voice was suddenly firmer and harder. "I went through living your way. The dissatisfied way. Doing things and getting rich and living well. And I don't care if I never taste that lifestyle again. Because I'm very happy with the way things are, here, do you understand? I'm content. And one reason I'm content is that I don't worry about all that crap you've been talking about."

Bobby shook his head. He avoided Michael's eyes, as if embarrassed.

"There's an old question," Michael went on. "Would you rather be happy and poor, or dissatisfied and rich?"

"I'd just rather be rich."

"Yeah, sure." Michael turned, walked to the windows, and stood looking out at the night.

"It's that woman, that Lisa," said Bobby, after a while. "She done it to you. She was always screwed up. You was all right till you met her."

"Sure, I was quite content till she came along." He went on looking out of the windows.

"And now you ain't even got her to yourself, seems like she's sharing herself with you and that guy Reid. She's done a real job on you, Mike."

Michael walked back along the aisle, catlike, moving silently across and around the piles of cans and cartons. He paused for a moment beside Bobby's improvised bed on the floor. "Sex is three-way like everything else, in a close relationship of three people, else our group wouldn't work. But I don't expect you to understand that. I don't expect you to understand anything. So there's no point in talking any further. But just remember that *I* understand *you*, and I always have."

Then, before Bobby could answer, Michael moved on quickly down the aisle, sure-footed as an Indian guide, disappearing into the blackness, behind the display shelves where Lisa and Reid had gone.

Bobby squirmed around uncomfortably. "Crazy bastard," he muttered to himself. He cursed Michael, cursed the cold air, cursed the lumpy packages of towels under him. A few things Michael had said came back to him briefly; he mentally threw them out, like garbage.

Later, as he started drifting off to sleep, he heard renewed sounds of sex and wondered briefly who was making it with whom. If it were Michael doing it with Reid, it wouldn't have surprised him.

Outside the supermarket, the moonlit clouds drifted on across the sky, over the silent, abandoned city.

The Old Woman

Bobby woke suddenly, feeling someone shaking him. He opened his eyes and found Michael beside him. The supermarket was full of gray dawn light.

"What is it? We moving on already?" His throat was rough, his eyes sore. It had been a cold, restless night, and his limbs were aching.

"Look out there. Go on, sit up."

Bobby got up on his elbows and squinted out through the supermarket windows. The powerpath that they had followed the previous day was just visible bridging the street a few blocks away. As Bobby watched, a figure walked across it, and paused to scan the scene on either side.

"There've been several of them in the last few minutes," Michael commented.

"Peace force people? Jesus, how did they follow us out here?"

"There's no way they could have."

"They're taking an awful lot of trouble looking for you, if that's what they're doing," added Reid.

Bobby rubbed his eyes and massaged his face, trying to wake himself up. "But from this distance you can't tell—they might be just people like you who live around here. Not peace force men at all. Did you think of that?"

"They're carrying guns," said Michael.

"So? Don't you have people out here who own guns?"

"Never seen any. People turn up in New Vista with nothing but their clothes, usually. And none of the warehouses stocks anything other than consumer goods."

"You serious?" He saw they were. "Oh Christ."

"Was there something you forgot to tell us, Bobby?" said Michael, with an edge of cynicism.

"No, man, I told you all there was to tell. Hell, maybe the peace force ran across one of your warehouses yesterday, and now they're spreading out all over, looking for more."

"Maybe, maybe. Come on, get up, we're leaving."

"Where to?"

"Somewhere safer, if possible."

"We should give him to those men out there," said Reid. "Then maybe they'd leave us alone."

"I don't think it's quite that simple," said Michael.

"It's worth a try, isn't it?"

"No." His voice was quiet but left no room for argument. "I have to find out exactly what's happening. Coming, Bobby?"

He hesitated. Then, "Yeah, you bet your ass I'm coming." He started putting on his shoes.

Outside, the air was sharp and painfully cold, biting into

Bobby's cheeks and making his eyes water. The wind had risen and dark, ragged clouds were moving low over the apartment buildings. "Snow by this afternoon," said Lisa, pulling gloves over her hands. "Can't you feel it?"

They started zigzagging through back streets away from the powerpath, sprinting across wide boulevards where the wind funneled down between the bare faces of the buildings, driving dust and garbage in stinging flurries. Bobby's skin grew raw and red, and he felt alone and insignificant in the cruel weather among the bleak, withdrawn shapes of the buildings, offering no comfort against the emptiness.

Michael abruptly motioned everyone to stop. They stood a moment, silently.

"What's the trouble?" Bobby was clutching his hands together under his coat, shivering.

"Life up ahead."

"Yeah? That's good."

"It isn't. I told you last night, this neighborhood was settled, originally. We avoid it. The old residents . . . see the windows up there, the top floor? The curtains? They just moved. Someone's watching. We'll have to make contact."

"I don't get it."

"If we just walk on through, we could get any kind of shit dumped on us."

"Ain't there some other way out of the neighborhood?"

"The powerpath. But we can't use that now. Reid, you and Lisa take the far set of stairs. I'll go with Bobby up the nearer flight. It'll only take ten minutes to check this out."

They entered the building. Reid and Lisa disappeared up the far set of emergency stairs. "See the tracks?" Michael pointed to patterns in the dust on the floor. "Just one person. But living here regularly. Come on."

They climbed flights of concrete steps, up the claustrophobic stairwell. "These people *got* to be crazy living on the top floor, with no elevators," Bobby muttered.

"Possibly."

Finally they reached the twentieth floor, at the top of the block. "How about if this character turns out friendly?"

"We'll warn him or her about the peace force people, and move on." Michael started along the corridor. Reid and Lisa were already waiting outside one of the apartment doors. Tracks led to it through the dirt on the corridor floor.

"Meet anyone?" Michael asked.

"No," said Reid.

"So they have to be up here." Michael knocked on the door. "Hello, inside. We come non-violent."

There was no answer.

"We know there's someone here. We just want to make peaceful contact."

Still no answer. Tentatively he tried the handle. He glanced up in surprise as it turned easily and the door moved in a fraction.

"Kick it," murmured Reid.

Michael shifted his weight, then booted the door, sending it swinging open. It revealed a small, smelly little living room. Broken-down furniture stood on a tattered carpet. Shelves of salvaged scrap wood were laden with old photographs and worthless ornaments. The drapes either side of the dirty window were fashioned from old bedsheets.

Michael and Reid walked cautiously into the room. It was cold and empty, yet had the feeling of being recently inhabited. "This was the window we saw from the street," said Michael. "I counted the apartments we came along the corridor. Check the kitchen; I'll check the bedroom."

They split up, quickly searching through the place. It smelled bad—a mixture of dust, dampness, and unwashed flesh.

They met up back in the living room, where Bobby and Lisa were waiting. "I don't understand it," said Michael.

"Let's just split, okay?" said Bobby.

"Did you check the bedroom closet?" said Reid.

"No," said Michael.

"I'll go look." He went into the other room.

"I guess whatever kind of hermit lives here could have hidden down on a lower floor when they saw us come in the building," said Michael, "but I still don't . . ."

He was cut off by a sudden yell from the bedroom. He and Lisa exchanged a startled look, then went running in the direction of the sound.

Reid was grappling feebly with an emaciated, wild-eyed figure, white hair straggling down to its waist, the body draped in filthy rags. As Michael got in the room he saw Reid stagger back clutching his stomach and moaning. Blood pulsed out from under his hands.

The white-haired figure turned and saw Michael and flew at him. He caught a brief glimpse of a wrinkled, old woman's face, bloodshot eyes, rotten teeth bared like an animal's. He brought his knee up and kicked out, catching the withered creature in the groin. She screamed horribly and came at him again. He grabbed an old wooden chair, swung it, and felled her. He swung it again, in frustration and anger, smashing it into the back of the old woman's head where she lay on the floor. She gasped, twitched, and lay still.

He dropped the chair. He found himself breathing hard and trembling. It was suddenly very silent in the room. Lisa had run over to Reid and was crouched beside him where he had slumped down in the corner, still clutching at his stomach. Blood was oozing out in a bright red patch, saturating his clothes.

"Came out of the closet at me," he gasped. "Some kind of a knife." He winced.

"Lay him out," said Michael.

"The knife's still in him," said Lisa, her eyes wide with anxiety and a kind of disbelief in the sudden horror of the situation.

Michael swore. He got his arm around Reid and helped him to lie flat on the floor, as gently as possible. Reid screamed, then lost consciousness, his breath coming in shallow gasps.

Michael grabbed the knife handle and pulled it out. It was a ten-inch carving knife. He threw the bloody weapon aside. "God damned crazy fucking old woman," he shouted suddenly, standing and turning and kicking the withered figure, lying where he had felled her.

"Looks like she's dead," said Bobby.

"We've got to stop the bleeding," said Lisa, crouched over Reid, trying to cover his wound. "The knife went in so deep."

Michael strode to the closet where the old woman had been hiding. He reached in and dragged out some clothes. The first garment was a yellowed, rotten, ancient wedding gown. He started ripping it into strips. "Use these as bandages."

Bobby had retrieved the knife. He wiped the blood off it. "Shit, Mike, look at this."

Michael turned, "What about it?"

Bobby showed him the weapon. "It's filthy." The blade was spotted with rust and crusted with food remnants. "There's going to be infections in the wound."

Michael leaned against the wall for a moment, regaining his control, thinking the situation through. He consciously slowed his breathing, made himself relax a little. "I'll go see if I can find medical supplies," he said. "Bobby, you stay here with Lisa, okay? There's a warehouse not far from here. It may have antibiotics, other drugs." He walked over to Lisa. "I'll be back in an hour, maybe less, all right?" He squeezed her shoulder.

She looked up at him with a weak smile. "Be careful."

"Of course. Here, give me that knife." He took the weapon from Bobby. "See you later." He strode quickly out of the apartment.

Silence closed in. The room filled with Reid's painful breathing. His face had turned very pale, and he was shaking.

"He's in shock," said Lisa, not bothering to look up at Bobby. "Pass me some blankets."

Bobby turned to the bed in one corner of the room and stripped the covers off it, handing the blankets to Lisa. He laid a bedsheet over the old woman lying on the floor. Michael's blow seemed to have broken her neck.

"It's snowing out there," he commented, glancing at the window.

Lisa didn't answer. She stayed crouched beside Reid, holding him, watching the blood well up and flow easily through each new dressing as she applied it.

They waited. Each minute dragged on interminably, while outside the snow started falling more heavily, a soft slow-motion waterfall, smothering the city.

An hour passed. Finally Lisa stood up, wiping hair out of her face. Bobby saw she had been crying. She turned and walked aimlessly across the room, then back again.

"He's dead?" said Bobby.

"No, but he's dying. He won't stop bleeding."

"Well, I seen guys in terrible shape who pulled through. You got to keep trying."

"Look at him, he's dying!" she shouted at him suddenly. "What am I supposed to do? Say a prayer? It's a *reality*, don't you see that?"

"Okay, okay." He shifted uneasily. "You act like it's my fault or something."

"Of course it's not your *fault*." She turned away from him. "Things were so peaceful, so easy before we found you," she murmured, half to herself.

"Lisa, I didn't do nothing!"

"Not directly. Nothing you should be blamed for." She glared at him.

He spread his hands. "Come on, listen, I want to help, do what I can with you people."

At that moment there were gunshots, out in the street. Lisa ran to the window. She tried to see out, but the snow cut visibility. "Oh God, not him too."

More gunshots, echoing between the lines of buildings.

"Want me to go down to the entrance hall?" said Bobby.

"Do whatever you like." She stayed at the window, clutching the frame. Her knuckles were white.

Bobby hesitated. Finally he sat down on the floor, leaning against the wall. He noticed that some of the blood around Reid had congealed and darkened.

The silence closed in again. They waited.

Then, footsteps, running along the corridor outside. "It's me!" Michael's voice.

Lisa ran to the door just as Michael came falling into the apartment, covered in snow, gasping for breath.

Lisa embraced him. "You all right?"

"Yeah. They shot at me but the snow made it hard to see. I think there were five or six of them." He shook snow off his clothes and wiped his face. "How's Reid?"

"It's hopeless. Did you find anything for him?"

Michael clenched and unclenched his fists in frustration. "I tried two places. There was only first-aid kind of stuff. Useless. Look, we have to get out of here fast. They saw which way I ran. The snow makes it easy to follow tracks."

"Right." Lisa walked through to the drab, dingy living room where she'd dumped her backpack and picked it up. She handed Michael's pack to him.

"You're really sure we can't do anything for Reid?"

"He won't stop bleeding. It's a matter of hours, maybe less." Michael sighed. "All right, come on."

"Hey, you going to leave the guy?" Bobby stood up.

"Carrying him would hold us back."

"He ain't dead!"

"He will be, especially if he's moved. All right, do what you want. No time." He took Lisa's hand and they went into the corridor.

Bobby hesitated, standing alone in the living room. He made a move toward the bedroom where Reid was still lying unconscious, then stopped himself. He cursed, went to the window and peered out. Nothing to see but snow.

He cursed again, strode to where Reid was lying, grabbed the limp figure and hauled him up, over his shoulders. Tottering under his burden, he made it into the corridor. "Michael!" he yelled.

"Here," said Lisa, from the emergency exit at the end.

Bobby broke into a stumbling run. He found snow blowing down the stairs from the open roof door. "You up there?"

"Yes. Come on."

Bobby staggered up the stairs and out onto the roof. The snow hit him, swirling white, icy cold. Bobby gasped and almost dropped Reid. "What's the idea, up here?"

"Peace force men were already in the building. Heard them coming up the stairs. No way to get down past them." Michael pushed Bobby aside. From his backpack he took out two of his little woodcarvings and used the old woman's knife to split them, making wedges.

"But we're trapped up here," said Bobby. "We're going to fucking freeze to death."

Michael ignored him. He slammed the roof door and started hammering the wedges in around its edges.

"You're crazy, man!" Bobby persisted. "They'll see the snow on the stairs, they'll know we're up here."

"No point in hiding in the building. They'd find us in a floor-by-floor search. Take off your clothes." Michael started shedding his own. "Make a rope."

"We're twenty stories up!"

"Do it!"

Bobby laid Reid on the snow and obeyed. The square platform of the roof was a lonely island in the snowstorm. Its edges were the edges of reality.

Lisa stripped herself naked. Michael added her clothes to the knotted rope he was making, then took Bobby's. He strode to the steel parapet rail and knotted one end of the clothes around it, then threw them down over the side.

Bobby stood shivering, with snow melting and running over his pale thin flesh. "So what do we do now, fly?"

Michael held up his hand, listening. Footsteps climbing the emergency stairs were slowly coming nearer. There were shouts of men down in the building, calling to one another.

"Over the side." Michael strode to the balcony rail and quickly went down the rope of clothes hand-over-hand. He swung at its end, then let go and fell into the balcony outside an apartment on the floor below. He reached up, caught his pack from Lisa, then hers, then helped her down after him.

Men started thumping on the exit door.

Bobby dragged Reid to the edge of the roof. "You got to take him from me!" he shouted. He hauled the unconscious body over the edge. Grudgingly, Michael reached up and accepted him.

Then, trembling with cold, Bobby climbed over himself. His fingers were numb and clumsy. He hung over the sickening drop to the street. He started shivering uncontrollably. His hands slipped. He half fell, twisting, landing painfully on the balcony, beside Reid, where Michael had dumped him.

Up on the roof the exit door began to yield to the combined efforts of the peace force men.

Michael immediately smashed in from the balcony to its apartment, then through to the corridor beyond. Bobby managed to get a grip on Reid and hauled him after them. Footsteps sounded faintly on the roof above.

Michael and Lisa made for the other set of emergency stairs, opened the door, and paused just for a moment to listen. "We're maybe half a minute ahead of them." Michael glanced down at Reid, then felt the unconscious figure's neck. "You can drop him, he's dead."

"He is?" Bobby hesitated, then let go of the body. Michael and Lisa leaped away from the stairs. Bobby followed. Abandoned on the corridor floor, Reid lay lifeless, blood spreading slowly under him.

Dizzy and breathless they made it to the ground floor. Heavy booted footsteps were hurrying down the stairs a few flights above. Michael raced out of the building's exit and threw himself on a sentry outside. The man's gun went off, but he fell with Michael chopping at his neck, then kicking him in the head. Michael quickly grabbed the man's rifle, then hoisted him onto his back and started out of the building, naked, into the snow.

Why the guard and not Reid? Bobby wondered, running with Lisa after Michael, into the white wilderness of the storm.

It was slippery underfoot. He almost fell. They turned a corner, hopelessly unprotected against the blizzard. From behind them came gunshots. The bullets kicked up snow in the street. Then one hit the man on Michael's shoulder. Redness started spreading across his chest. Shouts sounded in the distance, muffled by the curtain of whiteness.

They turned another corner. Then down an alley. Michael dropped the man from his shoulder, reached down and searched for something in the drifts. He cursed, moved on, searched some more.

Bobby and Lisa stopped nervously alongside him. Bobby's skin had turned pale blue and all he could feel was a cold-burning pain all over his body. He was trembling uncontrollably. Lisa stood shivering, clutching her backpack and Michael's.

Michael found what he was looking for. He heaved up a metal-mesh cover. "Subway system," he said. "Inspection hatch. Get down, quick."

There was a ladder inside, with ice on its rungs. Lisa went down it, into darkness. Michael threw the backpacks to her. Then he lowered the wounded peace force man.

"Why you want that guy?" said Bobby.

"You'll find out. Come on, you next, you're staying with us."

"Where the hell else you expect me to go?" Bobby started down the ladder, slipping and falling. Michael followed and slammed the hatch. In the darkness he found his pack and grabbed the flashlight from it.

The beam showed a narrow, stained concrete passage slanting down. They ran along it, the wounded man once again across Michael's shoulders. The passage led into a much larger tunnel, faced with concrete slabs that curved up to meet in a roof twelve feet above. Water trickled down the center. Rusted steel track lay stacked at either side; it had never been installed.

Michael ran along the tunnel, feet splashing in the water, the yellow circle of radiance moving with him, leaving the rest of the tunnel dark and threatening. Bobby struggled to keep up, his heart thudding, the tunnel echoing with splashing noises and the sounds of their breathing.

They reached a half-built station where the tunnel widened into a cavernous chamber. Abandoned machinery stood bulky and mysterious in the shadows. Heaps of excavated earth and cement bags stood up against the walls. Michael took a ramp into another passage off the main one. There, finally, he stopped and set down the wounded man. He paused, touching a finger to his lips.

They stood beside him, trying to slow their breathing and listen. For a moment they heard nothing but the trickling and dripping of water. Then, very faintly, a far-off shout. Then, nothing.

Michael leaned against the wall and closed his eyes for a moment. He let out a long, slow sigh. "Okay, even if they figure we're down here, I'm betting they won't have flashlights, so we have the advantage." He opened his pack and pulled out a blanket, then took another from Lisa's bag. They started drying each other.

"You got anything for me?" said Bobby. "I'm freezing, man."

"That's too bad, Bobby."

"Mike, for Christ's sake, I been trying to help you. Shit, I risked my life for your friend back there."

"You're a slimy little ingrate, Bobby, and you don't fool anyone." His tone was matter-of-fact.

"*What?* But I did it for you!"

"You did it to try to make us trust you."

Bobby stood for a moment. Then he went for Michael, his fists clenched. "You bastard!"

Michael turned and met him swiftly and easily, grabbing the flailing arms, kicking him away. "Times have changed, Bobby." He picked up the knife and held it meaningly. "Now you just stay there and freeze a few minutes longer." He turned and shone his flashlight at the wounded peace force guard, lying on the ground, his back against the wall. "We have some things to sort out here."

"Mike, for Christ's sake!"

"Shut up." Michael squatted down beside the peace forcer. He saw the man's eyes were open. "Hurt bad, mister?"

The man groaned. "You know I am. What you bring me down here for?"

"Information. You tell me what I want to know, and maybe I can help you. Deal?"

"You know it is. If you leave me here I'll die. Make it quick." He grimaced with pain.

"Right." Michael swung the flashlight beam on Bobby. "Do you know that guy?"

"Yeah. Bob Schwartz."

"No, he's crazy!" Bobby shouted. His voice echoed in the underground chamber.

Michael ignored him. He concentrated intently on the peace force man. "Tell me about Bobby."

"It was him brought us out here. He turned up some records back in town. Seemed there was supplies out here. So him and the rest of us come here to clean the place out."

Bobby suddenly sank down against the wall, hugging his frozen flesh.

"How'd he end up on his own, away from the rest of you?" asked Michael.

The man grunted with pain. Talking was becoming difficult for him. "Christ knows. We got here yesterday. Dawn. Spread out. Reconnaissance. Regrouped an hour later, Schwartz didn't show up; we figured he maybe got hurt somewhere, so we went looking for him. Didn't find nothing. Spread out further . . ."

"He told us he was running from you guys," said Michael. "Said you were after him."

"Bullshit! This whole thing was his idea. Help me now, for Christ's sake, will you? I'm *dying,* man!"

Michael sighed. "How do I help you? Carry you back up there and give you to your friends? They'd kill me."

The man's eyes widened in fear. "But you said—you promised!"

"I promised nothing. And I owe you nothing. You people came here and started shooting at us."

"It was orders! We had orders to shoot at anyone, stop 'em spreading word around and organizing any kind of resistance here. Man, you got to help me!"

"I've told you, I *cannot* help you. Shall I shoot you now with your rifle or leave you to bleed to death from your wound?"

"You fucking bastard!"

"It's dog-eat-dog, isn't it? That's the way you people live. Grab all you can and kill anyone in the way."

"You bastard!" the man started sobbing.

Lisa covered her ears. "If he has to die, he has to die *now.*"

Michael stood up. He hesitated, fingering the rifle. Finally, hopelessly, he shook his head. "I can't do it."

Lisa grabbed the gun. Before he or she had anymore time to think or hesitate, she shot the wounded man in the head. The flash and bang were blinding and deafening in the tunnel. Luminous after images lingered in their eyes and their ears sang.

Lisa stripped the overcoat off the dead man, avoiding looking at his head. She threw the coat to Bobby. "Dry yourself with this. Use just the outside of the cloth."

Dumbly he did as she told him. She and Michael wrapped themselves in their blankets, and watched him. "Now put the coat on," Lisa told him, when he was through.

"So what were you aiming at, telling us that dumb story yesterday?" Michael said finally, sounding no longer hard and angry, just weary.

"Wanted you to get to trust me," Bobby said dully. He seemed totally exhausted and crushed.

"Why, so you could later betray us to your friends?" said Lisa.

"No!" His eyes widened. "Shit, no! Listen, I fell off that bridge and knocked myself out, where you found me. Must've dropped my gun as I fell, don't know . . . anyhow, you found me, I didn't know what the fuck to do, I didn't know you guys were living here. Then I saw the warehouse with all that stuff in it, I figured maybe I should throw in with you people, 'cause things looked easier here, easier than back in town. But I thought if I told you I was with the other peace force guys come to clean this place out, you'd never trust me. So I made up a story . . ."

"Which I never believed from the beginning," said Michael. "Dumb, Bobby. Really dumb."

"I really wanted to work with you guys." His sincerity was painful. "Sure, there was times I almost changed my mind— 'specially back in that old woman's apartment when they was coming in the building for us. I could've switched back to them and saved my neck."

"Except that they might have shot you before they recognized you."

"Well, yeah, I thought about that."

"Okay, at least you're making sense now."

"We can still do it, Mike," he went on, his voice becoming a thin, irritating whine. "Get organized here, from the center, your headquarters. Defend your supplies. . . ."

"There is no center. There's a dozen little independent groups of people wandering around and a handful of crazy old folks like that senile woman back there. That's all."

"Nothing more than *that?*"

"Who needs anything more?"

Bobby shook his head. "I don't get it."

"No, and you never will. Lisa?" He turned to her, putting his arm around her. They embraced briefly. "See if we can make it to the east side, get ourselves some clothes," he murmured to her.

"All right," she said.

Flashlight in hand, Michael picked up his backpack and the peace force man's rifle. Lisa shouldered her pack, and started walking away with Michael, into the continuation of the subway tunnel.

Bobby watched them uncertainly, then started after them, pursuing the receding light. "Hey, where you going?"

They walked on, ignoring him.

He clutched the overcoat around himself. "Hey, Mike! Lisa! I'm coming with you, okay?"

They just went on walking.

The Final Encounter

They trekked through the tunnel for twenty minutes, Bobby cursing under his breath at the cold and the dampness.

"You don't have to stick with us if you don't like it down here," Lisa told him.

"Listen, I ain't got nowhere else to go right now, and I don't know where the hell I am or where the nearest food is or anything, all right?"

After that, they let him alone.

Eventually they emerged from the subway up the unfinished concrete steps of an exit, onto a desolate street corner. Snow was still falling. The light was fading. The city was silent; they seemed to be alone and unobserved.

Keeping close to the buildings, in the safety of twilight, Michael found the way to a nearby warehouse. The three of them ransacked the place for clothing, picked up extra blankets, then found food.

"That hotel near here," said Michael. "Remember it?"

"Yes," said Lisa. "It'd be fine."

"Sure, we might as well stay overnight in style," said Bobby. They ignored him.

The hotel was just two blocks away. They climbed a few flights of stairs and broke into a room at the back. In the faint light from outside, the room looked eerily perfect, a TV in one corner, two double beds made-up and ready, a bureau, a closet, a thick carpet. But paint was flaking off the ceiling, water had leaked in at the edges of the windows and across the floor, and when Bobby sat down on one of the beds a cloud of dust rose and the fabric made ripping noises.

Michael dumped his backpack, took out his knife, and started to hack away a circle in the carpet, then the underlay, till he reached bare concrete beneath.

"What you doing?" Bobby asked.

"If you don't get rid of the carpet before you light a fire, it stinks." He started breaking up one of the chairs. Lisa pulled drawers out of the bureau and smashed them into kindling. They piled it all in the center. Finally, Michael ripped paper packaging off the food he'd taken from the warehouse and used that and some hotel stationery from a bureau drawer to start the fire.

The flames quickly engulfed the dry wood. Lisa opened the window a crack, then the door out to the passageway, so that smoke was carried away in the cross-draught. The flames hissed, filling the room with flickering warmth. Bobby crouched close, savoring the heat.

Gradually, with the fire in front of him and a pack of food in his hand, he started to feel more human and less depleted. His hands and feet were painful with frostbite, and his skin was raw, but a new warmth was spreading out from his belly.

"You know, Mike," he said, finally, "I got to apologize; you're right, I should've been straight with you guys from the start."

Michael said nothing. His face was hard to read, opposite Bobby, the other side of the fire. Beside him Lisa had slumped down with her head on his shoulder.

"But I didn't mean no harm," said Bobby. "And I didn't cause you no trouble. And you sure as hell wasn't straight with *me*. Letting me think there was some kind of an organization out here." He laughed sourly, and shook his head.

"What difference does it make," said Michael.

"Difference? Hell, man, I told you, when I came over to your side, I risked my fucking life."

Michael thought for a moment. "You only committed yourself with us because you thought things would be easier, 'on our side,' when you saw the supplies and the city."

"Well, yeah. But anyhow, I didn't want to be working *against* you. I mean you and me been through a lot together."

Michael shook his head. "We've been on opposite sides of the coin all along. Always disliked each other, underneath. You know that."

Bobby shifted uncomfortably. He shook his head. "You're so down on everything." He brooded, watching the flames. "Shit, we shouldn't be sitting here like cavemen, burning up the furniture."

"What should we be doing?" said Lisa, sleepily.

"There's this whole damned city, everything brand new, just waiting to be fixed so it works. You still got water, you could easily get electricity, there must be a generating station . . ."

"Yes, we've been in it," said Michael. "It's nuclear. No one knows how to run it."

"So we can *learn!* Get some books on it, get some guys working on the problem. Get people moved into the buildings, get the whole system operating here. When I first saw that warehouse, I figured you people must be way *ahead*, compared to how we've been scraping by, back in the old town."

"We are ahead of you," said Michael, smiling faintly. "Years ahead. You'll see."

"What's this, more of your dumb pragmatism?"

"If you like." Michael stood up, went to the remaining chair, and started smashing it, throwing the wood on the flames.

Bobby scowled. "You're a messed-up case, Mike. You lied to me, you left your friend Reid to die, you did a really rotten thing to that peace force guy in the tunnel, and then you tell me I'm an ingrate. You act like *I'm* the one who's unscrupulous."

"You forced me to do that to the peace force guard, because

you wouldn't tell me the *truth*." Michael threw a large piece of wood on the fire, raising a cloud of sparks, making Bobby flinch out of the way.

"Cop-out," he said.

Michael sat back down. His momentary anger had died as quickly as it had risen. "Turn it around any way you like."

"Well, the way it looks to me, your pragmatism's just a fancy word for good old-fashioned self-interest."

"No, it's not the same. Self-interest was what led to the whole collapse. People exploiting each other, till there wasn't enough left to go around. When I talk about pragmatism I mean more than that. Reacting independently, doing whatever works, for survival in the broader context. Functioning in harmony with the world. Progress, achievement, luxuries—they're all obsolete. They no longer fit the way the world is."

"Yeah? Well, living like this, don't sound like it's what I want."

"What *do* you want, Bobby?" said Lisa. "You want to go back to being a rock star? You want a fancy car and little kids who scream at you?"

"No, for Christ's sake, that was just . . . that was juvenile, that wasn't—all right, I'll tell you what I want. If no one else has got the guts to do it, I want those peace force guys to take over this place, this New Vista. I want 'em to clean out all the bums, get this city operating, so people can live in it decently instead of running it into the ground."

"I admire your newly discovered values," she said.

"They sure as hell are better than yours, sweetheart."

"You're still missing the point," said Michael. "We don't *have* any values. Values are part of what causes the trouble. So long as there's an end, it'll be used to justify a means." He sighed, wearily. "You haven't matured, really; you've just found a new way to manipulate people, that's all. Your audience isn't pre-teen anymore, but it's still an audience—the people, the electorate you've been bossing around as a member of the peace force. You just want civilization back because you want to go on manipulating, you want your power games, your comfort, and your security."

"Oh, yeah? That's it, huh?"

"Yes." Michael gazed at him steadily.

Bobby threw an empty food pack aside. "You know, I think I've had just about all I can take from you."

"You've been asking for it, all along."

"And I think maybe you're asking for a punch in the face."

"Oh, go to hell, Bobby," said Lisa. "You've done nothing but upset our lives, since we found you."

"Amen," said Michael. He and Bobby looked at each other, Michael solid and muscular and cool, Bobby thin and exhausted and edgy with anger. "All right, goddamn it," he said, finally. "I'm leaving."

"Back to your peace force friends?"

"Maybe. I'm warning you, you and Lisa here, those guys *are* going to clean out this city, and if you're among the bums who get swept up with the garbage, tough shit. As of tomorrow you and me are back on opposite sides of the coin, like you said. Like you wanted, right?"

"It really doesn't matter either way." Slowly, thoughtfully, Michael reached out and picked up the rifle he'd taken from the peace force guard. "I'll keep this, though."

"All right, you keep it. Maybe you'll need it. Just remember, you brought this on yourself. I was willing to go more than half way with you, Mike."

"Sure, to get what you wanted."

"Up *yours*, man." He threw his remaining packs of food into the center of a blanket, picked it up by its corners and swung it over his shoulder. "I'm going to spend the night some place where I'm out of range of your half-assed preaching, that's all I know. And in the morning it's every man for himself." He walked to the door, turned and looked at them. "All I can say is, it's a goddamn shame to end a friendship like this."

"It ended a long time ago," said Lisa. "If it ever began."

"I ain't got nothing else to say to you. Except 'goodbye.'"

"Goodbye," said Michael.

Bobby went out of the room.

The hotel was almost totally dark, but he remembered his way well enough, counting doors till he came to the emergency exit, then feeling his way down the stairs and into the hotel lobby. It had stopped snowing outside; faint moonlight filtered in. One of the big windows fronting the street had been smashed long ago, and snow had drifted over the lush carpeting. The place was drab, ruined.

Bobby walked out. He shivered. He realized it might have been tactically better to make peace with Michael and Lisa, so he could stay the night by their fire. It wasn't going to be any fun sleeping in one of the other buildings, on his own, in the cold. But damn it, there were limits to how much abuse he'd stand.

The wide avenue was so empty and desolate, it spooked him. He turned and walked around the hotel, through the snow drifts, to a narrower street at the back. The buildings stood dark and immense, walling it in like a canyon. The snow was soft, ghostly white in the moonlight.

The wind rose briefly, howling between the buildings, and Bobby shivered again. He thought he heard a faint noise behind him and whirled around, his pulse accelerating; but there was nothing there, and nothing to be heard except the singing in his ears. He rubbed his eyes, making luminous patterns flower and disperse under the lids. He tried to unwind his muscles and his nerves. He started walking down the street.

The wind rose again, cutting through his clothes. Ice fragments fell from a high ledge, pattering into the drifts of snow. His skin prickled. He felt as if he were being watched.

Slowly, this time, he turned, to convince himself that he was imagining things.

A dark figure came running at him out of the night. A shadowy form, it threw itself at Bobby. It thudded into him. Sudden shock of physical contact. Falling, arms flailing, he hit the ground. He shouted. Felt cold wet snow. Pain from his elbow. His pulse hammering. Who? . . . Was it Michael?

Hands grabbed his throat. Someone's breath in his face. He was on his back in the snow on the street. He kicked, struggled, choked.

"Bring a light," shouted the black shape, still holding Bobby down.

Footsteps. A kerosene lantern. Yellow, flickering light splashed over Bobby's face. He squinted, dazzled, caught a glimpse of tall uniformed figures gathering around him in the night, buckles and boots and rifle barrels gleaming, faces looking down at him.

"Is he armed?"

Bobby's attacker let go of him and felt quickly down over his body. "No."

Bobby struggled to sit up. A foot kicked him in the chest, over on his back. More snow mashed into his face. "Hey, I'm a peace forcer myself! Bob Schwartz, you got to know me!"

"Shine that lantern again."

He shaded his eyes from the yellow flame. He tried to see the faces around him, to find one he could name, to prove his story. But they were all strangers. Then he remembered—there was to have been a second group of men sent to New Vista, the day after the team he'd been in himself. This must be them. He knew none of their faces.

"You got to listen . . ."

"If you're in the peace force," said a scornful voice, "where's your uniform?"

"I lost it. I—was captured. I had to . . ."

"Your rifle? How about your papers?"

"I recognize him, sir," said a young voice. "He was one of the people we chased and lost in the storm today. I saw him run out into the snowstorm with the other two."

"All right, put him against the wall."

"No!" Bobby screamed. He started to panic.

"Tie his wrists."

He started struggling wildly. The dark street and the yellow lantern swung around him as he wrestled with rough hands reaching for him in the night. He bit, he fought, he kicked. Then someone kneed him in the groin and someone else punched him in the belly and he gasped with pain, doubling up. Everything wavered. He felt his hands being lashed behind him with a belt. He felt himself being dragged across the street. His feet scuffed through the snow. His body was throbbing with pain. He hurt, he hurt all over.

"I can name all the men on the city council back in town," he tried to say, but his solar plexus was paralyzed, and all that came out was "uh—en—ouncil." There could be only seconds left before they shot him.

Then, suddenly, he realized where he was, behind the hotel. Just a couple of stories up, in the wall above him, was the room he'd been in a few minutes before. Michael and Lisa were still up there. He *knew* they were there.

"Any last words, prisoner?" said the man with the lantern.

"Michael!" Bobby shouted. His voice echoed up and down the street. "Mike, help me! Get them, Mike! Shoot them with the gun!"

He slumped back against the building. Frosty air billowed from his face as he gasped for breath. The sergeant lifted the lantern high. Five peace force men raised their rifles.

"Aim."

"No, Jesus Christ, no! You got to believe me—I'm from—I can tell you the name of every guy in the—Mike, please help me!"

"Fire!"

He despaired and turned to run, just as the guns fired and the bullets ripped into him. He screamed and fell into the snow. The gunfire echoed away from building to building, across the sleeping city, until once again there was nothing but the sound of the wind.

The sergeant waited a moment. Then he walked over and shone the lantern on the body. One bullet had gone cleanly through the head.

"Peace forcer," he muttered, grimacing, nudging the unshaven, scrawny figure with his boot.

"He seemed to be shouting for help, sir," said one of the men. "Maybe his friends are nearby, and we should . . ."

"Go and look in all these buildings?" said the sergeant. "We're in enough danger as it is, here in the street. In any case, his friends obviously weren't where he thought they were, else they'd have helped him."

"Yes sir."

"All right, back to the temporary base. We start at sunrise tomorrow."

The light was doused. The men spread apart a little, moving cautiously back along the dark street, their footfalls muffled by the snow. Within a few minutes they were gone, leaving Bobby's corpse lying under the clear light of the moon.

Up in the hotel room, looking down from the window, Lisa watched the men depart. She touched Michael's arm. "We could have helped him," she whispered.

He fingered the rifle in his hand. "Yes, we could." He blinked. His eyes were stinging; he'd smothered the fire in the room with a blanket, when he'd heard the first scuffle outside in the street. The cloth had scorched, and now the air in the room was tainted with fumes. He turned away from the window.

"Do you think it's safe enough to stay here tonight?" she asked, going to him.

"Yes."

"What shall we do, tomorrow?"

"Tomorrow is tomorrow."

Ignoring the dusty beds, they lay down together on the floor, embracing.

"I'll miss Reid," she said, after a moment.

"So will I."

"But what has happened, has happened."

THE FROZEN CITY

The fire that they had built the previous night was a heap of ashes in the center of the ruined hotel room. The air smelled of soot and charcoal.

Michael was awake soon after dawn. He looked out of the window at the cold freshness of the morning. The sky was cloudless and the sun was bright, and the city was white. Dazzling snow edged every balcony, covered every rooftop, and filled every street.

He woke Lisa and together they heated their breakfast on the little camping stove, drank coffee, and ate, wrapped in blankets. Without speaking, they looked at each other and felt closeness and understanding. He embraced her, and they clung together for a long moment.

"You know we have to leave the city," he said quietly.

Still hugging him, she nodded.

"There's really no alternative, now."

"I know," she said.

Together, then, they dressed, and started stowing their possessions. "It feels wrong," she said, filling her backpack, realizing that this was to be the last time she would go through that particular ritual in New Vista. "Things were so good, and so simple, before . . ." she trailed off, reluctant to refer to Bobby or mention the peace force men that were still somewhere out there, prowling through the city.

"Things can be good again," he told her, "and we'll be seeing the countryside; you always used to be so determined to get out of town and live off the land, remember?"

"Of course I remember." She buckled the strap and swung her pack over her shoulders. "But the real reason I used to want to get into the countryside so much was that it seemed the only place, then, where I could be free to live as I wanted, with peace of mind. As things turned out, I've had more peace of mind and freedom here in New Vista than I ever would have had living on a farm." She walked to the window, where he'd stood a little earlier. "It's really beautiful outside, isn't it."

"Yes." He went over to her. "I figure we're so close to the east edge of town, there shouldn't be any trouble getting out from here. If we're careful."

"I hope you're right."

And so together they left the room, walked down through the hotel, and out across the derelict lobby. They paused at the front entrance of the building, peering cautiously into the main avenue outside, but its mantle of snow lay undisturbed and the city was totally silent.

In the narrower street behind the hotel, they both knew, Bobby's body must still be lying where the men had shot him the previous night. But that was something that neither of them wanted to see or think about, so they walked quickly out of the front entrance and away along the sidewalk of the main avenue, stepping through the snow that had settled like a frozen tide, smothering the street, sparkling smooth and soft in the sunlight.

They climbed a flight of steps that had been reduced to a pattern of gentle ripples, like a white waterfall caught and held in stasis. They crossed a glittering bridge, frost-patterned and encased in ice that refracted the light into flashing jewel colors. And then they took a white-carpeted boulevard that curved out from the city. They walked through rectangles of glaring sun and abysses of shadow, and they left the apartment blocks standing as timeless as giant rocks, lonely islands lapped by a wind-caressed sea of frozen time.

Out at the edge of the city, heaps of excavated earth had been transformed into sugar mountains, dotted with snow-shrouded, rusting earth movers, bulldozers, and cranes, abandoned two years previously.

And beyond that, the open country began, clothed in snow

like the city, yet softer, gentler, and less austere. The drifts were crisscrossed with animal tracks and the trees swayed in a slight wind. Michael heard birdsong and felt the ground's unevenness under his feet, unlike any city street or sidewalk.

Feeling that they had at last reached a zone of safety, he and Lisa stopped at the crest of a hill and looked back at the city. Its buildings stretched into the distance, vivid in the frigid air.

"Strange to be looking at it instead of being in it," Lisa said. "As if I've somehow walked outside of my own self."

"It was our world. It was us." Michael paused. "It was our Garden of Eden. Abundant food and water, shelter, peace, protection, harmony. That must be why the bands of wanderers never got together into a cohesive society, and never settled; we all liked the illusion that each of us was alone, owning the city as privately as a fantasy world, free to wander anywhere through it."

"If New Vista was the Garden of Eden, was Bobby the snake?" Now that they were out of the city, away from the scene of his death, she felt able to refer to him.

"I didn't mean it too literally. But certainly the peace force coming in, signified a loss of innocence. They debased our paradise. And yet, maybe, it isn't so bad to be forced out of the womb."

"Why? To do what?" She looked up at him with the same unaffected directness that he remembered from years ago, when he'd first met her and felt she was challenging him all the time.

"I don't know," he said. "To do what . . . to do . . . well, all I know is that in one way Bobby was right—we were living off the past and it couldn't last forever. So maybe, now, we can find a way of life that's more permanent but still in harmony with whatever has happened to the rest of the world."

"Maybe we could join a farm around here, with decent people running it, we could . . ."

"I suppose so." He sounded doubtful. "The simple rural life has always seemed to lack something, to me."

The wind gusted across the hillside suddenly, making the trees bend and shiver, their branches creaking, shedding snow like white powder. Lisa drew her clothes around her. "Well, whatever it may lack, we'd better find a simple rural place to stay in pretty damn soon, else we're going to freeze and starve to death out here."

"True."

"You know I seem to remember . . . wasn't Laurence's farm not far away? I went by car but I think it was less than ten miles from New Vista."

"Yes, that's right. God, do you think he and Sheila ever made it work? Wouldn't it have been repossessed by the government, anyway?"

"From what Bobby said, the government gave up on areas around here a long time ago. And it's worth a try, isn't it?"

So they set off, across the fields, leaving the frozen city behind them.

INTERIM: THE COMMUNE

When they finally reached the farm, it was evening. The driveway was overgrown with weeds that poked up through the covering of snow. The automatic gate was gone; in its place was a mound of earth topped with barbed wire, and behind the barbed wire was a shaggy, bearded man with a shotgun.

"That's far enough," he shouted, when Michael and Lisa were still at least twenty yards away.

"We're looking for a guy named Laurence," said Michael.

For a long moment the figure with the gun didn't say anything. Then: "Yeah? What about Laurence?"

"We're friends of his. Does he still live here?"

Another long pause. "What're your names?"

They told him. Without taking his eyes off them he reached into a wooden box and took out a phone. He talked into it, too quietly for them to hear. Then he put it back in the box. "Laurence is coming down here," he said. "You dump your weapon on the ground, and your backpacks, and make sure you're not carrying anything else. We've had a lot of freeloaders trying to move in on us, here, and there ain't going to be anymore."

"At least he still lives here," said Lisa, putting her pack on the ground.

"If it's the same Laurence," said Michael, sweeping snow off a rock and laying the peace force guard's rifle on it.

They waited in the cold evening air. Lisa found herself remembering the day when she'd first come to the farm, with Bobby, when it had been a hot summer day and the shafts of sunlight had struck down through rich green layers of leaves, and she had still been just a little under the spell of Bobby's charisma. It seemed so long ago.

"Hey, Michael!" came a familiar voice. "And Lisa, is it?" Laurence's head come into view, above the barrier. He climbed up and over it, then came striding to meet them, dressed in a patched-together overcoat and ancient jeans. He had grown a beard and his face was weathered by sun and wind. He shook hands with them, and his palms were calloused. "Good to *see* you!"

"Was wondering if you'd still be here," Michael was saying.

"Yeah, I'm here." He laughed. "Although it isn't really my farm anymore. But they let me stay. Do you want to come on back to the house?"

"Are these people okay?" interrupted the hairy figure still guarding the barrier. "How about if they leave their things here, till Harris has talked to 'em?"

"Oh, all right, if you like," said Laurence, with some of his old vagueness.

They went with him to the house. Its aluminum facings were scarred and dented, and one wall was blackened, as if by fire or explosion. The Astroturf lawn had been plowed up and planted with a grain crop. Laurence's Cadillac was still in the driveway, but it had sunk onto flat tires and was beginning to show patches of rust.

"That's where I live, now," he said, gesturing to the car. Michael saw that it had curtains in the windows, and a doormat was on the ground in a patch that had been carefully cleared of snow.

"They kicked you out of your own house?"

Laurence shook his head. "Not exactly. I started letting people move in and stay with me, and it got out of hand. Then this fellow Harris turned up, and he knew a lot more about running a farm than I did, so I let him take over. I never really liked the house that much anyway. There's a guy here now who's good at electrical things; he got the geothermal generator working, so we have electricity. And last summer we got a good harvest."

"Where's Sheila?" asked Lisa.

Laurence was quiet for a moment. "She died," he said, as if to mention it still left him feeling puzzled or confused. "She and Chris. They committed suicide. Together. Shortly after everything . . . you know?"

"And Sheldon?"

"He ran away last year when Harris took over. I don't know where he is. Here, come inside, tell me what you've been doing with yourselves." He held the door open.

Inside the house the contemporary furniture was still there, worn and battered, and under the layers of mud the floors were still of white plastic. In the living room ten or fifteen men and women in their twenties and thirties were sitting around a fire in a fireplace that had been built originally as an ornament, but converted to be functional. Music was playing on the stereo. It looked as if a commune of hippies had moved into the plush residence of a movie director.

"My name's Harris," said a large, acne-scarred man with an orange beard. He had a barrel chest and wore a brass earring in one ear. The last knuckle was missing from the little finger of his left hand, and there were thin white scars on his arms.

Other introductions were given. The group was reserved, though not as paranoid as the guard outside had been. And they opened up more as it became clear that the visitors weren't hostile, weren't armed, and weren't freeloaders.

Lisa and Michael told their story about New Vista, and the invasion of the peace force. "And now we just need somewhere to stay," Michael finished.

Harris laughed. "That's what everyone needs, isn't it? You wouldn't believe the shitheads I've had to kick out, to get this place working." He scrutinized them. "What you got to offer, for your board and lodging?"

"We don't have money, if that's what you mean."

"Money! What the hell use is money?"

"I see. Well, I guess I've got a gun you could have. And some packaged food."

"Got any spare ammunition for the gun?"

"No."

Harris shook his head, as if both saddened and amused by such naivety. "Are you willing to work?"

"Of course," said Michael.

"Know anything about farming?"

"I was raised on a farm," said Lisa.

Harris shrugged. "All right, seeing as you're friends of Laurence's, we'll try it—temporarily." Harris thrust his hands in his pockets, standing with his legs spread, like an old-fashioned ship's captain. "We got enough food stocked up, really, and we need help right now—there's a couple people sick. But remember, you're temporary."

"He has to be strict," Laurence said apologetically, "because otherwise it wouldn't work here. I mean if *I* was still running things, the place would be full of all kinds of ridiculous people, anyone with a hard-luck story. I just can't seem to say 'no.' "

"I'll call Ray at the gate and get him to bring your things up," said Harris.

"It seems so magical that you have electricity," said Lisa.

"Yes, how did you ever get parts to fix the generator?" Michael asked.

"Traded for 'em, of course. You don't know *anything*, do you? See, weather permitting, we take produce from the farm—and anything else we can make, like clothing—and trek into the old town center, to trade for stuff the people there salvage from the offices and warehouses. Electric wiring, light bulbs, tools, metal sheeting, you name it."

"Gasoline?" asked Michael.

"Gasoline!" Harris roared with laughter. "Ain't been any gas since the federal people cleaned it all out, three months after things originally collapsed."

And so Michael and Lisa stayed at the farm, for a few days that became a week; then two weeks.

As their usefulness was proven, they became accepted into the communal system, they adjusted to the routines, and they started learning all the aspects of surviving in the country.

Lisa seemed content enough, but as weeks became months, Michael felt increasingly uneasy, like a guest becoming a permanent resident in a spot he would never have moved into by choice. His old dissatisfactions and restlessness were resurfacing. He thought they had died after he'd met Lisa and had settled in New Vista; but he realized now that they had only been assuaged, not resolved at all.

Time passed and winter eased into spring. The snow melted, making it once more possible to travel over long distances by foot or bicycle. And Michael realized with growing certainty that he was going to have to deal with his restlessness—define it, explore it, and resolve it once and for all. Though he didn't know where to find what was missing, he did know that if there was an answer, it lay outside of the farm.

PART THREE

SprinG

◑

2000

The noise woke him instantly. He listened to its last echoes dying into the distance and lay for a moment staring up at the sky, trying to recapture exactly what it was that he had heard. It had sounded like thunder, and yet. . . .

He stood up slowly, easing stiffness out of his muscles. It was still dark, with stars showing overhead, but there was a ragged line of pale gray-green light at the horizon, over the buildings in the east, heralding dawn.

Michael shivered. His hands and feet were numb. He brushed soot and grime off his clothes and started picking his way cautiously through the jungle of ventilators, pipes, catwalks, and inspection ladders cluttering the rooftop where he had spent the night. He had arrived in the old urban center the previous day. He'd felt alienated and vulnerable, and when darkness came, a rooftop had seemed a safe place to retreat to.

He reached the parapet and peered over its edge. Twelve stories below was the town square. On its opposite side stood City Hall, its old stone facade eroded by many seasons and scarred by riots, demonstrations, and power struggles that had taken place in the square during the last couple of years. But the old building retained some dignity and authority, even now. It still seemed to be a headquarters for city government, insofar as any was left. Faintly, in the darkness, Michael could make out two peace force men in uniform, stationed at either end of the wide flight of steps up to the stone columns in front of the building's entrance. A kerosene lantern burned; a tiny point of yellow light.

And then the noise that had woken him suddenly sounded again—a great booming concussion, in the distance. Definitely not thunder, he realized. His skin prickled; just once in his life he had heard a similar sound, near a quarry when high explosives were detonated to open up a new rock face. Who was letting off bombs, now, in the old urban center? And why?

He saw a third peace force man emerge from City Hall and confer with the two already on the steps. In the light from their lantern he could see their faces turn anxiously in the direction from which the sound had come.

And then came another noise, more familiar and yet in a way more surprising, for he had not heard it in years. Michael leaned over the parapet, looking along one of the main avenues that led out of the square. There was a roaring of gasoline-powered engines, and in the dark distance he saw brilliant white lights moving, coming closer.

More guards began appearing on the steps of City Hall, carrying rifles. And then moments later the vehicles came swarming into the square, like a horde of sinister black insects, their headlights sweeping across the pockmarked streets and the soot-stained buildings. The first few were salvaged automobiles, stripped of bodywork, right down to their skeletal frames. They raced around, swerving at random, horns blaring. Tires squealed and unsilenced motors bellowed in the night, and the stinging, acid-sweet fragrance of exhaust fumes rose in clouds.

Then came bulky black shapes of five armored personnel carriers, chugging into the square toward City Hall. By this time the steps were crowded with peace force men, rifles raised.

One of the cars swerved in a screaming power slide and stopped with its headlights shining straight at the old building. Something was thrown, glimpsed for a moment spinning through the white beams of light. It exploded with a flash. The concussion seemed to hit Michael in the chest, hurting his ears, making him flinch back.

The noise died away, echoing into the distance. Smoke billowed up, drifting slowly. All the vehicles in the square stopped in a circle around the crater that the bomb had excavated. And then from one of the stripped-down cars a figure in a scarlet cape jumped out, caught in the headlights like a ballet dancer on a ravaged floodlit stage. He ran flamboyantly across the asphalt, through the dust and smoke and a cacophony of car horns. He handed something to one of the peace force men—a document? A message?

Michael squinted into the glaring lights. Even at this distance there was something very familiar about that caped figure.

Impulsively he turned and stepped quickly to a rusty fire escape that led all the way to the street. He leapt down the iron-mesh steps, dislodging showers of rust and soot and dirt. The fire escape shook and creaked under him. In the square he could hear the cars re-starting their engines and beginning to move out.

He reached the sidewalk, his palms raw from clutching the eroded handrails of the escape. He ran in the direction of the engine noise and reached the avenue just as the first car came around the square, leading the rest. Michael shaded his eyes against the headlights. "Sheldon!" he shouted, as loudly as he could. He waved his arm.

The car came straight at him.

"Sheldon!" he shouted again.

At the last moment the driver hit the brakes and the car fishtailed to a halt, burning rubber, its engine still revving impatiently. Michael ran forward to it. "That you, Sheldon?"

Sitting in a passenger seat bolted on the bare oily chassis, the caped figure turned his pale face. "Get on!" Sheldon cried, above the roaring of the engine.

Michael hesitated, then climbed up and squatted where the back seat had been ripped away. He grabbed two cross-members of the car's frame. The propeller shaft whirled inches beneath his fingers as the car accelerated, spinning the rear wheels, sounding its horn, taking the procession of vehicles out of the square.

He was deafened by the noise of the motorcade, blinking at swimming after-images of the headlights. Cold air roared past at fifty miles an hour. He struggled to keep his grip as the car careened wildly down the avenue, dodging lumps of masonry and gaping potholes, heading toward the line of dawn light opening wider above the dark shapes of the buildings.

Sheldon turned and looked at him. "Michael?"

"Yeah. Haven't seen you since . . ."

"This is Neal," Sheldon shouted above the noise of the car, and gestured to the other kid driving.

"Where are you going?" Michael asked.

Sheldon just laughed, opening his mouth wide, revealing decayed teeth.

"What were you doing, back there in the square?"

"Flashing. Flashing what we got."

"An ultimatum," put in Neal. "Gave them a written ultimatum. We got the power, now."

Michael shook his head, giving up on making any sense out of the kids. The car lurched and jerked under him, and the icy wind forced past his face. Neal leaned on the horn and the long, blaring note echoed down the ruined avenue.

Michael squinted ahead, his eyes watering in the wind. It had been more than two years since he had been in the center, before the collapse. But he realized they were heading for the river. The night's darkness lightened to gray as they drove, the rest of the convoy still following. Then the river came into view, mirroring the strip of pastel dawn light. An ancient bridge hung like a cobweb from bank to bank. Neal accelerated, the car jumping over the uneven road, almost out of control. *Power,* Michael thought. Already people had forgotten how power felt—the roar of a V-8, the thrust of acceleration, so effortless and easy.

The wind ripped at Michael's clothes and lashed his hair into his face. The bridge loomed ahead. Then suddenly girders were flashing past in a blur, the exhaust note hammering and resounding among them; and then Neal hit the brake, locking the wheels in a screaming four-wheel drift, and Michael was thrown forward as the car slid around a corner at the end of the bridge, then headed down a riverside boulevard, where old ships lay half-submerged and the air was rich with the smell of stagnant water.

A large building came into view ahead. It was the pleasure palace, long since abandoned. Neal slowed the car, letting it coast easily.

"Where you been?" said Sheldon, looking back at Michael.

"Out of town, the last two, three years. At New Vista, and then . . ."

"What you doing here now?"

"I wanted to find out—I've been staying with your father, Laurence. He didn't know you were . . ."

"That asshole."

"I was told Jamieson came to the city. Jamieson, do you remember him?"

"Yeah, he's an asshole too."

"Is he here?"

"You ask too many questions." Sheldon said it with the presence and style of a 1920s gangster. He looked at Michael with lowered lids, tough and mean. Then suddenly he laughed his crazed laugh again, head thrown back at the sky.

Neal swung the car across the street and parked outside the old pleasure palace. Sheldon jumped out, ran up some steps, and watched the rest of the convoy coming in. His scarlet cape fluttered in the cold dawn wind; he looked like some juvenile comic-strip super-hero.

Neal turned in his seat. He was a serious-faced, pimply, scrawny kid with disheveled short black hair. He wore glasses improvised from a couple of mismatched lenses, held together with wire and tape. "You want to see Jamieson?" he asked quietly.

"Everyone inside!" Sheldon was shouting, up on the steps, as other kids started getting out of their vehicles. No one was more than fifteen years old. Many carried guns and knives, hand grenades and homemade bombs.

"Yes, I want to see Jamieson," Michael murmured to Neal. "I

heard a man of his description was in town, here. I heard interesting things are happening. I want to find out more."

Neal's eyes were invisible behind his spectacles, reflecting the
brightening sky. He nodded briefly.

Michael waited. Neal remained in the driver's seat. The other
kids went on up to the pleasure palace entrance, leaving their
vehicles scattered carelessly across the street. Leading his army
into his headquarters, Sheldon disappeared into the building.

"Okay," said Neal. "Come on." He got out of the car. "It's
only just across the river. Your name's Michael?"

"Yes."

"I guess if you know Sheldon, and Jamieson, it's okay."

JAMIESON

They walked back to the bridge, and across it. Everywhere that
Michael looked he saw signs of past street violence, and the terminal breakdown of the old urban center. The sidewalks were
littered with mounds of rubble and garbage: rags, cans, paper,
smashed furniture, barbed wire, bones—human bones, he realized. Lean, mean-looking dogs picked through the refuse. Cryptic, barely-legible slogans were painted on walls. And almost all
the buildings were now abandoned, their windows shattered.

He looked at Neal. "Not many people here in town?"

"They went out, most of 'em. How come you know Sheldon?"

"I know his father. Till a year or so ago, Sheldon lived with
him out in the country."

"Yeah? He don't talk 'bout that."

They left the bridge and Neal led the way up a confusion of
riverside streets, old warehouses crumbling and collapsing, raw
bricks and eroded stonework picking up the first faint rays of
morning sun.

"What exactly was the ultimatum you gave, in the square?"

"We got the cars, the trucks. The gasoline. The guns. They

don't. We showed 'em, those peace force guys, we can do what we want now." Neal's young face looked earnest and mean.

"But what *do* you want?"

"To take over, of course."

"Take over what—the city?"

"No, the trading. The peace forcers think they own it. We want it. The whole thing."

"Isn't there enough to share?" said Michael.

"Maybe now, but not in two, three years." He looked up at Michael, warily. "You're a weird guy. You don't know nothing. And you ain't afraid of us, are you?"

"I'm not sure."

"Better make up your mind. Which side you're on. Here, this is Jamieson's place." He pointed at an old tenement in a row overlooking a couple of lots where warehouses had collapsed into mounds of broken brick and rusty girders. Beyond was the river, the pleasure palace visible on the opposite bank. "Hey, Jay!" Neal shouted, his preadolescent voice piercing and shrill. He put his fingers in his mouth and whistled.

They waited. "Why didn't Sheldon want to tell me anything about Jamieson?" Michael asked.

"Sheldon does what he does, moment to moment. You never know. He don't know himself."

A window on the second floor slid up in its rotten frame. Jamieson's face appeared. There were a few more wrinkles, and the hair had receded further, but the face still showed the same serious preoccupation and intelligence that Michael remembered. Jamieson blinked in the morning light. "Neal?" He fiddled with his spectacles. "Who's that? Who's with you?"

"Me, Michael. Remember?"

"Michael!"

"Yeah, tracked you down."

"Well, well. Wait there." The window slid shut again. A moment later, the street door opened. "You come visiting at ungodly hours," Jamieson said, with an ironic smile.

Michael almost shook hands, then remembered Jamieson's prosthetic arms. He clapped him on the shoulder. "Been a long time."

"It has, it has." The pale, stooped man looked at him curiously. "Come upstairs. Place is a mess, but. . . ." He led them up to the second floor. "I find it's more practical to do everything in one room, though I suppose I could use the whole building if I wanted to." He showed them into a room crowded with papers, sacks of flour and rice, a cooking stove working off cylinders of bottled gas, a typewriter, a mattress, a pair of ragged armchairs, and an old table. "I suppose it's all a bit primitive, but . . ."

"Forget it, stop apologizing, it's good to see you. I'm used to being primitive myself." He sat down on the mattress. Neal joined him.

Jamieson carefully lowered himself into one of the chairs. "Well, well. So where have you been, for the last two years?"

"In New Vista, then at Laurence's farm."

"Were you in New Vista when the peace force went to ransack the place?"

"Yes. That's when we had to leave. We met . . . Bobby turned up there. He was in the peace force, did you know?"

Jamieson shook his head. "I've been here in the old center almost a year, now, but I've tried not to deal with those people; they remind me too much of old-style politics and capitalism."

"Well, out at New Vista, Bobby turned up, told us a story full of lies, and we went through some difficult times. He ended up dead, for which I was, I suppose, partly responsible."

Jamieson raised his eyebrows.

"Yeah, well, so here I am," said Michael. "Came into town yesterday with Harris, from Laurence's farm, with produce to trade. Harris wouldn't stay here after dark—said it was dangerous. So he set off back home on his own. But he told me a lot of rumors about the way things are here, and I decided to see what was really happening."

"I see." Jamieson transferred his attention abruptly to Neal. "Were you responsible for those explosions? Just before dawn?"

Neal looked evasive. "It was Sheldon."

"What was happening?"

"Gave 'em the ultimatum. The peace force guys."

"Oh. Oh, you did, eh?"

"That's right."

"That's bad, too bad." Jamieson stood up. He paced to the window and back. He seemed to have temporarily forgotten Michael. "I did *tell* you, it wasn't the best way."

"Yeah," said Neal, "but Sheldon, you know?"

"Sheldon, always Sheldon. He still refuses to talk to me?"

"He don't trust you, Jay. Whose side you're on."

Jamieson sat down again. "Hm."

Neal fidgeted, sitting on the mattress. "Look, can you give me those figures you talked about yesterday?"

"Hm, I suppose so." Jamieson went to the table and poked among the papers, pulling out one sheet in his plastic fingers. "Here. As well as I recall, this is how you calculate the output in watts. But you tell Sheldon, if he expects anymore electrical or mechanical advice from me, he'll have to start following my political advice more seriously. Violence doesn't solve anything. You need a *treaty* with the peace force. I'll be glad to negotiate one for you, I've told you."

"Yeah, right, I'll be sure and remind him." Neal took the sheet quickly and headed straight for the door. "See ya, Jay."

"Tomorrow?" said Jamieson.

"Maybe." The kid left.

"Hm, hm," said Jamieson, sitting down again. He looked out of the window at the pleasure palace, across the stagnant river. It was very quiet in the room. In one corner an old pendulum wall clock ticked slowly. "Those children stumbled on a real prize a few months back," Jamieson said, vaguely. "An old military store. The main armories were cleaned out years ago, of course, by the federal people. But this one had been missed. Records listed it as having been dismantled, but in reality it wasn't. I think it was for civil defense use after a nuclear attack, some fool contingency plan. Anyway, there were several hundred gallons of gasoline there, a lot of armored vehicles, and some weapons."

"How could it all be in working order, after three years?"

"Wasn't. I've been giving them information, helping them to renovate the equipment."

"What? Why? Jamieson, they're wasting all that gasoline, they're making Molotov cocktails, they're crazy."

He looked carefully at Michael, as if evaluating his intentions. "You must realize, for every item of information those children have obtained from me, they have also been given a fair amount of indoctrination. I've been pressing upon them the pointlessness of using force to get a monopoly of diminishing resources. You see I have in mind a social structure where there is equitable sharing of resources in the context of shared rural-urban . . ."

"Yeah, and how's it going?" Michael interrupted.

"Hm, hm?"

"You getting anywhere, preaching nonviolence to kids like Sheldon?"

"Sheldon *is* a problem. Quite psychopathic. But Neal and some others have been listening to me, and I'm hoping that through them I can reach all the children. It was a gamble, but when they understand what I'm saying, they'll soon lose interest in ever using that salvaged stuff for aggressive purposes."

"You've got to be kidding," said Michael.

"Hm?"

"They've taken you for a ride. I know those kids, I used to write songs for them, remember? They're brain-damage cases. Your so-called indoctrination won't work, in a million years."

Jamieson looked irritated. "It has to work! There has to be an end to destructive competition and exploitation."

Michael nodded. "It'd be nice, I agree. But talking to them won't do it."

"Well, I certainly don't intend to *force* my philosophy on them. The philosophy itself condemns all use of force."

Michael sighed. He massaged his forehead. He was tired from

his fitful sleep on the roof, and confused by Jamieson. How could a man who'd had such foresight three years ago be so out of touch with reality now? Was it premature senility, or just the idealism of a recluse who had lost touch with practicalities? "Tell me more about what's been happening in the center here," Michael said. "I mean, why are all the buildings empty? Where did everyone go?"

"Ah, yes," said Jamieson. Faced with a direct, factual question, he lost some of his reserve toward Michael. "For a while the peace force employed a lot of labor in surrounding areas, producing food. A few services were restored in town, and so on. But last summer the harvests failed and the farm labor force became disenchanted with toiling for their new masters. They ran off. When winter came the peace force ransacked anywhere they could, for food—including New Vista, which I think was completely emptied. But there were perhaps half a million people living in the center here, and they soon consumed all the supplies that came in. Faced with famine, in midwinter, they began leaving, to survive as best they could in the country. I imagine many of them perished. We're down to around ten thousand now, I estimate—the hard-core city dwellers who seem unable to face a retreat to rural life. Peace force people, most of them. They run the market, living off food that's traded in town by farmers from outlying areas. I've got it all summarized in chapter thirty-five of my book, if you want to read it." He rummaged among the papers on his table. "Was working on it just last week."

"Perhaps I could look at it later," said Michael.

"Hm, all right, as you wish."

"What about the federal forces?" Michael asked.

"Oh, they pulled out years ago, as soon as everything was in a shambles, with no coal or gasoline or electric power to speak of. They're a thousand miles away in their superhavens, insulated by the great distances across the American continent. We have no means to reach them and no means of attacking them to appropriate their wealth. Well, those children have some transport now, simple weapons, and a little gasoline, but not much—not enough."

"I see." Michael looked out of the window, thoughtfully. "They've sure as hell got enough to make a nice little war with the peace force, though."

"I am doing all I can to prevent that."

"Yes, I understand, I understand." Michael paused. "I think I'll go out and wander around a little, I only just got here, I need to see how it feels. Maybe come back here later—could I stay the night in your building?"

"Certainly. Goodness knows, there are enough rooms. And I have food; the children gave me some of a large stock they stole from a peace force stockpile a month ago. Of course I didn't approve of their night-time thievery, but since it was already a fait accompli. . . ."

"Sure. All right, I'll see you later, Jamieson."

"Very well. Er—later you must tell me, where you stand."

"What do you mean?"

"The ethical questions. The social structure we should be trying to rebuild."

Michael sighed. "I'll try. Sure. Later." He walked out.

The Marketplace

There was still a smell of burned earth and asphalt in the town square, but the bomb crater was hidden from view by dozens of market stalls that had been quickly erected during the morning. Now the place was packed with out-of-towners, pushing farm produce on carts improvised from bicycle wheels, scrap wood, and beaten-out auto panels, going from stall to stall, examining merchandise offered for trade. There was everything from electric motors (convertible to low-wattage generators) to razor blades; string to kerosene; and less-likely salvaged

stocks such as ballpoint pens, briefcases, deodorants, old magazines, and a million other items left over from civilization before
the collapse.

The traders all wore peace force uniforms, many of them
scuffed and ragged, fitting loosely around bodies that had become
gaunt and bony. It had obviously been a hard winter. But now
the spring was here, the sun was warming the streets and the
people, and the atmosphere was alive with the sounds and
rituals of trading.

The old dollar currency was no longer used, and nothing else
had taken its place. Hoarders of gold prior to the great collapse
now found themselves out of luck; the emergent economic system was still young enough for people to trust nothing but
physical necessities such as food and clothing. So each trader
exhibited a table of relative, arbitrary barter values: one stall-
holder might value a pound of wheat flour at "4"; a pound of
beans at "3"; a pair of gloves, "5"; a bicycle wheel, "10"; an electric motor, "15"; and so on, so that a farmer could get the electric
motor in exchange for five pounds of beans or, if he happened to
have them, three pairs of gloves, or various combinations of commodities. It implied a system of convertible currency, but without
the currency.

Figures varied from one trader to another, but Michael saw
that there were few substantial differences. The peace force
maintained the illusion of a free market, but in reality there was
the uniformity of a monopoly.

Suddenly, above the noise of dealers crying their wares and
buyers haggling over prices, an amplified voice started shouting
from the other end of the square. Michael looked up. He was
surprised to hear electric amplification, and in addition the voice
sounded familiar. He started in its direction.

He emerged from the market in front of the steps of City Hall.
On a simple platform, dressed in a tattered denim suit and the
remains of a clerical collar, was the Reverend Isaacs. His Spartan disciples had been reduced in number, to a single pathetic

figure wearily turning the handle of a little electric generator, powering the Reverend's bullhorn.

"Friends, people!" he was preaching. "You are still following the Old Way. The Bad Way. The way of technology. Material wealth. You do not *need* to own, to possess, to hoard. You must sacrifice, and share—share freely with your neighbors. Instead of trading you should be giving. Only in frugality can peace of mind be found. Do not try to follow the evil road back to affluence!"

Michael watched him, and felt a familiar surge of irritation. But now, years after he had last heard the Spartans, he was better able to define his feelings. It was not that the Reverend Isaacs was wrong. It was that he was so nearly right. The "evils" he condemned—greed, selfishness, material wealth—*had* played a part in promoting the great collapse. But there was no logic behind the Spartan credo. It was entirely a matter of faith. Doing-without was Good. Technology and wealth were Bad—in *any* form. A wind-powered generator to light a farmhouse in the evening was just as bad as a luxury automobile taking a kid on a joy ride. Farmers trading for necessities were as evil as rich men hoarding wealth in superhavens. Simplistic anti-technologists like the Reverend Isaacs ultimately undermined their own causes; men like him had helped to discredit the ecology movement of the early seventies. In a previous century he would have been a luddite.

". . . offer you a token of my sincerity," the man was saying. "I know that it is best to give; but before you can believe me you must see it is so, and that you may see, I must show you. Here," he held up a large glass jar. "These pills are a herbal compound made from natural substances known to those who live in simplicity and harmony with nature. These simple pills will cure arthritis, ease depression, end insomnia, and alleviate pain. We are giving them to you—free!—for it is best to give and to share. You may, if you wish, give to us the gadgets, the devices that we urge you to renounce. We will take them and destroy them. My follower will now move among you."

The crowd had doubled as soon as people heard the promise of free medication. Men and women and children pressed forward, Michael among them. He put out his hand and a haggard woman in rags gave him one of the little white pills. "Do you wish to donate?" she asked, holding a sack up.

"No," he said, as unpleasantly as he could.

She moved on.

He pushed his way out of the crowd, looking at the pill she had given him. It bore no pharmaceutical name or imprint. Cautiously he tasted it.

The taste was familiar. "Aspirin," he muttered.

"Hey, Mike," said a young voice, beside him.

He looked around. Neal had come up to him, moving quickly and quietly through the press of adults in the square.

"Over here." The thin, serious-faced boy jerked his head.

"What do you want?" said Michael.

Neal glanced around quickly. "Sheldon. Wants to talk."

Michael cautiously followed the kid, away from the market, across an avenue, leaving behind the center of noise and activity. He glanced behind him, and the marketplace was a mob of humanity dressed in salvaged and home-woven clothes, milling around under the faces of the old, decaying buildings.

"In here." Neal gestured at an alley between a couple of looted, burned-out store fronts. Broken glass had long since been crushed to powder on the blackened sidewalk.

Michael paused carefully outside the opening of the alley, far enough out in the street to be able to run if anyone came out at him. But his suspicions seemed unfounded; Sheldon was standing alone, his pale face watching Michael.

"Talk up on the roof," said Neal. "Got to be careful. Sheldon don't like being seen in town during the day."

"All right," said Michael. He walked into the alley.

Quickly Sheldon climbed onto some garbage cans, then leaped to the bottom rung of a fire escape ladder. He went running up the corroded metal, agile and fast, like a spider.

Michael followed, with Neal. They reached the roof. It was not unlike where Michael had spent the night, overlooking the square. He glanced around, taking in the scene—an old, wooden water tower, rusty iron railings, rotting roofing asphalt puddled with dirty water. The newness and cleanness of the untouched buildings of New Vista seemed a whole world away.

It was very quiet. The noise of the market was screened by intervening buildings. A pair of pigeons strutted around the rim of the water tower, looking down at Sheldon, Michael, and Neal, alone on the roof under the sky.

"So what do you want?" Michael asked again.

Sheldon walked close to Michael and squinted up at his face, as if evaluating him. "Neal says you killed some peace force guy," he said, finally.

Michael frowned. "Me?"

"Yeah," said Neal. "When we was over at Jay's this morning, you said you did it, when you was in New Vista. I heard."

"Oh, you mean Bobby." Michael paused, thinking carefully. The beginnings of a strategy were coming to him; a solution to the situation involving the kids and the peace force. "Yes, it's true," he said, grateful that he had talked carelessly earlier and made it sound as though he had killed Bobby with his own hands. "I shot him. And two others, as well. They were in New Vista stealing our food."

Sheldon was still watching Michael with narrowed eyes. Abruptly he turned away and spat on the roof. Then he looked at Michael some more. Michael looked steadily back at him.

"So," said Sheldon, "how about Jamieson?"

"Jamieson? What about Jamieson?" Michael couldn't follow the kid's intuitive, internal thought patterns.

"He trust you? You trust him?"

Michael shook his head. "I don't understand."

"He your pal?"

Michael hesitated. "Jamieson's changed," he said noncommitally. "He seems different from when I used to know him."

Sheldon turned and looked at Neal. Neal looked back at Sheldon. Sheldon turned back to Michael. "Want to help us?"

"Help you do what?"

"Neal says you talk like you know a bit. Like you got educated."

"Yes, I was educated."

"You know how to fix cars, make bombs?"

"Some."

"You come with us." In the kid's head, all questions had been suddenly settled.

"Wait," said Michael.

Sheldon stopped. "What?"

"You want me to help you knock out those peace force people? You have enough weapons to do it, if you get yourselves organized?"

"Yeah," said Sheldon. He grinned. "Last night was just show. Next time real. Fix those cocksuckers." His crooked teeth glinted yellow. His stringy hair blew in the wind. His crinkled-up eyes looked dark and evil.

"And you don't trust Jamieson to help you anymore," Michael went on.

"Old guy's full of shit," said Sheldon. "He'd sell us out. Or something."

"And me?"

"You, we keep you with us. From now on."

Under observation, Michael realized. He shook his head. "That won't work—if I disappear into your building permanently, Jamieson will get suspicious. He'll know you're up to something."

There was a long pause. Sheldon's expression clouded. He scrutinized Michael some more. Then he grinned again. "Yeah, is right," he said, as if the matter had just been confirmed by a message only he could hear. "You're a smart guy. So we let you go see Jamieson, once a day, keep him okay. But we watch you, all the time."

"All right," said Michael. "You know, I hate those peace force bastards as much as you do. In fact the one I killed once slept with my woman," he added, with a faint smile.

"Woman?" Sheldon shrugged as if irritated by something that was irrelevant. "Okay, Michael. You and us, fix those motherfuckers." Practically the only polysyllabic words he knew were obscenities.

Michael nodded. "We'll fix them."

Sheldon threw his head back and gave one of his manic, animal laughs, his face contorted, his arms spread out wide. Then he leaped across, swung around the fire escape, and went down it like an acrobat.

THE GARAGE

Two young kids in ragged clothes stood guarding the doors of the pleasure palace. One held a rifle, the other loitered close to a machine gun set on its tripod pointing at the street. Their eyes were sullen and brooding, their faces were blank. They barely looked at Sheldon as he strode in past them, his red cape fluttering behind him. He turned and beckoned to Michael. "Here, show you what we got fixed up."

The special effects in the building had been inoperative ever since the city's power had failed. The entry lobby was a bare metal and concrete space, littered with garbage, smelling of urine. Cryptic symbols and obscene drawings were daubed on the walls, like cave paintings. Kids of ten, eleven, and twelve were loitering munching army rations in a desultory way. Some were throwing stones at a target. Others were cleaning their weapons with obsessive care. Michael noticed that there were as many girls as boys; they seemed to be treated as social and sexual equals and had mannerisms identical to those of the males, as if gender was irrelevant. Maybe sex itself had become irrelevant, in their world. The rock concert audiences of three years ago had been already heading in that direction.

"Downstairs," said Sheldon, leading the way down an escalator that was choked with old food wrappers, discarded ammunition clips, empty bottles and cans, and other detritus.

They emerged in what had been the underground garage. It stank of exhaust fumes from a gasoline-powered electric generator chugging away in one corner, supplying light bulbs strung at intervals across the low concrete ceiling.

The space was a junkyard of salvaged technology. Against one wall stood sheets of steel, plastic, glass, aluminum, brass, and alloys. Old car frames littered the oil-stained floor. Ten-gallon cans of gasoline were stacked in the shadows beside a mess of auto parts, tools, spare tires, and electric cable. Shelves were piled high with cogwheels, levers, bolts, switches, and electronic control systems. Somehow the kids had managed to drag into the garage bulky items like a power hoist, an oil-burning domestic hot-water furnace, and the shovel off an earth mover.

"Where the hell did you find all this junk?" Michael started wandering through it all, fascinated. The kids had grabbed anything mechanical or electrical, as unselectively as a flock of jackdaws filling their concrete nest with baubles. A rack of telephone exchange switching equipment stood next to several cooking ranges, and a pile of TV sets.

"Found it all over," said Neal, walking close beside Michael. The kid had come alive in the mechanical environment. He started eagerly pointing out special objects, asking the names of others, asking functions, principles, historical uses. What was it, Michael wondered, that drew some people to technology like a starving man to food? What was the source of the obsession? It was nothing to do with intelligence; some of the best mechanics were semi-literate and seemed to operate more on intuition than logic.

He briefly explained some of the gadgets, digging back into vague memories of electronics courses he'd taken at college and times when he'd tinkered around with cars, before he'd ever considered getting into the music business. Neal's eyes were wide, behind his homemade spectacles, and his expression was intense, focused on Michael's mouth, as if he were watching the words coming out.

"But we ought to do something about that generator," Michael pointed to the gasoline motor belching fumes into the underground space. "Pipe the exhaust outside. So we can breathe in here."

"Hey, yeah, that's an idea," said Neal, as if such a cause-and-effect idea had never occurred to him. "This is great, this is going to be real easy with you here. Jay, he used to give out facts like he was giving away food. Mean old bastard. Never came over here, never would. And always talk, talk, talk to me about what we *ought* to be doing."

"Did you ever pay attention to that part?"

"Fuck, no."

"Do you think the peace force people know your stuff is all here?" Michael asked.

"Yeah, they know, just like we know where *they* are, in City Hall. But they ain't got enough to knock us out. Just rifles, mainly."

"When you say they're in City Hall," said Michael, "do they live there? Do they have *everything* in there?"

"They live in it, keep the weapons there. But the food and gadgets and stuff they trade in the market, they keep that spread around in places all over. Safer from us that way."

"I see. Makes sense. So, at the moment, it's a stand-off."

Neal frowned. "What you mean? What's that mean?"

"A stand-off? It means neither you nor they are going to make a move just yet, because you're too equally matched for either side to be sure of victory. You're watching and waiting."

"Right, right."

Michael turned it over in his head. His plan was set; he could see no alternative. If he didn't intervene, the kids would eventually run out of food and a confrontation would be forced anyway. Or they'd just attack for the hell of it and get themselves massacred. All that was certain was that there was no peaceful compromise possible, no matter what Jamieson would like to believe. "All right," he said, "let's get to work and sort out the junk from the stuff that's useful. That'll take a couple of days to start with."

"Yeah!" Neal's eyes were bright. "Let's do it!"

Michael found himself becoming drawn into the task. In a sense it was the first real work he'd done in years; the chores at the farm hadn't been his idea of work, since they had not in any way exercised his mind. He'd always been interested in electronics, serving him well when planning effects in Bobby's stage act and devising new music. And he remembered some engineering. In the basement with Neal, he felt himself regressing, remembering simple, peaceful times when he'd been a kid himself, living at home, playing with a chemistry set, or making elementary digital computers, or building a robot with his erector set and surplus electronics parts. You could lose yourself, in work like that.

After a few hours, someone brought a meal and they took a break to eat. The food was in plastic packages stamped with Civil Defense codings. Emergency rations. Tasteless and heavy, but nutritious enough. He sat on the bottom step of the escalator, chewing thoughtfully.

A kid walked down and sat beside him. He turned and realized that it was a girl.

"You're Michael," she said.

"That's right." He examined her face. It was sallow with grime and dirt—none of the kids bothered washing. Her hair was tied back behind her head. She might have been around thirteen. Her breasts were beginning to show under her clothes. Her eyes were serious, her mouth was delicate, she could have been quite pretty. Bruises across her cheeks suggested a recent fight. She was carrying an M-16 rifle; he wondered how someone her size could possibly handle a gun that big.

"What's your name?" he asked her.

"Carol. Sheldon said I should come talk to you."

"He did? Why?"

"I don't know." She shrugged. "Told me to ask if you wanted anything." She looked at him again. "How old are you?"

He had to think for a moment. He'd been twenty-four in the year of the collapse. "I'm twenty-seven, I think."

She studied him, with more than simple curiosity. "Do you like to fuck?"

Michael paused. He smiled. "Why are you asking?"

"Want to with me?"

"Did Sheldon get you to ask me that?"

She hesitated. Then she shrugged.

"Are you Sheldon's girl?"

"Kind of. He keeps me around."

Michael nodded slowly. "So Sheldon wanted you to check up on me, did he? He told you to come here and talk to me, then go back and tell him what I said."

She frowned. She looked at him suspiciously. "Why do you think that? Someone tell you?"

"No. It's clear enough."

She looked at him strangely. "What you doing here with us kids?"

Michael bit off another chunk of the survival rations. "You and I both have the same thing we want to do," he told her. "Get rid of the peace force. That *is* what you want, isn't it? To go and kill them all?"

"Right." There was no emotion; it was very matter-of-fact.

"Do you enjoy firing your gun?"

"Yeah!" Now, for the first time, the eyes became animated, the voice showed excitement.

"You like that best of all, huh?"

"That's right. Hey, can I have some of your food, there?"

"Sure." He broke off a hunk and gave it to her.

"Thanks." She chewed on it. "You know I can't tell if you like me or not."

"Perhaps," he said.

"So do you want sex?"

"Maybe later."

"Okay, I'll be around." She stood up to go.

"Come down here again," he said. "I'd like to talk to you some more."

"I'll do that." She disappeared up the escalator.

He thought for a moment, trying to imagine what a kid like her would be doing in three years' time. He couldn't. The kids themselves had no conception of the future. No direction, and no sequential thought. Their instincts, too, were scrambled. He was sure, somehow, that they were the logical product of human love-hate involvement with urban life and technology; their forebears had been urbanites who hung out in slot machine arcades bumming dimes so they could play pinball all day. And the strange aspect was, a part of Michael empathized with it—the depersonalization and detachment from simple life-force instincts. He was drawn to it, even as it repelled him.

MISSIONARIES

In the evening, Michael walked up the escalator, feeling pleasantly tired, physically and mentally. His hands were stained with grease, his ears still heard engines revving and backfiring, and his eyes still saw the white sparks of a welding torch. But it was a good feeling.

A few youths were still hanging around in the building lobby. "You going out?" one of them asked him.

"Yes, I am."

"I come too. Sheldon says."

Michael shrugged. "Okay."

Together they walked down the steps into the night. The moon was shining, over the river. Beyond its opposite bank the old office buildings and apartment blocks towered up in a formless black mass, not a single lighted window among them. Like New York City during the blackout.

Michael walked along the street with the kid beside him, rifle in hand. Neither of them said anything. It was as quiet as a little road in the middle of the country.

Crossing the bridge, Michael thought of Lisa, and missed her. She had understood his restlessness and need to revisit the urban center. But she would not understand why he was doing what he was doing now. She was always so willing to let events go their own way, without her intervention. And for a while he had thought he could be like that himself and be easily satisfied.

When he reached Jamieson's house he saw a faint glow of light up in the second-floor window. He shouted up to the man, and waited.

"I stay here, watch the house," said the kid, retreating out of sight.

"I may be here all night," said Michael.

"Is okay. I wait."

Michael turned as the front door opened and Jamieson appeared. "Ah," said the man, seeing Michael but not noticing the kid in the background. "Was wondering when you might turn up. Come in." He led the way back up the stairs.

The room was lit by an enormous flickering candle, set on top of an empty cooking-gas cylinder on the old table. Fresh sheets of paper were stacked beside the typewriter. "Don't let me interrupt your work," said Michael.

"No, not at all, not at all. I don't often have the chance for some intelligent conversation." And that was part of the trouble, Michael realized—Jamieson had been on his own too long, with only the kids to talk to. It would have divorced anyone from reality. "Have some oatmeal." He was already spooning some out before Michael could refuse. "And tell me what you've been up to."

"Been over at the pleasure palace." Michael sampled the gray paste; the oats were gritty, not sufficiently cooked, but the taste was good and it was hot.

"Hm, hm. So how are the childrens' warlike preparations?"

"I've been encouraging them to lose interest," Michael lied. "They've got enough food there for months." Another lie. "I've come to the conclusion there's no real reason for them to attack the peace force. Last night was just high spirits."

"You really think so?" Jamieson frowned.

"Right."

"Why, *that's* good news," he said, thoughtfully. On a personal level the man was an easy con, Michael realized. He could disentangle web upon web of political deception, but he tended to trust the innate decency of his fellowman. "Those children are our hope for the future," Jamieson went on. "If we can only communicate to them the logic of survival."

"What's that, exactly?"

"It's elementary. If everyone acts positively to help society as a whole, each individual will subsequently benefit *from* that society. Whereas if individuals try to exploit society, society eventually becomes depleted and everyone suffers—except perhaps a tiny minority who are better at being exploiters than anyone else." He sat down in one of the old armchairs. His face was half in shadow from the flickering candlelight.

"Sounds like an old socialist argument," Michael said, finishing his oatmeal and setting down the bowl. "Help your fellowman and he'll help you in return, right? But don't you think in practice it tends to be more like, rip off your fellowman before he takes what you have first?"

Jamieson shook his head. "It *has* been that way, but it needn't be. Especially now that we have fewer resources to fight over."

"You mean, now that almost everyone is poor, we're more

nearly equal, so there's less to excite greed? Maybe there's some truth in that." Michael thought back to his trip across country into town, from the farm. He and Harris had made it on bicycles, taking turns pulling a homemade trailer loaded with farm goods. It had taken three days stopping off at small towns on the way. People had been cautious and guarded, but the hard times being experienced by all did produce some sense of sharing. "Still I think the selfish instincts, to grab what you can from the other guy, are still there," Michael said. "Especially in cases like the kids, who have no conception of being members of society, or the peace forcers, who are so reluctant to give up on the old urban lifestyle and values."

"Those tendencies aren't instincts," said Jamieson. "More like habits. Bad habits. We simply have to break them."

Michael laughed. He leaned back against the wall, stretching his legs out on the old mattress. "Yeah? How?"

"Educate them away, of course."

"We've reached our point of disagreement, Jamieson. I think those bad habits, or instincts, can't be eradicated so easily."

Jamieson leaned back in his chair. It creaked under him. Behind him on the wall the clock ticked, slowly, regularly. "Well, how else can it be done? Suppression is out of the question, obviously. It must be done with *suggestion*."

"Oh, come on, you're reminding me of the Reverend Isaacs. All he's ever done is preach, and . . ." Michael broke off. "Did I say something wrong?"

Jamieson had stiffened suddenly, looking away from Michael. "The Reverend Isaacs is a corrupt fraud."

"What do you mean?"

Jamieson cleared his throat testily. "The Spartans were supported by laundered government funds back before the collapse, because the government wanted people to be happy with less— the Spartan message. And now the peace force is supporting them."

"The peace force? Are you sure?"

"Yes." His voice was cold and clipped. "Isaacs encourages people to share and be less possessive. Such people are easier to trade with and exploit, wouldn't you agree? Those gadgets the man collects supposedly to be destroyed—they're back on the market the next day. The peace force orchestrates the whole thing."

"Oh."

"Isaacs is despicable, twisting a basically good and just philosophy to satisfy the ends of exploiters of the common people." Jamieson sounded as though he were reading a prepared statement.

"Yeah, well, really, I didn't mean *you* were like that."

"No, no, I quite understand." Jamieson stood up. He walked to his table. "Actually I should get back to work on my book. I don't want to seem unfriendly, but it is getting late."

Michael got up off the mattress. "You really shouldn't take offense about what I said. I didn't mean . . ."

"I haven't taken offense," Jamieson said, distantly.

Michael sighed, feeling impatient with the man, unwilling to try to humor him further. "All right. I'll go and see how the accommodation is upstairs."

"You'll find it comfortable. The occupants were unexpectedly massacred in a street demonstration, I believe. They left all their possessions in their apartment."

Michael laughed. "That's a lucky break."

"Hm, hm," Jamieson said, still screening him out. "Goodnight."

"Yes, goodnight." Michael walked out of the room. Angry, and once again disillusioned by the man, he felt his way upstairs through the darkness of the house. The apartment on the next floor was unlocked, and moonlight filtered through its dusty windows, showing the rooms untouched and perfect—ornaments on a mantelshelf, old but comfortable furniture, shelves of books, a TV in the corner, pictures on the wall. Michael walked through to the bedroom and found it as comfortable as the living room. He kicked off his shoes, then crawled under some blankets on one of the beds. They smelled of dust and were cold and damp, but it was a better place to sleep than on a rooftop. The softness of the mattress was almost disconcerting.

He lay staring at the ceiling. Why were all the idealists so theoretical and impractical and out of touch? And all the practical people so lacking in ideals? Not a very new question, and it had no answer. Well, of course, if everyone had Lisa's matter-of-fact, undemanding, easygoing relationship with the environment. . . . But everyone didn't.

Michael knew that it was clear, what had to be done. He didn't like it, because it involved manipulating groups of people for the sake of abstract ideas dangerously close to "building a better society" and "protecting the future."

But he had to do it.

CAROL

Days passed. Michael spent hours in the garage with Neal and other kids, fixing machines. He went and located a city branch library, dug out chemical reference books, found an old copy of *The Anarchist's Handbook,* and learned about explosives. And each night he regularly went back to Jamieson's, often with Neal, to preserve an illusion of normalcy and make Jamieson believe the kids were coming around to his ideas about pacifism, socialism, and survival.

The peace force eventually answered the kids' ultimatum by offering them a twenty-five percent cut of the trading market. Sheldon laughed his manic laugh and tore up the message. He demanded to know, from Michael, when he would be able to move in and destroy the peace force headquarters at City Hall completely. Michael estimated it would take another seven days of preparations. Meanwhile, there were skirmishes every night between crazed teenagers joyriding in cars and peace force snipers hidden in the old buildings.

One afternoon, a week after he had started working with the kids, Michael went wandering through the old pleasure palace, taking a few hours away from the garage. He walked along dark corridors, through rooms and chambers that had once glittered with special effects and were now grimy, sordid retreats, concrete bunkers where the child-guerrillas slept and ate and lived. And he went into what had once been the Love Garden.

A hole had been blown in its roof—kids testing Molotovs, he guessed—and dim light filtered through, across the man-made landscape of plasticized hills and hollows. There was some litter, and the place smelled damp, yet it looked basically as it had years earlier.

Then Michael realized he was not alone. Twenty feet away, in a dip near the middle of the area, two of the kids were lying together on the artificial grass.

Quietly, he crept closer. The girl's back was turned toward him, but he could see that the boy she was lying with was Sheldon. He was fingering her body, his face earnest, yet blank, as if observing something that he didn't entirely understand, and that didn't require his participation. Michael had seen expressions like that on kids watching TV. Sheldon's hands moved over the young breasts, waist, thighs. His fingers clenched on flesh; the girl gave a yelp of surprise and protest. Sheldon pinched her again, holding her down, watching her flinch. He smiled faintly. He drew back. He slapped her, hard. She didn't struggle.

Then, as if losing interest, Sheldon rolled away onto his back, naked, fondling himself lazily, his eyes staring at the roof where there had once been an electric moon and stars.

The girl reached out and started touching Sheldon. After a moment he knocked her hand away. He stood up and dragged his clothes on over his young, skinny frame. Shaking his blond hair out of his face he turned and wandered away across the plastic grass, toward the exit, while Michael remained hidden in the shadows.

Sheldon left, and the door slammed.

The girl sat up. She started dressing herself slowly. She yawned, as if bored. Michael saw it was Carol, the one he had talked with before. He moved quietly forward.

She stood, pulling her shoes on, then turned and saw him. She paused. "Michael?"

"Yes."

She started across to him. She walked very easily, very naturally, as if quite unconscious of her own body and how she might look. "You been spying on me?"

"I guess I have," he said.

She shrugged indifferently. "Come for a walk."

"All right, if you like."

They left the ruined Love Garden, walked down through the building, and out of it, to the boulevard by the river. The kids were no longer so insistent on always having Michael accompanied by an armed guard, now; seeing him leave with Carol, none of them bothered to follow.

"How's it going, down there with the machines and stuff?" she asked him.

"Pretty good."

It was a warm spring day, and even strewn with garbage and debris the street looked better in the sunlight.

"When we going to go get those peace forcers?" she asked.

"Soon, now. In a few days." He looked at her. "I suppose you'll want to be there, when it happens?"

She grinned. "You bet!"

"It may not be as easy as you expect," he said carefully. "There may be a lot of fighting. People may get hurt."

She picked up a brick and hurled it at one of the old ships half submerged in the oily river. Rusty metal resounded with a clang. "We'll beat the shit out of them," she said.

"You could get killed. Think about it."

"Me?" she looked up at him and smiled, playful, child-like. "I got my M-16."

"I mean it." He put his hand on her shoulder, gripping hard, trying to make her listen. "In fact I think you should stay out of the attack."

She frowned. "Come on, you sound like that guy Jamieson."

"I suppose I do." Michael sighed. "Yes, and God knows no one ever listens to him." He looked at another of the ships, tied up to a pier. "Ever been on a freighter like that?"

"No."

"Come on." He led her down to the pier, across its rotting wooden planks. The ship had sunk low in the water; they could easily climb aboard.

They explored over the rusting steel decks, up onto the bridge, then lower down where water had flooded some of the cabins.

"If we could get one of these ships seaworthy," said Michael, "where would you go?"

They finished looking around, and sat down out at the stern, on the deck, in the sunshine.

She shrugged. "I don't know."

"You could cruise around the whole world. Do you wonder what's happening now, in other countries? Britain, Denmark, Russia."

"My mom and dad took me to England once. When I was little. We stayed in a hotel. It was cold and all the people wore raincoats and looked hungry. It was a fucking waste of time." She turned and looked at Michael, her face close to his. "You talk about weird things."

"No, I was just thinking. . . ."

"Yeah, thinking ain't worth the bother."

"You're some kind of pragmatist," he said, half smiling, half sad.

"A what?"

"Just a joke," he told her.

"Oh." She lay on the deck for a while, saying nothing. Then she rolled closer and reached between his legs. "You want to, now?"

"All right," he said. Then, gently and slowly, he kissed her, lying there under the sky on the boat that was going nowhere.

"You don't know how to kiss," he said a moment later.

"No? Then show me."

He had sudden memories of being back at high school. He laughed. "All right."

She picked it up quickly, but seemed uninterested. "I thought you wanted to have sex," she complained, tugging at his clothes.

He lay back and let her undress him. Her hands moved randomly over him, learning his body. With curiosity she stroked the hair of his thighs and his arms; ran her fingers through the hair on his chest and his groin.

After a while he started undressing her. She looked deceptively small and frail. He held her to him and then made love to her, as he would to a sensitive, mature woman whom he was fond of. He was firm, but gentle; he moved purposefully but easily. She looked up at him with clear eyes that seemed puzzled, questioning. She didn't seem to know how to respond.

When it was over she just lay staring at him. She touched his penis. "You ain't like Sheldon," she murmured.

"No?"

"No. For a start he don't often go inside me."

Michael frowned. "What *does* he do?"

"He jerks himself off, or he gets me to touch him, or do it with my mouth, or most often he doesn't come at all. He don't get interested enough."

"It looked like that today, when I saw you."

She nodded. "Yeah. But you're weird, you really get into it, and you're so, so . . ."

"Gentle?"

"I guess that's it."

"I'm not always like that," he told her. "I've been with

women where sex was more like a fight, and we hurt each other as well as pleased each other."

"Yeah?" She looked more interested.

"But I think that that's the only kind of sex play you've ever learned," he went on. "I wanted to show you, that there are other things, subtler thoughts and emotions, in sex and everything else, that you don't know about."

"Yeah? What's all this stuff I don't know, that's so important?"

Michael felt embarrassed. "I suppose I shouldn't preach."

"I am what I am. Don't you like it?" she looked belligerent.

"I like what I think I see in you," he said carefully, sincerely.

"So stop talking shit and do it to me like you said just now, like a fight. Or ain't I worth it or something? Because I'm just a kid?"

He sighed. He looked across the river at the buildings on the opposite bank. He wondered if Jamieson were peering out, watching him at that very moment. Not that it mattered. "I don't feel like doing it that way with you, Carol."

"Well, shit." She started putting on her clothes.

"I'm going for a walk into town, to the square," he said.

She didn't bother to answer.

"I've maybe got to see someone there. Do you want to come?"

"No."

Michael started putting his own clothes on. "All right, maybe I'll see you later," he said.

She walked ahead of him along the deck of the ship. "Maybe." She jumped down onto the pier.

He followed her. When they reached the street he stopped her, with his hand on her shoulder. She turned and looked up at him, a little sulky, a little resentful.

He took her grimy face between his hands and kissed her hard on the mouth, forcefully yet with some tenderness. Then he turned and walked away down the street.

She stood watching him, her toe scuffing the dust, her hands in her pockets. She frowned, as if trying to think about something that she had no words to deal with. Then, with a shrug, she turned and walked back to the old pleasure palace building.

The Attack

The basement was packed with kids. Manic faces, wild eyes; tonight was the night. Pale skin was blackened with soot and grease. Young bodies were wrapped tight under dark clothes and improvised glass-fiber armor. Several hundred of the children were swarming around with their guns and their knives and their homemade bombs, cramming themselves into the forty-odd personnel carriers that Michael had managed to make operational. Drivers started their vehicles and revved the engines mindlessly; the garage started filling with fumes. Not a single child would be left behind in the pleasure palace. Every one was going to be in the attack force.

Sheldon danced down the escalator and leaped onto the hood of a car that had been given a body of bolted-on armor plates. It stood like a mechanical dinosaur, daubed with red paint and arcane black symbols.

"Gonna kill 'em all!" Sheldon shouted through an amplification system that Neal had hooked up, loud enough to hurt and so distorted that the words were almost incomprehensible. "Kill all those cocksuckers in City Hall. Bomb 'em and shoot 'em and stab 'em. Kill, kill, kill!" The sound cut through even the noise of the revving engines, till every little soldier was caught up in the hysteria, screaming with excitement.

Michael cranked open the garage exit door, his eyes smarting from the fumes, his ears hurting from the din. Sheldon jumped off the hood of the armored car and swung into it, and Neal started its motor. "Come on!" Sheldon shouted.

Michael stepped over to the vehicle and got in on the passenger side. There was only room for three, sitting up front; all the space in the back was packed with explosives—bottles, pipes, and cylinders nesting in cases packed with crumpled paper.

"Go!" Sheldon shouted, and Neal accelerated forward up the ramp into the street, the rest of the convoy following.

Michael kept his shoulder against the passenger door, his fingers tight around its handle. His pulse was fast; his skin and mouth felt dry. Sounds and images impinged as if from somewhere else. He felt like an observer. And yet he knew what was going to happen, knew how real and violent it would be.

They moved down the riverside boulevard, the white lights of the convoy stretching out behind. It was a cool spring night. The sun had just set, leaving a splash of red in the west, like streamers of blood across the sky.

Sheldon leaned forward, sitting between Neal and Michael. He held a pistol in one hand, a rifle in the other. His eyes were wide, his teeth bared. "Come on!" he shouted above the hammering noise of the engine. "Go faster!"

"We'll leave the others behind if we go faster," said Neal. But it didn't matter; Sheldon wasn't listening. He was staring into the night as if he could already see City Hall in flames.

The convoy rumbled across the bridge. Michael started counting the number of blocks remaining to City Hall. Thirty; twenty-nine; twenty-eight. . . . He glanced back through the tiny rear window and saw personnel carriers peeling off to right and left, to circle and converge simultaneously on the square from all four sides. All as he had planned.

Through the windshield he watched worn, weathered buildings move past the armored vehicle, bleached by the touch of its headlights. It shook and rattled, and it stank of oil and gasoline. The bombs in the boxes in the back trembled and clinked together as the car lurched over potholes and debris on the avenue.

Michael wanted to get out, wanted to run, but he knew he had to wait, had to follow his scheme. Twelve blocks remaining: then eleven, then ten. He squinted at the rooftops, as if he might see peace forcers hiding up there in the night.

Five blocks to go. City Hall coming into view. Four blocks. "Sniper up ahead!" Michael shouted suddenly. "Up there!" He gestured wildly. "Slow down!"

Neal slowed a little, uncertainly. Sheldon looked confused, distracted from his obsession. "Don't matter," he started to say.

"I'll get him," Michael shouted. He grabbed a gun and kicked open the door.

"No!" shouted Sheldon.

But Michael was already out. He hit the street at twenty-five miles per hour and fell. Instant jolting pain in his head and shoulder. The world spun. He slid, clothes ripping, grit tearing into his outstretched hands. As soon as he could, he rolled and scrambled up and ran blindly for the nearest cross-street.

"Come back!" Sheldon was shouting from the passenger door of the armored car.

Michael made it to a building, threw himself into the shadows and stood gasping for breath. He knew what Sheldon would be thinking—that the other three attack forces were converging on the square. Sheldon couldn't stop now. He had to get there. And anyway, he wouldn't understand what Michael was doing. Too much hysteria, too much confusion.

Michael heard the scarlet-caped figure shout curses above the roaring of the engine, then saw him disappear back into the armored car. The door slammed. And the convoy moved on, down the avenue, headlights parading past.

Michael tried to slow his pulse and his breathing. He swallowed hard and checked where he was. He ran from doorway to doorway, to the building he'd investigated two days previously. He kicked its door open and ran up the dark emergency stairs, two at a time. He knew he had to reach the roof before the kids reached the square.

He finally made it, sixteen stories above the street, his chest and legs aching, his head throbbing, his eyes buzzing with sparks of color. He stumbled out across the roof and saw a figure waiting there for him.

"Jamieson," he gasped, joining the old man standing by the parapet.

"Michael—what was the reason for your message?" In faint moonlight Jamieson's pale face was creased with worry and suspicion. "I found your note on my typewriter—why the cloak-and-dagger secret meeting place? Is that the children down there on the avenue?"

"Yeah, it's them." Michael gripped the parapet, feeling the stonework rough and solid under his raw palms. He steadied himself against it, still breathing hard, still tense and apprehensive. Down in the street he saw the first vehicles of the convoy moving into the square.

"What are they *doing?*" Jamieson said, his voice high-pitched with anxiety.

"Attacking."

"Then we must get down there!"

"Don't be an idiot," Michael told him. "There's no stopping them now. I wanted you up here so you'd be safe from what's going to happen."

The other fleets of the kids' vehicles were closing on the square from the other avenues. The engines roared in the night, echoing down the empty streets. So far, City Hall remained dark and lifeless.

"But what's going on?" said Jamieson, agitated and confused. "Did you *know* this was going to happen?"

"Yes, I knew."

"Then you must have been lying to me!"

"Yes," said Michael. "I lied to you. I told you I was encouraging them not to fight, when really I was fitting out their army."

"Why? In heaven's name why?"

"If you weren't such a dumb idealist you'd see those kids are a lost cause. They're never going to change. They would have staged an attack eventually, no matter what anyone said or did. Their heads were fucked up years ago. Permanently. I've just moved their confrontation ahead of schedule, that's all." A sud-

den burst of gunfire crackled from the square. Michael's hands
clenched harder on the parapet.

"But this is terrible!" said Jamieson, his eyes wide, taking in
the scene below.

The personnel carriers and armored cars had formed a semi-
circle, headlights focused on City Hall. Kids were throwing
bombs, firing rifles at random. The arena flashed brilliant
yellow and there was a pounding thump of explosives det-
onating, scattering shrapnel. Smoke billowed. Then a fireball
flashed crimson, right among the building's pillars. There was
a rush and roar of cascading masonry. Shrill screams of excitement.

But not a sign of life from within the building.

"Where are the peace force men?" Jamieson was shouting,
above the snapping of gunfire and the booming concussions of
the bombs.

"Down in the avenue, there," said Michael, pointing.

Jamieson looked. Quietly, through the darkness, black-uni-
formed men were running along the avenues toward the town
square, converging from all around. They didn't have vehicles,
they didn't have bombs, but every man carried a rifle—and
there were several thousand of them.

"I tipped off the peace force that something might happen,"
Michael said. "Told the Reverend Isaacs, last week. He must
have passed the word. They evacuated City Hall. Now they've
got the kids surrounded."

"My God," said Jamieson, "those children will be caught—
massacred!"

Michael didn't answer. He just stared at the square. Unaware
of the closing circle of peace forcers, the kids were getting more
daring, running and flinging bombs directly into the City Hall
building, through its ruined facade. There was a renewed thunder of explosions and flashes in the night. The roof of the old
building caved in. Slowly, slowly, one of its walls leaned out-
ward and cascaded down into rubble.

And then the peace forcers struck, completely encircling the kids. Rifle fire came in waves, sharp and deafening and cruel. Jamieson covered his ears. Bullets ricocheted off armor, struck soft flesh, ignited bombs and grenades. Kids panicked, running around in confusion. The armored vehicles backed off from City Hall, looking for a way out.

Michael took from his pocket a little box the size of an electronic calculator. He levered off a plastic blister that had covered a single button. He pulled out a telescopic antenna.

In the square, the vehicles drove wildly, ramming into each other, smashing into storefronts, mowing down tiny black figures running like trapped insects among the headlight glare. The peace force men were everywhere, shooting and killing.

Michael found himself watching with teeth clenched and every muscle knotted. He laid the little box on the parapet in front of him and turned on a switch on its side.

Jamieson looked at him. "What's that? What are you doing?"

Michael saw that everyone—peace forcers and kids alike—was now within the town square. He pressed the button.

For an instant nothing happened, and he was afraid that all his scheming had failed. A hollow feeling caught his guts.

And then, all around the square, he saw the buildings collapsing.

The noise hit him in a painful jarring wave. The roof he stood on shook under his feet. Fireballs blossomed. The sky lit up yellow. Vehicles, kids, and peace force men were all lost, smothered as the bombs were radio-detonated in every building overlooking the square, and the old structures sank down as if too weary to continue standing, their tons of brick and stone and concrete fragmenting as they fell.

Fires burst out sporadically. The explosions boomed and boomed again, and then slowly died into the distance. And the night became suddenly, strangely silent.

A wave of heat wafted over Michael's face, as if an oven door had been opened. Then came smoke and dust, spreading out from the scene of the catastrophe. The entire square and everyone in it were smothered by the demolished buildings.

Feeling light-headed and dizzy, he turned to Jamieson. "It's time we left."

The man looked at him blankly. Stiff-legged, he let himself be led to the emergency stairs. He began descending them like a robot. "All those people dead," he said, stupidly.

"Yes, probably almost all of them."

"You let the kids destroy City Hall, you let the peace force destroy the kids, and then you yourself . . ."

"Yes, Jamieson. Now all the bombs, the guns, and the exploiters are buried in that heap out there. And the peace force's hidden stores of food and salvaged technology are still scattered around town, unharmed, available to everyone. Farmers won't even have to trade anymore. Just come and get what they need. See?"

They went on walking down the stairwell, feeling their way through the darkness. The footsteps resounded in the enclosed space, but Michael hardly heard them. His ears were still ringing. His eyes still saw the fire of the explosions. It had been easy, in a way—easy to fool kids who were too simple-minded to guess at motives above their own animal-instinct level. Easy to filch from their unsystematic stocks of explosives. Easy to slip out behind Jamieson's house each night and lay the charges in the empty buildings around the town square, while peace forcers were skirmishing and sniping at tearaway kids in cars. Easy to figure out the radio-controlled detonator. All he had had to do was follow his own plans, step by step, as if the instructions had come from someone else.

At last he emerged onto the street. The air was thick with drifting dust and the smell of smoke. "Deceiver," Jamieson was mumbling. "You're a murderer, do you realize that? You're a cold-blooded . . ."

"All right, Jamieson. You don't need to go down the list."

"So what now? You declare yourself the new dictator? In control of the city?" The man's face looked haunted and a little crazy.

"Don't be a fool," Michael said. "No one controls the city,

now. No one has the means to do so. Look, I'm not going to waste time debating with you. I'm going back to the farm, to Lisa. There's one car that I kept for myself at the pleasure palace, with enough gasoline. And you, you might just as well go home and write another chapter of your book."

Jamieson shook his head. "I hope you can live with yourself. If there were any justice . . ."

"Goodnight, Jamieson." Michael turned and started walking away, leaving the man standing alone in the street with the smoke and dust and flickering yellow flames burning in the debris that filled the square.

All Michael knew, now, was that he wanted to get out of the city as soon as possible. Not once did he look back at the heaps of rubble behind him—the rubble that had buried the peace force men, the weapons, and the children—kids like Sheldon, and Neal, and Carol.

THE OPEN FUTURE

He set out from the city in the car that he had retained for himself at the pleasure palace. It ran erratically, never faster than forty miles an hour, and the Interstate had been washed out in several places, forcing him to detour. So the drive back to the farm was long and arduous, and by the time he got there it was past four in the morning.

The guard on night duty was full of questions when he saw the stripped-down automobile, but Michael was in no mood to talk. He left the car by the barrier that blocked the track, and walked from there up to the house.

Everything was silent, dark, and peaceful, and he felt the mood of the place settle over him, dulling the vivid images of the city that still crowded his mind. He paused outside the building and rubbed his eyes, weary yet still tense. Then he opened the door and walked upstairs, stepping quietly, finding his way through to the room that had been assigned to him and Lisa.

She awoke the instant that he walked in. He heard her sit up in the darkness, and heard the rustle of blankets as she scrambled off the mattress in the corner. He saw her come quickly across a patch of diffuse moonlight, and then she was hugging him. Her body was suddenly soft and real and warm against him, and for a moment he thought he would be able to forget all that had happened in the last two weeks.

But that was too simple and even as she kissed him he felt himself mentally stiffening and drawing back from her.

She sensed it. "Michael?" she whispered, touching his face. "I've missed you so much."

He led her back to the mattress on the floor in the corner and they sat down side by side. "I missed you too," he said, truthfully, yet mechanically.

"Where have you been? What have you been doing? God, I'm glad you're back. It seemed so long. I . . ."

He put his hand on her arm. "Easy, take it easy," he said. "I'm very tired."

There was a silence. "Aren't you pleased to be back?" she asked.

"Yes. Yes, of course I'm pleased to be back. Just very, very tired."

"Oh." She sat up close to him, holding onto him, waiting for him to say something more. But where could he possibly begin, he wondered, to explain everything to her? Maybe he should say nothing. But that would not be right or fair.

"What's the matter?" she asked.

"A lot happened, in town."

"Harris said he left you there, you wanted to make contact with the peace force people and some others; he was kind of vague about it, but he said no one with any sense hung around in the old center after dark. I was worried."

"It's all different now," he heard himself saying, wearily.

In the moonlight he saw her face looking up at him, concerned. "Different? What do you mean, different between us?"

"No. God, no." He squeezed her hand. "I mean, different back in town."

She waited for him to go on. Then, when he didn't: "Well, are you going to tell me about it?"

"I'll try. It's been traumatic. I've always been so much a loner, detached from things, never involved."

"I know that."

"Well, as soon as I discovered how things were in the center, I found myself in the middle. Between two sides. I had a position of power. And I just went ahead and used it."

"You're not making much sense, Michael."

"I'm sorry. It's difficult to make sense of it myself. I'm never going back there, that's all I know. I just staged the last-ever suicide rock concert, except it wasn't in a concert hall, it was in the street, and the act was for real." Mentally he saw the fire boiling up again and the buildings sinking, smothering it in rubble and dust. He massaged his face and sighed.

"You can talk about it tomorrow," she said quietly. "Maybe you should get some sleep."

"Yes, I need sleep, but I want to talk if only to capture how I feel now, before it gets blurred. Events lose their sharpness, the more time passes. In a way things are very clear at the moment. I had a lot of time to think, driving back here through the night. You know, three years ago, before I met you, I was so complacent about everything; I believed in an open future, I was part of the status quo, and I didn't question the way things were. I exploited the entertainment market and got rich, and I enjoyed staging things without ever really being involved myself. Then at that party, on the night of the presidential speech, I realized the future *wasn't* open. Everything was being used up. People were exploiting a diminishing supply, and there was no way of evading a decline. Well, if there wasn't going to be a future, the only sensible thing to do seemed to live only in the present moment. And that's what we did in New Vista. For us, progress and wealth and future had become nonexistent. It was an ap-

propriate philosophy for me, because I've always tended to re
treat, and that was the most perfect retreat of all. And you
wanted to be undisturbed and free to do as you wished, so it
worked for you, too."

"I think I know all this," she said, still close by him. "I don't
see what you're getting at."

"Well, after the peace force moved in on us, we came here,
and I couldn't exist in retreat anymore. I realized gradually that
the rest of the world still existed and things were happening.
Some kind of new social structure would emerge. There *was*
going to be some kind of future, offering various different alter-
natives. Meanwhile I was still a spectator, uninvolved, but restless, not knowing what I should be doing. So I went back to the
old urban center, almost like going back to my roots. And I
found things happening: a gang of kids who'd found weapons
and vehicles and gasoline, and a hostile last-ditch group of peace
forcers running a cutthroat market economy. People from surrounding farms were coming into town and trading their valuable
food for simple technological necessities that the peace force
controlled. I realized that the farms and small communities are
the way that society is going to develop next. But they were being
inhibited, by the people in town hoarding what was left of salvaged parts and materials. And at the same time those damn
brain-damaged kids were threatening to screw things up in some
kind of battle or confrontation that they might actually *win*, and
either way, it would mean things were going to be wasted and
conflict would drag on. Stupidity would reduce the chances of
a whole lot of other peoples' survival. So there I was, and I suppose I could say I felt a kind of moral indignation, but it wasn't
really like that. I just got angry and felt, to *hell* with you people
and your squabbling for power and your dumb games. To hell
with all of you. And I was angry with myself for never having
participated more in the real world. So I decided to stop being
a spectator. I worked out a simple way to pit the two sides against
each other so they would wipe each other out."

He finished abruptly.

"What do you mean?" she whispered.

He shrugged uncomfortably. He straightened his legs, realizing that he was tense and cramped. "I told you. It was the last suicide rock concert."

"I don't understand."

"I can't talk about it, Lisa. It's too much. All I know is, people will be able to go into town now and get what they need. The city's dead. The little communities are growing and flourishing all around. I saw them two weeks ago, on the way into the old city with Harris. Small towns with a few technological remnants, centered around agriculture, producing just enough to allow their children an education, and to run a few simple services."

"You make it all sound so important. Something to work for. But you always used to say that so long as people believed in an end, they'd use it to justify a means, and . . ."

"I know, I know. But our so-called pragmatism in New Vista only worked in New Vista. Outside, things are more complicated than that. Maybe if everyone were as undemanding as you, that wouldn't be so. But life isn't like that."

"Still, you sound optimistic, somehow."

"Yes," he said, "in a way I am, because people can't exploit other people so easily anymore. The basic resources are all gone in this part of the country: no more oil, no more easily smelted iron ore, no more metals outside of scrap metal in the garbage dumps. All there is is coal and wood for energy, and soil and water to grow food. There's room for cottage industries, now, but no real growth anymore. No way to get rich at someone else's expense. No way to build industrial empires. Things will stay small. They have to."

She sighed. "It all sounds very theoretical. All *I've* ever wanted . . ."

He hugged her. "I know, peace and freedom to do what you want to do."

"You make it sound trivial."

"No, I've just been preoccupied with my own problems, that's all."

"But do you think you've resolved them?"

"Hell, is anything ever resolved? All I can say is, I broke some barriers, put to rest some of my dissatisfactions. But there's still the question of my fitting into life back here on the farm. I don't like farm life, it's repetitive, uninteresting, hard, and communal. The land dictates what we do every day, and the social organization of our co-workers dictates how we do it. What I'm hoping is that I can move around more, going to neighboring communities, getting more involved in the way things are going. Maybe I can get rid of the restlessness in harmless ways, building things, meeting people, working out answers to problems. I have to face it, there is an element in me that needs that kind of gratification."

"It doesn't sound a very peaceful life, Michael."

"It's a compromise, don't you see? A way to satisfy that persistent need to *do* things."

"Well, if that's what you need."

"I think so. I must admit, I've never been very good at knowing what I need." He stretched, feeling some of the tension draining from his muscles, for the first time in days. "You know, it's good to be with you again."

She looked at him. "I was afraid you weren't going to say that. You seem strange, as if you've changed."

"I've been through a lot. But I want to forget that now."

Faint dawn light was beginning to show through the window of the little room, invading the darkness. He saw her face more clearly, and he kissed her.

"We'll just see how it goes," she murmured.

"Yes," he said. "No more talking for a while, all right?"

"Mm. There are better ways to communicate than with words."

He smiled at her.

They embraced and then, on the mattress on the floor, they lay down and made love. And outside, in the fields that had been cultivated with such painstaking care and labor, the crops grew taller in the fresh spring air, and gray twilight gave way to daylight in the yellow radiance of the sunrise.